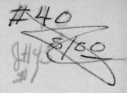

ENEMY FIRE

Wolf Who Hunts Smiling's Colt spat muzzle smoke. Touch the Sky watched as the lead freighter yelled and then sprawled in an ungainly heap in the middle of the road.

The freighters behind him had broken out their long guns and covered down when the attack commenced. Now Touch the Sky saw all of them excitedly point in his direction. The next moment slugs started buzzing past Touch the Sky's ear with an angry-hornet sound, forcing him to retreat. Clearly, they assumed he was one of the attackers.

Just as clear was the blood-soaked hair of the bullwhacker who lay sprawled in the road. Wolf Who Hunts Smiling's last shot had been fatal.

"You murdering, savage bastard!" one of the freighters shouted behind Touch the Sky. "Put at 'em, boys!"

CHEYENNE

GIANT SPECIAL EDITION!

BLOOD ON
THE ARROWS

JUDD COLE

LEISURE BOOKS NEW YORK CITY

A LEISURE BOOK®

July 2000

Published by

Dorchester Publishing Co., Inc.
276 Fifth Avenue
New York, NY 10001

ISBN 0-8439-4734-9

CHEYENNE

GIANT SPECIAL EDITION!
BLOOD ON
THE ARROWS

Prologue

The tall warrior named Touch the Sky had earned more coup feathers than any other brave in his Northern Cheyenne tribe. But his bloody struggles to protect his people could not defeat the many tribal enemies who constantly demanded his death, accusing him of spying for blue-bloused soldiers.

The ill-fated brave's tragedy began in the year the white man's winter-count called 1840. A U.S. Cavalry ambush killed the great Cheyenne peace chief Running Antelope and his wife Lotus Petal. Only one Cheyenne survived the Platte River massacre: Running Antelope's newborn son.

Pawnee scouts were about to brain the infant against a tree when the lieutenant in charge stopped them. The baby was taken back to the river-bend settlement of Bighorn Falls near Fort Bates in the Wyoming Territory. There he grew up the adopted son of John and Sarah Hanchon, owners of the town's mercantile store.

The Hanchons named him Matthew and loved him as their own blood. The first sixteen years of his life were happy ones. Early on he went to work for his parents, stocking shelves and delivering goods to the outlying settlers. Though some local whites hated this full-blooded Indian in their midst, many others eventually accepted and even befriended him.

Then his life's path took a fatal turn when he fell in love with Hiram Steele's daughter, Kristen.

The richest and most powerful rancher in the area, Steele caught the young lovers in their secret meeting place. He ordered one of his wranglers to savagely beat the youth and promised to kill him if he caught the couple together again. Fearful for Matthew's life, Kristen forced herself to a difficult lie: She told him she could no longer love an Indian.

Already humiliated and heartbroken, Matthew soon faced even greater troubles. A proud and arrogant lieutenant from Fort Bates, Seth Carlson, had staked a claim to Kristen's hand. He visited Matthew with a merciless ultimatum: Either Matthew pulled up stakes for good, or the Hanchons would lose their contract to supply Fort Bates—the very lifeblood of their mercantile business.

Thus trapped between the sap and the bark, a miserable but determined Matthew said goodbye to the only life he knew and lit out for the upcountry of the Powder River—Cheyenne Indian country. But his white man's clothing and language and customs doomed him. Captured by braves from Chief Yellow Bear's tribe, he was immediately accused of being a Bluecoat spy and sentenced to torture and death.

Two young braves especially hated him: Black Elk, the tribe's war leader, and his cousin Wolf Who Hunts Smiling. Black Elk's loathing of this intruder deepened when Chief Yellow Bear's daughter, Honey Eater, took too keen an interest in the accused spy's fate.

Wolf Who Hunts Smiling was about to plunge a knife deep into his vitals when an authoritative voice stopped him. The speaker was old Arrow Keeper, the tribe's shaman and protector of the four sacred Medicine Arrows.

Arrow Keeper had just returned from experiencing a crucial vision at holy Medicine Lake. In that vision, a mysterious youth—the son of a long-lost Cheyenne chief—eventually led the entire Cheyenne nation in its greatest battle victory. This mystery warrior would be recognized by a distinctive mark, and Arrow Keeper spotted it buried in the hair over the prisoner's right temple: a mulberry-colored birthmark in the shape of an arrowhead, the mark of the warrior.

Over the strenuous objections of many, Arrow Keeper and Chief Yellow Bear spared the prisoner's life. His old name was buried in a hole forever and he was renamed Touch the Sky. Even more shocking: Arrow Keeper insisted that this pathetic intruder must live with the tribe—and even train as a warrior.

Despite a constant campaign to destroy and humiliate him, Touch the Sky became the most formidable warrior in the tribe. But after Chief Yellow Bear died, Honey Eater was forced into a loveless marriage with Black Elk. Her star-crossed passion for Touch the Sky—which he returned—drove Black Elk to a murderous jealousy that his cousin Wolf Who Hunts Smiling constantly encouraged.

With the mysterious disappearance of Arrow Keeper, Touch the Sky was narrowly voted as the tribe's new shaman and Keeper of the Arrows. But Wolf Who Hunts Smiling joined forces secretly with Comanche and Blackfoot allies. He also selected another clever and scheming brave, Medicine Flute, and called him the tribe's only true shaman.

Now the tribe is deeply divided and the battle lines clearly drawn. Wolf Who Hunts Smiling and his allies are determined to murder this white man's dog and either convert or destroy his followers. Unlike his treasonous cousin, Black Elk remains loyal to his tribe, but is jealously obsessed with killing Touch the Sky. Hated by the white man, mistrusted by the red man, Touch the Sky places his last hope in the powerful medicine vision which promised that his destiny as a great Cheyenne leader would eventually justify this loneliness and suffering.

Chapter One

"Brother," Little Horse said quietly, "here comes a trouble cloud blowing your way."

Little Horse, Two Twists, Tangle Hair, and Touch the Sky were gathered around a willow-branch travois that was heaped high with beaver plews and elk skins. Touch the Sky was busy lashing the furs tight with a rawhide cord. He glanced at his friend, then looked in the direction Little Horse indicated.

Three braves strolled purposefully across the central camp clearing, heading toward the group preparing the travois for a journey to the trading post at Red Shale. Touch the Sky recognized the one with the deepest scowl as Black Elk. The smaller, furtive-looking brave at his side was his cousin Wolf Who Hunts Smiling. They were accompanied by the slender, heavy-lidded youth named Medicine Flute.

"Here come three trouble clouds," Touch the Sky corrected his friend.

"Three of them and four of us," muttered young Two Twists, whose preference for double braids had earned him his name. "Let them come, I am *for* them."

Touch the Sky finished knotting the rawhide and rose to his feet again. He was taller by almost a full head than any of his companions. A strong, hawk nose and straight, determined mouth dominated a face framed by unevenly cut black locks. The warm moons had begun, and like his companions he wore only a doeskin clout—pouched in the front—and elkskin moccasins. The knotted muscles of his chest and shoulders were pocked with burn and knife scars.

"Two Twists," he answered, "you would count coup on the Wendigo if you could. But you are too quick to rush into trifling danger. A warrior is not easily goaded by words and lets his weapons speak for his courage. Whatever chatter these three jays have in store, do not rise to their bait."

"Look here, brothers!" Wolf Who Hunts Smiling called out. "Once again the Headmen have foolishly trusted White Man Runs Him to take our furs to the traders. They have forgotten the time when his own friend, Little Horse here, caught our great 'shaman' swilling devil water with the hair faces at the post."

"The Headmen forget many things where *this*

one is concerned," Black Elk said with bitter contempt. His intense black eyes bored into Touch the Sky. The war leader looked even more gruesome and fierce as a result of the detached ear which he had crudely sewn back onto his skull with buckskin thread. Severed in battle by a bluecoat saber, the dead, leathery flap now hung crookedly.

"They also forget," Black Elk said, "how he deserted his own tribe to go fight for the whites who raised him. How he leaves messages in trees for the same white soldiers who kill us. How he helped white miners build a path for their iron horse across our hunting grounds. And they forget how he schemes to put on the old moccasin with our Cheyenne women."

Touch the Sky showed nothing in his face, but his companions scowled at the reference to putting on the old moccasin—the Cheyenne way of referring to an unmarried brave's desire to lie with a more experienced married woman.

Understanding what was troubling his brooding cousin, the crafty Wolf Who Hunts Smiling caught Touch the Sky's eye as he said, "Indeed, cousin, Medicine Flute here has told me a thing. He has told me that strong medicine exists in our camp. Strong *bad* medicine. Medicine designed to keep certain deserving warriors from successfully siring a whelp."

Touch the Sky knew full well that this barb was meant to fly straight to Black Elk's jealous heart. Everyone in camp knew he blamed Honey Eater's failure to bear him a son on her love for

Touch the Sky. For many believed that if a squaw loved a man other than her husband, her womb remained infertile to her husband's seed.

At his cousin's words, dark wrath twisted Black Elk's features. Alarmed at the turn things were taking, Touch the Sky knew he had to divert the attention from Honey Eater before Black Elk could get angry enough to hurt her again. That meant diverting the source of the problem—Wolf Who Hunts Smiling.

"Brothers," he said to his comrades, his tone friendly and relaxed, "have you noticed a curious thing? Have you noticed that our fierce warrior Wolf Who Hunts Smiling has not once ever held a woman in his blanket to make love talk?"

Little Horse, always quick to sense his friend's plans, quickly responded in the same tone. "I have indeed noticed this curious thing, brother. Yet, he claims constantly to know always what goes on secretly between men and women."

Tangle Hair pitched into the game. "Stout bucks! If I want tips on killing a man, I go to a Sioux, not a Ponca! As for our ferocious Wolf Who Hunts Smiling, he seems content lately with the company of Medicine Flute here. Truly, they often disappear together for long periods."

"As lovers will," Touch the Sky added in a stroke of brilliance that ruined Wolf Who Hunts Smiling's cold composure. Purple rage flushed his face and he started to speak. But in a rare

Blood On The Arrows

turn of events, it was Black Elk who restrained him.

"Mock, Woman Face," Black Elk shot back. He added cryptically: "Soon the worm will turn, and your mocking smile will be swallowed along with your teeth."

"Had you killed me every time you promised to, Panther Clan, I would need ten more lifetimes just to fit in all the dying."

Black Elk and Wolf Who Hunts Smiling exchanged a knowing glance.

"Killing a man," Black Elk said, "is less satisfying than humiliating him and then leaving him alive to steep in his shame. I say again, Woman Face, the worm will turn."

"You have all enjoyed calling me Woman Face," Touch the Sky said, "because you say I show my feelings in my face for all to see, as does a woman. Yet, look at you three now. Get to the sewing lodge and join your sisters."

"I no longer only call you Woman Face," Wolf Who Hunts Smiling replied. "I call you White Man Runs Him. And I tell you this, also. Soon you will know there is nothing of the 'woman' in my cousin."

Touch the Sky didn't like this. This was the second time now that his enemies had promised some new trouble. And just after Sister Sun rose from her birthplace, Touch the Sky had seen crows circle his tipi. Fresh treachery was on the spit.

During the brief silence which followed Wolf Who Hunts Smiling's remark, Medicine Flute

15

lifted a slim flute to his lips. Made from the hollowed-out leg bone of a tribal enemy, the crude instrument blew only a few monotonous notes. Now, his drooping eyes mocking Touch the Sky, he played his gruesome instrument.

Silently urging his comrades, with his eyes, to ignore the other three, Touch the Sky began tying the travois to his chestnut pony's rigging.

"Woman Face!" Black Elk shouted above the hollow piping. When Touch the Sky refused to respond to the name, Black Elk added, "Soon, Woman Face, the worm will turn. Soon, and the white man's dog will be kicked by the same boots he once licked!"

The trading post at Red Shale was located one full sleep's ride from the Cheyenne summer camp at the confluence of the Powder and the Little Powder Rivers. The camp, under Chief Gray Thunder since the death of the great peace leader Yellow Bear, traded at the post far less often now because the tribe received a generous yearly supply of trade goods delivered to them by packtrain.

That annual payment came from white miners as the ongoing peace price for allowing them to transport their ore by iron horse over Cheyenne land. Touch the Sky had served as a pathfinder for the railroad. He had outwitted the treacherous Wolf Who Hunts Smiling and defeated Sis-ki-dee, the crazy-by-thunder renegade Blackfoot. He and Little Horse had risked their lives for every foot of that spur line down out of the rugged Sans Arc Mountains.

And now, Touch the Sky thought bitterly as his strong chestnut easily made her way up the long uphill slope of the ascending valley, look what his struggles had earned him. His enemies used that expedition as further proof he was a Bluecoat spy or at least a white man's dog. Yet, did not Black Elk and Wolf Who Hunts Smiling and their Bull Whip troop brothers crowd to the front for best pick when the goods arrived?

It was the same every time he defeated a new enemy for his tribe. His foes within the tribe managed to paint him cleverly as tainted by the white man's stink. Even as his bravery and fighting skill won over reluctant admirers, still others were driven to deeper depths of hatred and mistrust.

Old Arrow Keeper had warned Touch the Sky long ago to spend less time talking and thinking, and more time listening, seeing, sniffing the wind—attending to the language of his senses. How often had that advice saved his scalp? And recently Touch the Sky's shaman sense convinced him he now faced an even more crucial and dangerous trial.

Whatever that trial was, Black Elk would be involved. His recent threats and hints in camp could bode nothing but some new calamity. If only Arrow Keeper were still here, his powerful medicine and deep wisdom once again guiding Touch the Sky.

"Brother," Little Horse's voice cut into his rumination, "do you have the Eagle Eyes that

17

Caleb Riley sent with the last packtrain?"

Touch the Sky nodded and slipped a pair of brass U.S. Army fieldglasses from the hide pannier sewn to the chestnut's rigging.

"What do you see, buck?" he asked. He squinted hard as he gazed in the direction Little Horse was facing—east, across a vast expanse of lush new buffalo grass. Touch the Sky spotted nothing that seemed out of place. Just a few gnarled cottonwoods with their wind-stunted limbs, scattered sycamore and willow thickets closer to the valley. But Little Horse was known for the keenest eyes in the tribe.

"What do I see?" Little Horse replied. "Perhaps only *odjib*, a thing of smoke."

He raised the fieldglasses, somewhat hesitant and suspicious of them, and clumsily adjusted the focus. Then he watched through them for a long time. Their ponies, momentarily halted, gratefully chomped the grass. They were taking turns pulling the travois, and now it was lashed to Tangle Hair's ginger mustang.

"No smoke this time," Little Horse announced triumphantly. "I spoke straight-arrow. Several wagons driven by whites. They are just now crossing the saddle on Lakota Ridge."

"Bone shakers?" Two Twists said, referring to the canvas-covered wagons of the frontier settlers.

Little Horse shook his head. "These are the open freight wagons they use for shorter journeys across easier country. Three of them. Piled high with the odd things Yellow Eyes keep inside their lodges. I see four palefaces. One appears to be a squaw. She—"

Abruptly, Little Horse fell silent. Touch the Sky watched his friend's normally impassive face suddenly tighten at some shocking recognition.

"She what, brother?" Touch the Sky demanded. "Hand me the eagle eyes so I may see for myself."

But Little Horse refused to surrender them. "Never mind, Bear Caller," he said, using the name Pawnee enemies gave to his friend after he had summoned a wild grizzly at Medicine Lake. "They are only more of these queerly dressed intruders from across the Great Waters. Our path will not cross theirs, and certainly they are no war party. Let us hurry to Red Shale! I wish to see these pieces of curved glass which magically focus the sun and start fires."

But Touch the Sky was not fooled by his friend's sudden enthusiasm for the white man's science. He nudged his pony up beside Little Horse and snatched the glasses from his hand.

"Brother," Touch the Sky said fondly, "you fight like ten men. But you are the poorest liar I have ever known. You should take lessons from the whites who write the treaties."

Little Horse looked utterly miserable, exchanging quick warning glances with Tangle Hair and Two Twists. As Touch the Sky adjusted the focus a little, Little Horse urged again: "Let us make tracks! You have seen plenty of white men for this lifetime."

"True enough. But these must be different,"
Touch the Sky said quietly, "if they can make
even you tell a lie."

Suddenly a man's grizzle-bearded profile
leaped into sharp focus in the glasses. He rode
a big claybank beside one of the wagons. A rifle
butt protruded from his saddle scabbard, another was propped across the tree of his saddle.

Touch the Sky did not know this face. One
glance convinced him he had never seen this
man, for he would not have forgotten that huge,
distinctive round dent in his beard where a
musket ball, apparently, had once torn through
his left cheek, leaving a knot of white scar tissue.

He scanned with the glasses until a second
rider came into view. He rode horseback on the
other flank of the wagon, his mount a large,
powerful cavalry sorrel. The man, like his
horse, was big and powerfully built. And like
the other rider, he was heavily armed. Between
rifles and numerous braces of pistols, the two
men would be capable of firing dozens of
rounds before needing to recharge a bore.

Still, both men were strangers. Touch the Sky
wondered what had upset Little Horse. He
trained the glasses on the man driving the lead
wagon. But all he could see at this angle was
the man's profile. It seemed vaguely familiar, as
did the thickset shoulders and the compressed
strength of his movements.

The woman Little Horse had mentioned rode
on the plank seat beside the driver of the lead

wagon, wearing a full skirt without hoops. A frilled sunbonnet hid her face. But Touch the Sky glimpsed a few loose tresses of hair the color of golden oats.

A memory chord within him responded. And just then, abruptly, the woman turned her face in his direction and peered as if straight into the other end of the glasses.

Touch the Sky felt his blood seem to stop and flow backwards in his veins. The glasses nearly fell from his trembling fingers. Then, recovering, he returned his attention to the driver and now recognized him immediately.

So his shaman eye had seen the truth, and trouble was indeed about to engulf him anew.

The man and woman in that wagon below were Hiram Steele and his daughter Kristen!

"Brother," Little Horse urged, "let us point our bridles toward Red Shale. Never mind what you see out there on the ridge. For whatever you see, it is best avoided."

Despite the fact that most whites looked alike to an Indian, Little Horse had easily recognized both Steeles. For he had accompanied Touch the Sky to Bighorn Falls to fight for his white parents when Hiram Steele tried to destroy John and Sarah Hanchon's mustang ranch. Little Horse had also fought at Touch the Sky's side against Steele in Kansas. That time, Steele had teamed up with an Indian 'policeman' named Mankiller to terrorize the entire Cherokee reservation.

By now Touch the Sky had recovered from the conflicting feelings caused by spotting, at the same time, one of his deadliest enemies and a young woman who still claimed a place in his heart.

Now he looked at Little Horse. "Brother, below, crossing our homeland, is one of the lowest enemies of all red men. Even if you had not seen him try to kill my white mother and father, it would be enough to count only the innocent Cherokees he caused to be sent under. Would *you*, Little Horse, the finest warrior I ever fought beside, so willingly flee from such as he?"

"In a heartbeat," Little Horse replied promptly, "when such as *she* is with him."

And suddenly Touch the Sky understood: Little Horse was thinking of Honey Eater. For the sturdy little brave considered her, as did young Two Twists, his sister. He knew full well the dangerous effect this sun-haired woman had on Touch the Sky.

"Brother," Little Horse hastened to add, seeing his comrade frown. "When I say 'such as she,' do not bend my words the wrong way. That brave girl defied her dangerous father and risked her life to help us fight him. You know I am not among those Indians who despise all whites because some are evil.

"Indeed, it is *because* she is such a fine woman that I wish to ride away. For another fine woman has suffered long for you. Even now she dreams of the day when she might be with you."

Touch the Sky would permit only Little Horse to take such a personal liberty in saying this to him. And so many words from the taciturn Little Horse amounted to a long speech. So Touch the Sky considered them carefully before answering.

"Brother, I am glad that this fine woman you speak of has such a friend in you, a friend who looks out for her. I have placed your words close to my heart. And I tell you this thing now. So long as the fine woman you speak of still waits for me, there is no danger of another capturing my heart.

"But I am riding down there, alone and under a truce flag. I am going to look into Hiram Steele's face and find out why he has come back here after so long. Brother, my white father and mother live only half a sleep's ride from this place! He tried to destroy them once and vowed he would yet. Do you understand that I cannot let this hair-face killer and thief ride back now unchallenged?"

Clearly Little Horse *did* understand. He nodded reluctantly. "But alone, buck? Can we not ride down together, all of us? Those two ugly buzzards with Steele would shoot you as quickly as they might swat a fly. Nothing but murderers ride for him."

"As you say. All the more reason I must go out alone. They would never let a group of red men approach. One they will not fear."

Despite his reassuring words, Touch the Sky knew full well that Steele nursed an aching need to kill him. Especially now that he had thwarted his ambitious schemes twice and cost him a fortune both times. Fueling this thirst to kill the Cheyenne was Hiram's abject humiliation—after all, had his own daughter not kissed a savage full on the lips?

But this had to be done. Touch the Sky would not let this brutal criminal intimidate either the local Indians *or* the Hanchons. Not without the bloodiest fight of his life.

He tied a white cloth to his lance and left his weapons with his comrades. He was about to heel his pony into motion when Little Horse called out:

"Brother! I know you are the shaman, not I. But I have a feeling you are making a deadly mistake. Therefore, hand me the eagle eyes before you go. I want to keep watch on you."

Chapter Two

Touch the Sky, like most warriors who faced
death constantly, had long ago learned to place
his fear outside of him lest it conquer him. A
warrior must expect death, he reasoned, and
hopes only that it will be mercifully quick when
it finally arrives.

Yet, even the boldest warrior dreaded most
what Touch the Sky did now: He rode closer
and closer to a treacherous, well-armed enemy,
unarmed himself. Worse, he was forced to pon-
der his own death in advance, to anticipate destruction at every moment.

But ride closer he did. In country this open,
they had of course spotted him, truce flag flut-
tering in a brisk northern wind, long before he
reached them. As Touch the Sky had predicted,
at first curiosity overcame fear—no one even

drew a bead on him as his pony cantered closer.

Raw fear warred with nervous anticipation. For despite his deep love for Honey Eater, he often thought of Kristen Steele. Not only had she dared to love him and befriend the red man, she had dared to defy a father who was as mean and dangerous as she was decent and kind. And now Touch the Sky was about to see her again.

He could almost feel the weight of their eyes on him. He saw his chestnut's ears prick forward as the pony whiffed the unfamiliar smell of whites. The little caravan had stopped, all eyes staring at the approaching rider.

Kristen recognized him first. Touch the Sky saw her face lose all of its rosy hue when the blood drained out of it.

But it was Hiram Steele who first spoke.

"*You!*"

The single, unbelieving word exploded the hushed stillness like a gunshot. In the few seconds of surprised immobility which followed it, Touch the Sky showed no fear while, with inner urgency, he surveyed his situation.

Hiram drove the lead wagon, Kristen beside him. A sheathed rifle lay across Hiram's lap, and knowing him well, Touch the Sky assumed he carried a hideout gun too. Two apathetic, down-at-the-heels teamsters, armed only with pistols, drove the other two wagons. They showed no zeal to fight, only high hopes of some diversion on these god-awful boring plains.

But the heavily armed guards still flanked the

lead wagon. And now, at a brief signal from Steele, they went for weapons.

The man on the big claybank, the grizzle beard with the musket-ball hole in one cheek, whirled his mount. Now Touch the Sky noticed a detail his earlier glimpse through fieldglasses hadn't revealed: A specially rigged saber belt held a shotgun with both barrels sawed down to twelve inches. Leaving the gun in its sling, he expertly aimed it from the hip at Touch the Sky.

"Mr. Fontaine, *no!*"

Kristen was halfway off the board seat, clearly intending to leap on the man with the shotgun, before Hiram caught her by one arm. Roughly, the powerful man slammed her back down onto the seat, rocking the entire wagon.

"Shut your cake hole, girl!" he ordered her in a voice made brittle with anger. "One damn time too many you've sold your own race out for the likes of that savage, criminal bastard. I'll see you on some stump ranch breeding shirt-tail towheads with white trash before I let you ever touch his filthy hand again!"

Steele turned to the rider with the shotgun. "Don't kill him just this second, Abbot," he said, excited at this unexpected opportunity. He stared at Touch the Sky. "The hell's got into you, Hanchon? Peyote? You must be tired of living."

To emphasize his contempt, Touch the Sky ignored Steele and his goading. But he couldn't keep his eyes from darting to Kristen's. The sun-bonnet had fallen off in her exertions, taking her hairpin with it. Now her hair tumbled over

27

her shoulders in a golden waterfall. She was as pretty as ever, only now it was the rounded-out beauty of a young woman, not a coltish girl.

"What's got into me," he answered calmly in English, "is you. This is the Cheyenne homeland you're crossing, Steele. This place doesn't want you."

"Whoa!" said Abbot Fontaine, feigning exaggerated fear. "This red nigger is about half rough, eh, Stoney?"

Stoney MacGruder nodded. "He's a nervy cuss."

Steele, calming down some and now fighting back a smirk, said, "No need to get your blood in a boil, Hanchon. You said the word yourself. I'm 'crossing' Cheyenne land. By treaty law whites have safe right-of-passage over Indian grantlands."

It felt odd to speak English again and be called by his old last name, the same name Arrow Keeper had buried in a hole forever. Touch the Sky stared at the heavily loaded wagons.

"*You* speak of treaty law? Will a fox guard the hens? You, who hire others to kill red men as if they were mere rabbits."

Steele winked at his hirelings. "Well now, that's not exactly true. You see, a man can eat a rabbit. An Indian isn't worth the powder it takes to blow him to hell."

There was a loud click when Abbot Fontaine thumbed back both hammers of the sawed-off scattergun. Contemptuously, Touch the Sky ignored him.

"Our law-ways do grant you a legal right to cross our land. But not to settle on it," he told Steele. "Nor to mine it, farm it, graze it or otherwise use or profit from it. You can't cut one tree nor kill even a prairie dog on our land. That's a law *your* people made, not mine."

"Hell," Fontaine said sarcastically, "I guess we can't even piss on your precious dirt."

"You're right, Hanchon," Steele agreed. "That's what the treaty signed at Fort Laramie says. You just reeled it off chapter and verse, Hanchon, because the white man taught you how to read and memorize. The white man's school taught you something damn useful, didn't it? Too bad you turned your back on civilization and went back to the blanket. But then, once an animal, always an animal."

"Funny," Touch the Sky said, "how you can drive a man out at gunpoint and talk about his 'turning his back on civilization.' Anyhow, there's no animal on earth lower and more cowardly than a white man."

"You don't seem to get the drift," Abbot Fontaine growled. "You best cut the guff, you ain't in charge here."

"Bend a gun barrel over his flea-bitten head!" the other gunman shouted. "Hell, I'll air him right now!"

"Stoney!" Hiram snapped. "Lower your hammers, both of you. All in good time. I've been waiting years for this moment. Now I've finally got this red sonofabitch pinned in the dirt, let me see him squirm a little before I step on him."

He looked at Touch the Sky, baiting him with another grin. "You keep using your tongue for a shovel, blanket ass, and you'll dig your own grave with it. There's something else that treaty says, too. It's called Article Eleven. Comes right on the last page. Right next to the spot where all the big Cheyenne and Sioux chiefs made their mark. You recall Article Eleven?"

Touch the Sky held his face impassive, saying nothing. But a strong premonition of disaster iced his blood as he read the malevolent depths of Steele's cold, flint-gray eyes. This was not just a mean, hateful, and hidebound man—he was on a mission of vengeance.

"Drew a blank on Article Eleven, huh? Let me refresh your memory."

Steele pulled a tow pouch from under the seat and removed a sheaf of papers. He sifted through them until he found the passage he sought.

"Article Eleven," he announced, "of a treaty signed on April 15th, 1859, by legal representatives of the Northern Cheyenne people, the U.S. Army's Department of Wyoming, and the U.S. Bureau of Indian Affairs. Listen up, Hanchon.

" 'It is further understood that all conditions of this treaty are contingent upon a good-faith agreement by both parties, to wit: The violation of any major clause of this agreement, by either party, invalidates the agreement and terminates the special legal rights of the signees.' "

Still grinning, Steele put the papers away and

looked at the Cheyenne again. "Once the commanding officer at Fort Bates certifies sufficient violations, all the land hereabouts reverts to the public domain. That means it also falls under the new Homestead Act. Whoever proves it up gets clear title."

"I know every clause of that treaty," Touch the Sky said. "My people have violated none of them."

Steele laughed outright, thoroughly enjoying himself. "Well now, Hanchon, things could change. That's why me and my darling little girl here are moving back to this area. I learned a long time ago that the first man on the scene always stands to profit."

"Especially when that man's got the morals of a scalp seller," Touch the Sky said.

In an eyeblink Abbot Fontaine's shotgun was aimed at Touch the Sky again.

"Quit sugar-talkin' this bastard, boss. Give me the word and he's stew meat."

"You got it. *Kill* him!"

"No!" Kristen screamed again, struggling against her father's iron grip furiously enough to edge into the line of fire.

Touch the Sky deliberately nudged his pony sideways so the shot pattern would miss her. He thought about rolling off his pony, a move he had practiced often, but he was too late. An eyeblink later a loud report echoed out across the rippling waves of grass, and Kristen shrieked in terror.

One of the mules pulling the lead wagon suddenly slumped dead in the traces. Abbot Fontaine's fingers froze before the shotgun went off.

Touch the Sky held his face expressionless and showed no surprise, hiding his relief at his comrades' quick thinking. Now he thanked *Maiyun* that Little Horse had asked for the field glasses.

"You have eyes to see. Rifle sights are trained on all of you," he announced. "Do as you please. But know this. Make sure my death means all to you. For the warriors of my tribe kill two enemies for every dead Cheyenne."

This last remark was directed at Abbot Fontaine and Stoney MacGruder. Touch the Sky tugged hard on the buffalo-hair reins, turning his pony and riding off.

"Freeze, you sonofabitch, or I'll hind-end you with buckshot!" Fontaine roared.

"Hanchon!" Steele shouted. "Hanchon, you bastard, I'm not done talking at you!"

But not once, despite the threats and curses and the sawed-off shotgun, did Touch the Sky pause or look back.

Chapter Three

Honey Eater loved these peaceful moments at dawn.

Cheyennes, like most of their Plains Indians neighbors, recognized no official "bedtime." When not on the war path or engaged in the annual hunts, braves often slept until sunset and then caroused all night throughout the noisy camp. They were insatiable gamblers, and bets were placed on everything from foot and pony races to stone-throwing contests.

But now the entire camp, even the dogs, lay wrapped in deep sleep. Shifting pockets of mist floated out over the river. From the surrounding trees grebes, willets, thrushes, and larks sent up their collective dawn chorus. Honey Eater moved slowly among the silent tipis and lodges, enjoying a few blessed moments of peace and solitude before the brutal misery of her daily existence once again caught up with her.

As always, Honey Eater had braided fresh white columbine petals through her hair. She was uncommonly pretty, with delicately sculpted cheekbones, wing-shaped eyes, and the supple body of young womanhood. No one had trouble believing this woman of such proud and gracious bearing was the daughter of the great chief Yellow Bear—Yellow Bear, who in his youth fought beside Arrow Keeper at Wolf Creek, when they smeared their bodies in Kiowa and Comanche blood and saved the Cheyenne Nation from destruction.

But now, the troubled young Cheyenne woman thought bitterly, her dead father's glory was worth less than smoke blown behind her. For if it mattered, how could her lot be so hard and miserable?

As if guided by a will of their own, her feet threaded their way toward a lone tipi which stood on a hummock apart from the others. Ever since joining them Touch the Sky had always been forced to live separately because he had no official clan circle to join. Nor had the independent loner petitioned to join one of the soldier societies as most young warriors did. He remained always loyal, but ever aloof.

Now, of course, with Arrow Keeper's abrupt disappearance he must live separately because he was the new tribe shaman and Keeper of the Arrows. Honey Eater had finally understood that it was his lonely destiny to be among them without truly belonging—not so long as his enemies had breath in their nostrils to play the fox against him.

She stopped in front of his silent tipi. Her eyes swept the ground before the closed entrance flap. Then she spotted it, just past the cooking tripod: a soft white glimmer like foxfire.

A smile touched her lips as she recognized the fist-sized chunk of white marble. Her throat pinching closed at the memory, Honey Eater recalled that terrible ordeal when she had been taken prisoner by Henri Lagace and his murderous whiskey traders.

All night long she had been forced to listen while they mercilessly tortured Touch the Sky, trying to force him to reveal where his comrades were hidden. And at the height of his misery, sure he was about to die, he had called out to her in Cheyenne:

Honey Eater! Do you know that I love you? I have placed a rock on the ground in front of my tipi. When that rock melts, so too will my love for you.

There lay the rock, she told herself as hot tears welled from her eyes. Unmelted, like his strong and solid love. But what did it matter? Thanks to Wolf Who Hunts Smiling and the others, Touch the Sky would never gain full acceptance—indeed, would never even be safe to sleep at night. Their love was clearly as ill-fated as the destiny of the Cheyenne people—a great promise that could never be fulfilled.

"Your randy buck cannot let you sneak into his tipi to join him," came a bitter voice behind her, making Honey Eater flinch hard and then whirl around.

There stood Black Elk, fierce and angry in the grainy light! "He has gone off to drink strong water at the trading post with his hair-face masters, remember? But pine not. Your honorary white man will soon return and put on the old moccasin with my squaw!"

"Black Elk," Honey Eater said quietly, her proud indignation warring with her fear of his jealous wrath. "How can this thing be? You are this tribe's war leader, and a good choice was made. Never have you let your tribe down when danger loomed, nor has a more fearless Cheyenne ever worn the Medicine Hat into battle. But do you hear your own words to me? The worm of jealousy has cankered at your brain. You have always been hard to Touch the Sky from the first days of his warrior training. But there was a time when you tried to be fair to him. You were better—you are *still* better— than your despicable cousin Wolf Who Hunts Smiling. But now you let him and that low coward Medicine Flute beguile you with their twisted words. He works on your jealousy, using it to further his own treasonous plans."

Black Elk had been momentarily surprised by Honey Eater's conciliatory tone when she genuinely praised his bravery. But now heat surged into his face.

"You treacherous she-bitch, ride herd on your disrespectful tongue before I cut it from your throat! How dare you question the affairs of men! My cousin has eyes to see what *every* loyal Cheyenne in this tribe can see.

"He was right when he aptly named this pretend Cheyenne White Man Runs Him. His white stink has twice ruined the buffalo hunts. River of Winds, the most trusted brave in this camp, swears he saw him leaving messages for Long Knives in the hollow of a tree. He also swears he saw him holding a white woman in his blanket for love talk.

"Yet *still* you deny me my son by lusting after Woman Face instead of a loyal Cheyenne like your husband! You accepted my gift of horses and married me. Now, by pining for him, you close your womb to my seed."

This was raving madness, and the crazy glint in Black Elk's eyes sent cold, numbing fear to the marrow of her bones. She longed with all her being to scream in his face: I was *forced* to marry you. For Touch the Sky had apparently deserted his tribe, and when her father died, Cheyenne law would not permit her to live alone.

But Honey Eater bit back any further reply, convinced that another word might provoke him to leap forward and kill her. He had already beaten her, bull-whipped her, cut off her long and beautiful braids to publicly shame her into doing her duty. Next time, his pent-up rage would kill her.

The thought of something else niggled at her. What was Black Elk doing lately that caused him to rise so early like this and ride out even before the old grandmothers sang the song to the new sun rising? Usually he and his fellow Bull Whip troopers were among the latest of the nightly revelers, seldom rising before Sister Sun was halfway across the sky.

As if he sensed her suspicion, Black Elk abruptly calmed himself. A mean smile twisted his lips. *This* was the fierce warrior who once routed thirty Apaches from breastworks, she thought with a shudder.

"You have denied me my son," he repeated. "You have chosen to cast your lot with a spy raised by our enemy. So it is, things are the way they are. Shaming you has not worked. Perhaps taking you out on the prairie and leaving you for any man to enjoy would teach you some humility, at least.

"As for your white man's dog, he once made great sport of humiliating me with paleface tricks. Soon you and this entire tribe will see your noble warrior groveling in the dirt—close to the worms his dead flesh will soon feed."

"Do not hit with just your fists," the Sioux brave named Sting Hands told Black Elk. "The best hair-faced boxers swing from their heels. And do not aim *at* an opponent. Aim *through* him. Pretend you are hitting a point well behind him. That way you strike with more force."

Sting Hands spoke in the combination of

Sioux and Cheyenne words that was easily understood by these two cousin tribes, longtime battle allies who often made camp near each other for protection. He was a huge man and, like Black Elk, heavily muscled for a Plains Indian, most of whom were slender of limb compared to white men.

"Also," Sting Hands said, "you are still fighting with hatred as your animus. Fury makes a man wild, true. But it needlessly wastes energy which should be applied to a quick defeat. A cold, emotionless fighter who punches with zeal will win every time over an angry opponent. Have you seen a wolverine close for the kill?"

Black Elk nodded.

"Well then, Cheyenne! Take a lesson, for the small and light wolverine is the quickest and most vicious killer of them all. Nor does this mighty fighter waste time in empty snarling and spitting. It homes in directly for the kill, all senses boldly pressed to one purpose, complete defeat."

Without warning, Sting Hands suddenly threw a hard right jab at Black Elk. With incredibly quick reflexes, Black Elk threw a perfect left-forearm block. But as taught, he didn't waste the block in a mere defensive movement. He turned the forearm block into a thrust to unbalance Sting Hands. At the same time, he punched up from the hip with his right fist and landed a solid uppercut on the point of the Sioux's jaw.

Sting Hands's head snapped back so fast that

his teeth clacked audibly. He landed hard on his back in the grass.

A cheer erupted from several spectators scattered around a makeshift boxing ring rigged from buffalo-hair ropes and young saplings. Among the Sioux faces were two more Cheyennes from Gray Thunder's camp: Wolf Who Hunts Smiling and his new shadow, Medicine Flute.

"Well done, Cousin!" Wolf Who Hunts Smiling shouted. "The Mah-ish-ta-shee-da have brought very little to our land that is useful. They brought their cholera to wipe out our villages. They brought their whiskey to unman our warriors. But this odd fighting called boxing—*here* they brought us something worthy. For like guns, it can be turned against them!"

Wolf Who Hunts Smiling had used the original Cheyenne name for white men, *Mah-ish-ta-shee-da* or "Yellow Eyes," because the first whites they saw were mountain men with severe jaundice. Black Elk nodded, reaching one hand out to help his friend Sting Hands stand up.

The Sioux still rubbed his sore jaw, an approving glint in his eyes. He beamed proudly at his apt pupil.

"Black Elk, place my words in your sash. It has been ten winters now since a fur trapper from across the Great Waters taught me this fighting. During that time I have earned fine trade goods by boxing in fights arranged by the blue-blouses. I am paid nothing if I lose, so usually I win. And never, Cheyenne brother, have I been hit better than you just hit me. I have taught you well. Indeed, you have grown beyond my instruction."

"But you will never grow beyond my gratitude or respect, Sting Hands. You have taught me another useful art of war."

Sting Hands was older than Black Elk. Thick scar tissue crowded his eyes, and his nose had been broken so often it was covered with lumps.

"You were an eager pupil. But never forget what I have told you about fighting from hatred."

Despite his genuine respect for this capable Sioux brave, Black Elk's obedient nod was not sincere. How could he *not* be consumed with hatred? How long now had he seethed, desperate for revenge, since the time Touch the Sky had used white man's fist-fighting to pummel him senseless?

But beating him to the ground hadn't been enough. That woman-faced mock Cheyenne had taunted him while he did it! *"See* what this dog learned from his white masters!" he had goaded as he rained jabs and punches on the helpless Black Elk. Now Black Elk was finally prepared to reward one humiliation with another.

Later, ready to ride back to the Powder River camp, Black Elk, Wolf Who Hunts Smiling, and Medicine Flute walked out toward the common corral where their ponies grazed with the Sioux herd.

Judd Cole

"Cousin," Wolf Who Hunts Smiling said, producing something from the pouch of his clout, "did Sting Hands show you these?"

Black Elk, lost in thoughts of his looming confrontation with Touch the Sky, glanced carelessly at the strange objects in his cousin's hand.

"Why would Sting Hands show me these? What are they?"

"These are the crooked nails hair-faces use to fasten shoes on their horses. The Sioux brave named Crow Killer explained it to me. See, look here. See how easily they slip over the knuckles? The white soldiers call them drinking jewelry."

Black Elk's famous impatience flared quickly. "Cousin, there was a time when you only mentioned white soldiers to call for their death. Now you tell me how they adorn their bodies when they drink their devil water. You have spent too much time with this lazy, skinny flute blower. You are losing the warrior's dignity and scorn for trivial matters."

Medicine Flute, lately aware of his growing influence as a shaman rival to Touch the Sky, scowled when he was insulted. But before he could protest this, Wolf Who Hunts Smiling shot him a warning glance.

"Cousin," he said patiently, "you miss the meat of my point. The soldiers wear these on their hands in a *fight*."

Suddenly Black Elk did understand. A rare grin slowly divided his face. "I would need nothing like these to defeat Woman Face," he boasted.

"No," his cousin agreed. "But each blow would hurt him more."

"Perhaps," Medicine Flute put in casually, "they might even kill him. In an unarmed fight, a death would not be called murder. Thus, the Sacred Arrows would not be stained or Black Elk shunned."

Black Elk liked the sound of this. He looked at Medicine Flute with a bit more respect. Touch the Sky dead! Pounded to death in front of Honey Eater and the rest—this prospect of revenge was sweeter to Black Elk than the lure of absolute power or the promise of great wealth.

"And with White Man Runs Him sent under," Wolf Who Hunts Smiling suggested carefully, "there would be no one to interfere if a certain brave chose to discipline his squaw, as men must occasionally do."

Black Elk nodded. His wily cousin was being deferential. But he was also tactfully reminding Black Elk of Touch the Sky's well known promise, made the last time Black Elk laid a hand on Honey Eater: Hurt her again, and Sacred Arrows or no, Touch the Sky swore to kill him.

Finally Black Elk extended his hand. Wolf Who Hunts Smiling dropped the lethal "drinking jewelry" into Black Elk's palm.

"Wait for me just a bit, bucks," Wolf Who Hunts Smiling said after they had cut out their ponies from the herd. He handed his halter to

Medicine Flute. "Hold my pony. I saluted the four directions with a brave and left my best pipe in his tipi. I will be right back."

Because he was always scheming and currying influence, Wolf Who Hunts Smiling visited this Lakota Sioux village often. He knew it, and its occupants, well. Their peace chief, Pony Saver, had married a Southern Cheyenne woman. Cheyenne visitors were free to roam the camp paths at will, as were their Arapaho allies.

It was a busy camp, and he was paid scant attention as he made his way quickly to a tipi standing in the Spotted Owl Clan circle. Unlike Cheyennes, the Sioux placed no privacy flap over their tipi entrances. Thus, after glancing carefully around him, it was an easy matter to duck quickly into the tipi of the brave named Crow Killer.

Wolf Who Hunts Smiling knew this young brave well. Often they had come here to share a pipe of fragrant kinnikinick and recite their coups. It was here that Crow Killer taught him about the horseshoe nails. So Wolf Who Hunts Smiling knew that Crow Killer had joined a Sioux raiding party that was now heading into the mountains to harass the turncoat Utes.

He also knew about a trophy Crow Killer kept hidden under his heavy sleeping robes.

He was forced to squint in the dim light slanting in through the smokehole at the top. Quickly, knowing Black Elk would soon be fuming with impatience to leave, Wolf Who Hunts Smiling threw the smelly, scratchy buffalo hides aside.

Relief glinted in his eyes when he saw the weapon lying there. It was a two-shot, cap-and-ball dragoon pistol that Crow Killer had captured from a blue-bloused soldier in the battle at Crying Horse Canyon. The customized weapon was too beautiful to ruin by regular use. Fancy hand-cut scrollwork covered the barrel, and the metal had been mirror-polished and then coated with silver.

Wolf Who Hunts Smiling was familiar with this model. It was extremely accurate for a side-arm. It fired a huge, conical ball so heavy and powerful that a hit to an arm or leg was often as not fatal.

Crow Killer would be gone for many sleeps yet. And best of all: No one at the Cheyenne camp possessed a gun like this.

So when Touch the Sky was found with a fist-sized hole blown through him, no Cheyenne would be suspected. It would be blamed on soldiers.

Never mind this boxing contest coming up, thought Wolf Who Hunts Smiling. Black Elk was in formidable condition to administer a beating—maybe he really could kill Woman Face. But how many times had Wolf Who Hunts Smiling watched this tall Cheyenne slip from Death's grip like a fish from a wet hand?

No. He was the only major obstacle now standing between Wolf Who Hunts Smiling and control of most of the Red Nation. Once Wolf Who Hunts Smiling raised high the lance of leadership, he would command a war of extermination. The bones of white men—and all Indians who cooperated with them—would be strewn from the Rio Bravo to the Marias.

Black Elk would get his chance. But even if he fails, Wolf Who Hunts Smiling thought as he hid the pistol in his pouch, this cat-and-mouse game was finally going to be over.

Chapter Four

At the trading post in Red Shale, the Cheyennes' various animal pelts were pressed tightly into standard "packs" for shipment back to the warehouses in New Orleans.

Beaver-fur hats were no longer the rage in London, so prices were down for those plews. But the braves had red fox and other long-hair furs of good value. Their worth was computed and taken out in powder, lead, ball, wiping-patches and bullet moulds as well as coffee, sugar, calico and medicines.

The proprietor was impressed by Touch the Sky's excellent English and sharp arithmetical skills. He made no attempt to hornswaggle the young Indians and even threw in some free peppermint candy for the children and a magnifying glass for Little Horse.

"Brothers," Tangle Hair said during the ride back to camp, "the traders usually treat us better than other white men do. We make them rich and they are wise enough to see this."

"As you say," Two Twists agreed. "But it is not always just the riches. Some of them take Indian wives and learn our language. A few are even initiated into our soldier societies and sit at council. These things are not necessary simply to earn gold. A few whites there are who admire us and choose to live as red men."

This truth silenced them all. For truly not one Indian here considered most hair faces their friends. Yet, there could be no higher compliment than these whites who lived as Indians. They were highly respected throughout the Red Nation, for they had mastered two cultures and were thus doubly formidable as warriors. Nor could Touch the Sky and the rest not be aware of it: He, himself, was a man of two cultures. Yet, unlike these respected whites, he was shunned in both worlds.

Touch the Sky said, "Arrow Keeper once told me that an entire people can never be our enemy. He told me that when you encounter a poisonous snake, you do not kill it for being a snake. For indeed, most snakes are friendly. You kill it for being *poisonous*."

Despite these conciliatory words, Touch the Sky was plagued by the question: What was a poisonous snaked named Hiram Steele up to this time?

Whatever it was, he knew Steele would do the

hurt dance on the Cheyenne tribe. And once again the flint-hearted "businessman" was dragging Kristen along to give his illegal schemes the veneer of family respectability. No man—white or red—could look into the depths of Kristen's bottomless blue eyes and believe she was spawned by an evil father. Steele banked on that.

Touch the Sky's comrades, especially Little Horse, knew the encounter with Hiram Steele and his daughter had left him in a gloomy, preoccupied mood. Wisely they held back from questions, for warriors were reluctant to broach private matters. But it was clear to all of them that, soon, they would face a new battle.

Touch the Sky's group reached camp just before sunset. They rubbed their tired ponies down with clumps of sage and turned them loose to graze with the herd. Then they left the goods with Spotted Tail, leader of the Bow String soldier society.

The highly regarded Bow Strings would portion the goods equally to the clan Headmen for distribution to the people. Touch the Sky had lived among Indians long enough to recognize one trait, especially, which distinguished them from whites: With rare exceptions such as Wolf Who Hunts Smiling, few Indians placed themselves ahead of their tribe. In times of plenty, all ate; in leaner times, all starved. The fate of one was the fate of all.

Touch the Sky saw no sign of Honey Eater as

Judd Cole

he crossed to his tipi on its lone hummock between the river and the camp. Nor of Black Elk or his wily cousin. Yet there seemed to be a feeling of tense expectation in the air. Small groups of men had gathered quietly throughout camp. Many of them studiously ignored Touch the Sky.

But at the moment his thoughts were of a coyote-fur pouch hidden in his tipi.

Touch the Sky borrowed a glowing coal from a nearby fire Then he ducked under the flap of his tipi and lit the kindling in his firepit. Soon the fragrant smell of sweet grass and osage wood filled the tipi.

He found the fur pouch where he'd left it, wrapped in oilskin and hidden under his sleeping robes. Touch the Sky unwrapped the soft fur to reveal the four ceremonial arrows within. Painted in blue and yellow stripes, the flint-tipped shafts were fletched with bright red feathers.

Arrow Keeper's mysterious departure left everyone unsure if the venerable old medicine man still lived. When he left, protecting the Sacred Arrows became the responsibility of his chosen apprentice in the shamanic arts— Touch the Sky.

At first Touch the Sky had hidden them outside of his tipi, fearing his enemies might otherwise harm them. But Wolf Who Hunts Smiling secretly stole them and gave them to his ally, the Blackfoot "contrary warrior" known as Sis-ki-dee. Only a harrowing quest to

50

Sis-ki-dee's fortress atop Wendigo Mountain had saved them—and thus, the tribe—from destruction. Since then, Touch the Sky could only trust to fate and leave the Arrows in his tipi.

Every Cheyenne believed that the fate of the sacred Medicine Arrows represented the fate of his tribe. Any crime against a fellow Cheyenne was a crime against the Arrows—and thus, a crime against the entire tribe. It was "the thought of the Arrows" that held many an angry brave back from a violent act against a fellow Cheyenne.

As the Keeper of the Arrows it was Touch the Sky's responsibility to keep the Arrows safe, forever sweet and clean. The darkest days in all Cheyenne history occurred when Pawnees seized the Medicine Arrows. All manner of disease and ill luck had befallen the tribe until they were recovered.

Assured they were safe, Touch the Sky wrapped the Arrows again and put them away. But he couldn't put away this other trouble—this new problem with the arrival of Hiram Steele. And Black Elk's recent words still plagued him: *Killing a man is less satisfying than humiliating him and then leaving him alive to steep in his shame. The worm will turn, Woman Face.*

Touch the Sky held the entrance flap aside and again gazed out over the camp. Clan fires now blazed here and there, loosing streamers of bright orange sparks. Far across camp, on the opposite side of the central clearing, he

51

could see a huge fire blazing in front of Medicine Flute's tipi. A knot of braves was gathered there, Wolf Who Hunts Smiling at the center of them.

Touch the Sky frowned so deeply that a furrow formed between his eyebrows. Here was more trouble about to erupt. For everyone knew that Wolf Who Hunts Smiling championed Medicine Flute as the tribe's only 'shaman.' The Cheyenne people placed great faith in supernaturalism and visions. Who controlled a tribe's medicine thus controlled its destiny—a truth Wolf Who Hunts Smiling had grasped firmly by the tail.

Medicine Flute was as wily as his new friend and much lazier. So far the two schemers held many in thrall with their clever deceptions. They had even once learned secretly of a comet that was due to pass overhead—Wolf Who Hunts Smiling announced that Medicine Flute would "set a star on fire and send it blazing across the sky." The subsequent "miracle" convinced many that Medicine Flute's magic was real and powerful—that it was Touch the Sky who pretended to shamanic skills.

In the midst of these reflections, Touch the Sky became aware of the hollow drumbeat of hooves. The camp crier flew by on his pony, spreading an urgent announcement:

"Meet in the common clearing! Our war leader would address the entire tribe! Black Elk waits for his people in the common clearing!"

*   *   *

In a heartbeat, Touch the Sky understood.

All the signs and portents: His medicine dreams, Black Elk's recent threats, the groups of men—mostly Bull Whip troopers—working hard to "ignore" him when he rode back from the trading post.

It all pointed to one truth, clear as a blood spoor in new snow: His enemies within the tribe were moving against him, and decisively.

In the leaping spear-tips of flame, he glanced toward his percussion-action Sharps rifle. The bore was charged and there was a cap behind the loading gate. But his intuition quickly assured him to leave his weapons behind.

Whatever they had in mind for him, he wouldn't defeat it with a lead ball. Nor would he make a mockery of everything Arrow Keeper taught him to believe. Taking up arms in camp against fellow Indians was a barbaric Comanche trait, not Cheyenne behavior.

Several huge fires served as giant torches, casting eerie yellow-orange illumination over the figures streaming into the clearing. Touch the Sky was joined by his friends as he entered the clearing. All of them appeared to sense, as did Touch the Sky, that a bold new move was planned against the hapless warrior.

So without comment, they made a pattern which had become almost second nature to them. Little Horse, Two Twists, and Tangle Hair formed a triangle with Touch the Sky as the center. When anyone threatened to enter the triangle, they quickly tightened up.

His lips set in a determined slit, Touch the Sky did not bother with hanging back. He pushed boldly forward to the place where Black Elk stood in the clearing.

Chief Gray Thunder soon arrived and also pushed forward. The still-vigorous warrior could not hide his curiosity. Nor could Spotted Tail, leader of the Bow String soldiers.

But Touch the Sky noticed something else: None of the Whips looked at all curious. Just expectant. Clearly, their barely suppressed smiles said, a fine entertainment is at hand!

By chance, Touch the Sky's eyes abruptly met Honey Eater's.

She stood with her favorite aunt, Sharp Nosed Woman, partly hidden behind one corner of the hide-covered council lodge. Her desperate eyes warned him to leave. But Arrow Keeper had taught Touch the Sky long ago that a boil would not go away until it was lanced.

Now he met Black Elk's triumphant eyes in the flickering firelight. Though they looked back at him with murderous rage, Touch the Sky reserved the true heat of his own anger for those mocking orbs of Wolf Who Hunts Smiling and Medicine Flute. It was *these* two who had pricked constantly at the open sore of Black Elk's jealousy, goading him to this madness now.

As if by previous accord, the assemblage fell silent. A few young children asked questions but were quickly hushed. Two dogs began a growling fight. But they raced toward the river, yelping in fright, when a Bull Whip soldier lashed them hard with his knotted-thong whip.

"Fathers and brothers!" Black Elk shouted. "Cheyenne people! You know me, all of you know me! I have smoked the common pipe with many of you. The same lips that touched that pipe speak now. Breathes there a Cheyenne among us who can say that Black Elk ever hid in his tipi while his brothers were on the war path?"

"Black Elk, count upon it. If *we* were on the war path, *you* were our scout!" a warrior shouted, and a chorus of approval backed him up.

Black Elk and Touch the Sky stared at each other with mutual defiance, neither willing to look away first.

"As you say," Black Elk resumed. "And when a certain white man's dog was allowed to drift in among us, I and my cousin, and some others, spoke harshly against his white man's ways."

The fire behind Black Elk suddenly whooshed higher as a dry cottonwood log caught flame. A swirling trail of sparks shot into the night sky.

"But we were wrong to show contempt for every paleface custom," Black Elk said, stepping closer to Touch the Sky. "Indeed, *this* one standing before me even showed me a useful white practice."

Touch the Sky never saw the punch coming and didn't realize he'd been hit until he was sitting on the ground, his skull ringing.

After the initial surprised silence, some of the people murmured their disapproval. But they were drowned out by a chorus of approving shouts from the Bull Whips.

Touch the Sky tasted the salt tang of blood and felt his lips already swelling. The hit had been powerful and it was hard to get his thoughts flowing. In that confused state, he made the mistake of standing up.

"Your face for my son," Black Elk said in a low, hateful voice meant only for Touch the Sky. An eyeblink later a powerful right hook, followed by a left and then another right, made bright orange lights explode behind Touch the Sky's eyelids.

A wild cheer exploded from the Whips as Black Elk waded in quickly, driving his overwhelmed foe backward. Two quick jabs to the middle sent Touch the Sky reeling to the ground again.

The powerful blows had come in quick, deadly succession. His thoughts raced about like frenzied rodents, and for a moment he wanted to give in and pass out. But the warrior in him rallied, and he shook his head a few times to clear it. Droplets of blood flew from his nose and mouth and from an ugly cut under his left eye.

Just before he rose, Touch the Sky glimpsed his three best friends. Despite the concern clearly etched into their faces, Touch the Sky knew they wouldn't interfere so long as the fight was one on one. They would rather see a fellow warrior die than humiliate him by fighting his battle for him. Instead, they kept an eye on Wolf Who Hunts Smiling, Medicine Flute, Swift Canoe, and certain others who daily prayed this tall Cheyenne into the ground.

This time when Touch the Sky stood up, he rose on the offensive.

He had been a fair boxer during his life among the white men. At 16 he had sent the cavalry officer Seth Carlson sprawling into the dirt. He threw a good feint at Black Elk with his left, then followed with his right.

With incredible speed and dexterity, mocking him with a smile the whole time, Black Elk merely rolled his head away from the feint. He easily blocked the right-hand blow with the outside edge of his left forearm.

The right he landed hit Touch the Sky so hard it sent off a spray of blood and saliva. The ground rushed up to meet him. Touch the Sky tasted blood and dirt, and felt explosions of pain with each heartbeat.

"Mighty shaman!" Wolf Who Hunts Smiling taunted. "All his 'visions' now are of twigs and dirt!"

"Oh, tall Bear Caller!" a Whip shouted. "Summon a grizzly to stop this killer elk!"

Another chorus of laughter. Touch the Sky struggled up from the dirt. His eyes met Honey Eater's again. Her worry had given way to near panic—the kill-glint sparked in Black Elk's eyes. Yet despite the concern of Chief Gray Thunder and others, no one moved to stop this.

Indeed, no one knew exactly how to handle this. No weapons were involved, so the usual camp police—the soldier societies—were reluctant to interfere. And truly, the camp had never been confronted with a fistfight.

Touch the Sky felt his will to fight seeping out with his blood. Then the words came back to him from the hinterland of memory—Arrow Keeper's words, spoken when Touch the Sky had nearly given up during his initiation ordeal at Medicine Lake:

As the twig is bent, so the tree shall grow. If you cannot endure this small thing here today, how will you stand and fight when the war cry sounds? When the blood of your people stains the earth?

How will you stand and fight?

. . . stand and fight . . . stand and fight . . . stand and fight!

When he came up this time, the desperate youth butted his head hard into Black Elk's stomach. Touch the Sky had the weight advantage and drove his adversary off balance. He followed up with a flurry of well-landed blows that drove the arrogant smile off Black Elk's face.

"Who held at Buffalo Creek?" Little Horse suddenly shouted—alluding to the heroic battle when he and Touch the Sky had stood back-to-back and held off a score of white buffalo hiders.

Hearing this, Touch the Sky set his mouth in its straight, determined line. A crashing right fist actually unwrapped Black Elk's braid.

"Who beat Sis-ki-dee on Wendigo Mountain?" Two Twists yelled, and Touch the Sky smashed a left jab into Black Elk's throat.

"Who counted first coup at Tongue River?" Tangle Hair roared, and the next punch put Black Elk on the ground.

Touch the Sky's foe was down. But the near-superhuman effort, on top of the savage beating Black Elk had given him, left Touch the Sky's calves weak as water. So much blood ran in his eyes that he could barely see.

Few paid attention when Wolf Who Hunts Smiling moved in closer. "Cousin," he said quietly, "don't forget. You can hit harder. Much harder."

Touch the Sky was too groggy to see anything sinister in the comment. He hardly noticed when Black Elk's fists disappeared for a moment inside the pouch on the front of his clout.

He came up quicker than Touch the Sky expected. The tall warrior ducked the first punch, side-stepped the second.

And then his world exploded to black nothingness as a fist like iron knocked him senseless.

For Black Elk, despite his elation, it wasn't quite over yet.

True, inside he was swelling with satisfied pride. As his worst enemy lay vanquished at his feet, he triumphantly met Honey Eater's eyes. Still holding them, he pulled his obsidian knife from its beaded sheath.

"No!" he shouted, even as Touch the Sky's

friends surged forward to stop him. "I am not going to scalp this dog! But move to stop me, and I *will* kill him!"

Staggering, he knelt, clutched the unconscious brave's long hair, wrapped it once around his wrist. Black Elk knew he would be severely punished by the Headmen for scalping this one. But custom was clear—it would be humiliation enough to take the proud warrior's long locks.

A cheer erupted from the Bull Whips when Black Elk severed the locks and crammed them into his sash. Mortified, Little Horse, Two Twists, Tangle Hair, and Honey Eater watched Wolf Who Hunts Smiling step forward for the final humiliating touch: He covered the downed warrior with a woman's shawl, for dressing a brave as a woman was the worst insult one warrior could inflict on another.

"Behold!" Medicine Flute shouted. "Thanks to Black Elk, our mighty shaman and Keeper of the Arrows lies napping! Good thing Wolf Who Hunts Smiling has covered Woman Face with a shawl. *She* will stay warm now while she dreams of her white masters!"

Chapter Five

"The Homestead Act didn't pass this year," Hiram Steele complained, "because the Quakers and the Indian lovers in Congress pitched it as the Devil's own work. But it'll pass soon, Soldier Blue, and you can take my prediction to the bank. Trying to stop frontier expansion is like trying to hold the ocean back with a broom."

Captain Seth Carlson, blouse unbuttoned for evening, picked up a carboy of bourbon from a sideboard and filled his glass. "Stop it? What, for a double handful of illiterate aboriginals who never figured out how to harness the wheel? The paper-collar cowards in Washington have taken the best chunk of this country and set it aside for thieving, murdering, soulless beasts who top their own mothers."

"Hear, hear! You and I, Carlson, are flying the

61

same colors on this land-set-aside malarkey. If a law is tarnal foolishness, a man has a right to break it."

The two men were conducting business over drinks in Steele's library. Steele had scoured the country until he found and rented this roomy frame house in secluded Blackford Valley. Strategically located close to Fort Bates, it was nonetheless well north of the river-bend settlement of Bighorn Falls. This way Steele had room for his bodyguards and could meet regularly with Carlson while avoiding the hostile residents of Bighorn Falls. He still faced vigilante justice there, if they caught him, for murder and attempted murder in his terror campaign to destroy John and Sarah Hanchon—a campaign thwarted by their Indian son.

"Now, you consider that huge tract set aside for the Northern Cheyenne," Steele resumed, pacing the room as his agitation grew. "The most fertile ground in this part of the territory! And damn the government's blind eyes if they didn't include *two* major rivers into the deal, thus depriving every hard-working white man of a drop of that water."

Spots of angry blood stippled his cheeks. Steele stopped in front of a huge Mercator map of the Montana and Wyoming Territories. One stubby index finger traced the winding course of the Powder River.

"Here, along this stretch between Sloan's Ford and Medicine Bend, is some of the most fertile soil in America. I've read the reports filed by Army topographers. It's rich Canadian top-soil, pushed down centuries ago by the gla-ciers."

Carlson said, "Can't tell you much about gla-ciers or topographers. But I know what the farmboys in my unit tell me. They say dirt where nut trees grow is the best farming soil in the world. A thousand times I've patrolled that stretch you just traced. There's so many nut trees thereabouts the men call it Gray Squirrel Trail."

Hiram grinned. "See there? Well, they better get used to calling it Grain Alley. To hell with feeding squirrels. That same dirt will produce the best oats and wheat and barley the world has seen. Only one problem. Rainfall. Once you get west of the 100th meridian, it drops off dra-matically and the short grass takes over. But thanks to the Powder, that can easily be cor-rected."

His finger tapped the map again. "Here, at Medicine Bend, a simple slope dam would re-route the Powder into an already existing net-work of dried-up creeks and rills. This would irrigate that entire stretch. Put it to good use, instead of letting it set empty just so a few buff can leave chips on it."

"The big herds are gone anyway," Carlson said. "The hiders have wiped them out around here."

"And a job well done. The quicker the buff

disappears, the quicker we'll get shed of the red Arabs, too."

"Speaking of which," Carlson said, "I take it you've got a plan for dealing with them?"

"*We've* got a plan, soldier. We. Let's not sugar-coat it, we've both been humbled and humbled bad by Matthew Hanchon. That filthy, stinking, gut-eating savage kissed my girl full on the mouth! God knows what else he's done to her. I couldn't be more ashamed if a daughter of mine whelped a darkie baby.

"And you! Why, man, she chose to love a Cheyenne over a graduate of West Point. One of Old Virginia's sons, heir to a tobacco fortune! I know that kind of mean treatment has to canker at you."

Carlson said nothing. But his jaw muscles bunched tighter as he recalled how Kristen wasn't the half of it. *That* shame was mostly private, at least. But there were also the times when Matthew Hanchon had humiliated him in front of his cavalry troop.

"Don't worry, I'll get to the Cheyennes directly," Steele said. "But first I want you to understand more of the actual plan. The Homestead Act *will* pass, count on it. But that act is only going to grant each citizen one section of 180 acres."

"That's a big farm back East, but not out here. How can we set up as land agents if all we got is 180 acres?"

"We can't. Which means we get set to acquire as many adjoining sections as we can."

"How, if there's only two of us?"

"Simple. The U.S. Army to the rescue. We'll pay selected, trustworthy men in your unit a small bonus for filing. Once they file separately, it's completely legal if they deed the land over to us later. Think they'll go along?"

"My men? Most of 'em would trade their peeders for a cup of 40-rod whiskey. But first we have to get the land rights back from the Cheyenne."

"That's where you come in. By the terms of the most recent treaty, a severe enough violation by the Cheyennes will invalidate the agreement."

Carlson nodded, catching on immediately. "Article Eleven. You're saying maybe we could *manufacture* a violation?"

"Or violations, plural. We'd need a good case to sway the Territorial Court. And from what I've heard of your new commanding officer, he's for pacifying the savages. It would need a string of incidents, I'm thinking."

"Colonel Thompson? You read him right. He's a good enough field soldier, commanded an artillery brigade in the Mexican War. He's not one for mollycoddling malcontents. But then again, he's also a devout Methodist. That spiritual crowd are convinced the savages can be converted by the Bible and the plow."

"Personally, I favor 'converting' redskins with bullets. But I plan to bring 'em plenty of plows. With your help."

Carlson's brow furrowed as he recalled

something. "Of course I'll help," he said. "Deal me in from here to harvest. But it seems to me that it's foolish to get a fox to play a coyote when real coyotes are available."

Steele's big, bluff face wrinkled in a frown. "No need to take the long way around the barn. I don't follow your drift."

"You say we want to make it appear that the Cheyennes have reneged on their treaty. Well, I can pick a few men and rub berry juice on their faces and teach 'em to loose a war whoop. Then we can attack way stations and whatnot. I worked with a gang that pulled the same trick up in the Bear Paw Mountains.

"But, Hiram, I'd call *that* taking the long way around the barn. It isn't just white men who hate this Indian. I got Indian scouts crawling all over this territory. They got their own Moccasin Telegraph, they hear things. And one of the things they hear is about a power-hungry Cheyenne named Wolf Who Hunts Smiling."

Steele followed all this closely, knowing Carlson was not one to speak for the sake of talking. "I like his name, anyway. It warns you right up front to watch your back-trail."

"So I hear. But the main thing is, he hates Matthew Hanchon. The only problem is, he can't figure out how to kill him."

"We haven't figured that out yet, either."

Carlson frowned, his eyes distant with some unpleasant memories. "No, we haven't. My Indian scouts swear Hanchon's life is charmed. I don't believe that pagan mumbo-jumbo. But sometimes, I wonder. . . . Anyhow, I got a Southern Cheyenne scout that knows this Wolf Who Hunts Smiling. Should I arrange a parley?"

Steele thought about it, then shrugged one beefy shoulder. "Hell, why not? We best face it now and be honest. We need whatever help we can get. Because you can chisel this in granite: If we *don't* kill Hanchon, this plan won't be worth dog meat."

"Kristen, I swear you're a godsend! You ever try to get a *man's* opinion when you're trimming a dress? 'Oh, it looks real pretty,' they say every time, no matter how terrible it really is. If you hadn't moved into this valley, my nearest female neighbor would be Holly Nearhood, thirty miles away in Bighorn Falls."

Laura Bishop interrupted herself long enough to hold up the emerald satin gown in her lap. "You like this scalloped lace, or is it too frilly?"

Kristen Steele, lost in reflection, seemed not to hear her friend at first. The two young women occupied wingback chairs in the cozy front parlor.

Kristen looked up from her own neglected sewing. "Hmm? Oh . . . too frilly? No, it looks very elegant."

"Well, it's simply impossible to know the fashions," Laura nattered on.

She was plain but pleasant and lively, with mischievous eyes and a mobile face that could go from silly to serious in a heartbeat.

"I try to read Godey's, when it's delivered," she added. "But by the time whatever I order is shipped out here, it's out of fashion. Do you know? Holly insisted that hair snoods were the latest thing. By the time mine arrived from St. Joe, Holly was telling me we can't wear our hair in chignons. La! Not that we have any reason to dress well. Oh, how I miss the cider parties and the hayrides back East!"

Kristen tried to attend to her friend while also listening to the drone of masculine voices behind the closed door of her father's library. Faint worry lines creased her brow. It had been a very unpleasant shock when Captain Seth Carlson had shown up this evening. Not only did his appearance revive unpleasant personal memories, but she knew it signaled new trouble for Matthew and his people.

Laura caught her glancing toward the door. Misunderstanding, she flashed her charming smile and lowered her voice confidentially.

"I can't blame you for being distracted. He's quite handsome. A bit arrogant, I thought, though he's clearly tamed by *you*. But the Army makes them arrogant. Do you know? My father says the enlisted Army is made up of common criminals. It takes tough officers to command such raffish trash."

"Sometimes," Kristen said quietly, "the raffish trash is commanding them. My friend Tom Riley is stationed at Fort Bates, too. Tom used to be an enlisted man. He served so honorably he was meritoriously appointed as an officer. The men under his command are certainly rough men. No doubt many of them *are* criminals—Tom says plaster saints don't live in tents or fight wild Indians. But crude or no, they're men of honor because their leader sets an honorable example."

Now her tone took on a bitter edge that made Laura go wide-eyed with surprise. "But Seth Carlson? He's in it for himself—just like my father. It isn't good enough to make a comfortable living. They are both mad with greed. And they've decided that they can't get rich without stealing from the Indians."

"Well," Laura said hesitantly, "your pa *is* a mean one, if you'll pardon my boldness. But do you know? That hireling of his, that Abbot Fontaine? That one has the snake eyes of a killer. His friend looks dumber, but I don't like him, either. I can't believe your father lets those crude men stay right here in the house."

"He has to," Kristen said grimly. "They're his bodyguards. My father's past business practices have ensured the need. I suspect his present plans will, too."

"La!" Laura said when her needle missed the thimble and pricked her finger. "Well, if you—"

The front door was abruptly thrown open. Abbot Fontaine and Stony MacGruder entered, boot heels trailing red clay across the rose-pattern carpet. Laura turned slightly pale, then tucked her chin and concentrated on her sewing.

"Well, now! Lookit here, Stoney. Two sweet young thangs sittin' all alone and goin' to waste like unplucked flowers. What say we pull up a chair and do us a little courtin' and sparkin'?"

Despite her abhorrence for Fontaine, Kristen's eyes stole an unwilling peek at that ugly musket-ball hole in his grizzle-bearded cheek. As always, he carried the sawed-off shotgun in its specially rigged sling. She had never seen him without it and suspected he even slept with it on.

"I wish," she said archly as the two huge, unkempt men flopped into chairs, "that you gentlemen wouldn't wear your spurs in the house. You've ruined that foot stool, Mr. Fontaine."

"Do tell?" He winked at Stoney. "Well now, that is a shame, a pure-dee shame, yessir, by Godfrey! Mrs. Fontaine's boy Abbot was raised to have real respect for quality folk like you, Miss Steele, he shorely was. But now your pa, see, he asked me and Stoney here to keep a good eye on you. He seems to think—ain't this a hoot?—that you're sweet on that-air tall Cheyenne buck we seen the other day."

Abbot winked at Stoney again. The latter was busy stripping Laura with his eyes. "Ain't that foolish of ol' Hiram, Stoney? I mean, thinkin' a *quality* woman like Miss Steele here would, ah, share her favors with a red Arab?"

"Why would a white woman even look at an Injin," Stoney said, "if there was white men to be had? 'Sides, does a dog mate with a cat? It ain't natchral."

Abbot nodded sagely. "There it is, Stoney, God's own truth." He stared hard at Kristen now. "Way this hoss sees it, a woman that cozies up to red men had by-God best be sweet to any white men who want her."

"That shines right," Stoney said. "Anyhow, nobody misses a slice off a cut loaf. If you ladies—"

"Laura," Kristen announced suddenly, her cheeks flaming at this outrageous and vulgar talk, "I'm sorry but I don't feel very well. I think I'll go to my room and lie down."

"La! I have to be flying, anyway," Laura said with hasty and desperate enthusiasm. "Pa will have a fit of dyspepsia if his dinner isn't on time."

Fontaine threw back his head and roared with laughter. "Good evening, ladies," he called out as they hastily gathered up their sewing materials. His eyes caught Kristen's for a moment. "Sleep tight, sugar britches," he added. "No need to fear them Cheyenne savages. I'm sleeping right across the hall from you."

Chapter Six

Although Touch the Sky regained awareness almost immediately after Black Elk beat him senseless, he bore the proof of his defeat for several sleeps.

It was not only his raggedly shorn hair, which Black Elk triumphantly bruited throughout the camp. His lips, nose, and eyes were grotesquely swollen; deep, grape-colored bruises covered much of his face; and that final punch had mysteriously left deep gashes that looked like the cuts made by Bluecoat canister shot.

"Brothers, have ears for my words!" Little Horse pronounced grimly two sleeps after the fight. He watched his friend bathe those odd gashes with a solution of yarrow tea and sassafras root. "This was the work of a weapon, not a fist."

"Black Elk's fists *are* weapons," Touch the Sky replied, wincing at the pain.

He and his comrades sat in warm sunlight near the river, filing arrow points. For Touch the Sky, nothing had changed after the fight. He merely resumed his normal routine as if nothing ever happened. Indeed, he spoke of the incident as if he had observed it rather than borne the brunt of it.

"They are weapons," he said again. "As surely as his lance or his bow. Where did he learn to fight that way?"

"No doubt from his friend Sting Hands, at Pony Saver's Lakota camp," Two Twists said. "The white soldiers put their best fighters against him. He defeats most of them."

"I, for one, believe it. He found an apt pupil in Black Elk," Touch the Sky said. The words were still slightly slurred by his swollen lips. "Brothers, I would rather have seen such skill demonstrated on another face than my own. But truly, Black Elk beat me. I only hope it sates his urge for greater mischief."

It was rare for Little Horse to show impatience with his friend. Yet he did so now.

"Brother, I have no ears for this. Is this Touch the Sky I hear? Or are you a white-livered Ponca who loads the very gun that kills you? When *you* defeated Black Elk with your fists, you did so for cause. And you fought him in private. You did not publicly humiliate him."

"Yes," Tangle Hair said, "nor did you dress him as a woman in front of the entire tribe. And

Little Horse speaks straight-arrow, only *look* in the water, see your face—it came up against something more deadly than knuckles."

"Bucks," Touch the Sky said calmly, "Arrow Keeper was right. He once defined men as creatures who walk on two legs and are ungrateful. All three of you are cracking your teeth on the shell and missing the tasty meat."

"Truly? But only look!" Little Horse said incredulously. "You are laughing at this even now. Or trying, for surely your face is too battered to cooperate. Brother, granted, I have never known you to seek a trifling revenge. But how can you pretend that Black Elk's attack is so unimportant?"

"Brother, I pretend nothing. It was very important. For you see, I had expected much worse to take place when I heard the camp crier gather us. My own death, at the least, the destruction of the tribe, at the worst. Instead, Black Elk sought only a personal revenge. It was far more petty than I feared it would be.

"And have you not eyes to see? He *has* that revenge. True it is, I can hardly strut about and describe my valor. I spent much time with my face in the dirt. I am more accustomed to taste victory, and now my pride is bruised along with my face. I admit it freely.

"But what of that? Brothers, have you counted my coup feathers? I need not fume over the loss of a twig when I already own a tree."

Now Little Horse *did* begin to understand. "A tree? Better claim an entire forest. As you say, brother. As you say. Black Elk has little cause now to continue in the plotting against you. And after all, *his* face is none too handsome as we speak."

"Perhaps even more important," Two Twists put in, thinking of his friend Honey Eater, "if his anger abates somewhat, he may stop making life so hard for his persecuted wife."

Now they all finally understood Touch the Sky's seemingly odd behavior since the beating. For his purposes, it was more of a victory than a defeat. But despite the prospect of at least a truce with Black Elk, Touch the Sky's hope was secretly tempered by a grim reminder: Trouble often arrived in a divided force. Wolf Who Hunts Smiling would *never* settle for a truce.

And even if Touch the Sky's tribal enemies were not poised for immediate treachery, Hiram Steele's recent return might prove worse than any beating.

Early the next morning, as a heavy fog drifted in from the north, Wolf Who Hunts Smiling rolled out of his robes with one thought singing in his blood: *Today, finally, I will kill Touch the Sky!*

With fingers that trembled slightly from anticipation, he picked up a stick and stirred the coals in the firepit to life. His hide tipi cover was stretched thin with age. So he took care not to build the flame too high—some early riser might see his actions within.

He removed the stolen dragoon pistol from a

parfleche hidden under his battle rig. For a moment he was transfixed by his own distorted image in the mirror polish of the silver plating. Even here, safe in his tipi, his furtive, quick-as-minnow eyes were constantly in motion, watching for the ever-expected attack.

Wolf Who Hunts Smiling had prepared carefully for this day. This weapon could never be linked to him, and he had closely studied Touch the Sky's daily habits. As shaman, certain rituals were unavoidable. This morning, as every morning when in camp, the tall Cheyenne would rise early. He would go down to the river and sweat himself in the lodge there while saying the ancient sunrise prayer for the tribe.

But *this* morning, unlike most mornings, Touch the Sky would do one thing out of the ordinary.

He would die.

The crisis facing the Cheyenne Nation was coming to a head. Wolf Who Hunts Smiling had lately been in secret communication with his allies: the Comanche Big Tree, to the south, and the Blackfoot renegade Sis-ki-dee, currently terrorizing white miners in the Tongue River country. Both had already lost too many braves to Touch the Sky's battle skills. And both now sent the same word: Kill this tall buck first. Then—and *only* then—would they return to help Wolf Who Hunts Smiling take over Indian country. But so long as *that* one walked above the earth, they refused to return.

Black Elk had given it a good effort, thought

Wolf Who Hunts Smiling. It was a glorious fight! But his cousin has stopped short of the kill. Ruthless against any tribal enemy, the thought of the Arrows held him back from drawing Cheyenne blood. He still, Wolf Who Hunts Smiling realized with a disdainful sneer, clung to some foolish remnant of 'honor.' Thus he would never be a powerful leader of ruthless men—the only kind who would survive in this pitiless land where the war between red men and white men was quickly becoming a war of outright extermination.

No. The only 'honor' was in achieving revenge against an enemy.

Wolf Who Hunts Smiling opened the charger of the pistol and filled it with grains of black powder from his flask. Once the bore was charged, he slipped a primer cap behind the loading gate. Finally he tamped home the huge, conical ball that made the dragoon pistol such a lethal weapon.

He stretched out one foot and lifted the flap over his entrance. This fog was thick, he told himself. Thicker than the usual morning mist. That could work for and against him. It would make it easier to hide, but also more difficult to draw an accurate bead. Well, no matter. Sister Sun's rays would soon heat up and burn some of it off.

For a moment he let his thoughts drift back to the most fatal council meeting in his memory: the meeting during which the Headmen had voted to strip him of his coup feathers. This harsh sentence—the worst imaginable for a warrior as proud as Wolf Who Hunts Smiling— was ordered as punishment for his schemes against Touch the Sky. Now, thanks to that white man's dog, Wolf Who Hunts Smiling wore a naked headdress—like some little reservation squaw-man who stood in formations and answered roll calls.

No. This thing would not stand. Black Elk was right: *The worm will turn.*

Wolf Who Hunts Smiling checked the dragoon pistol one final time. Then, anticipation stirring in his belly, he slipped the weapon into his legging sash and melted into the fog.

A curious thing happened to Black Elk after beating Touch the Sky. His feeling of triumphant elation gradually gave way to a nagging sense of guilt. Yes, all had seen him defeat his enemy. But Black Elk also knew what most of them did not: He had cheated to ensure the victory.

Honey Eater had refused to even look at him since the fight. However, there was little left to ruin between them. Some time ago they had stopped living as man and wife, each keeping to separate sides of the tipi's center pole.

But now, as Black Elk lay sleepless in the quiet tipi, her words sounded in his mind: *You are better than your despicable cousin Wolf Who Hunts Smiling. He works on your jealousy, using it to further his own treasonous plans.*

In the quiet moments of the morning, Black

Elk had to confront it: Honey Eater was right. His cousin, and that skinny coward Medicine Flute, had shrewdly been using him for their own ends. But was Honey Eater also right in her belief that these two schemers had bloody treason on their minds?

Black Elk did not like admitting to mistakes. Yet in his jealous blindness perhaps he had missed the clear signs. If Honey Eater was right, it would explain why Medicine Flute was able to describe Comanche camps from so-called 'visions'—the deception had been arranged by Wolf Who Hunts Smiling, cooperating with their enemy!

Bloody treason. The thought so agitated him that Black Elk rose and stepped out into the half-light of dawn. The fog lay moist against his bare skin and soothed his battered face—for even without horseshoe nails over his knuckles, Touch the Sky had inflicted plenty of damage.

Black Elk's pride was fierce, but that same pride had never tolerated a liar or a cheat. So he was forced to admit it to himself: Touch the Sky would have won the fist-fight had it remained fair.

This lie Black Elk found himself living. As he wandered down to bathe in the river, he asked himself how it was any different from lying about counting coup? His hatred for Touch the Sky was not the point. A warrior who took credit for an unearned coup was the scourge of his clan and tribe. Yet this hair dangling from his clout—was it not a sham trophy?

Abruptly, Black Elk stopped and cocked his head like a wading bird, listening.

There. There it was again. A rapid clicking sound. At first it took him by surprise. Then he remembered the lore of the old grandmothers and he relaxed a bit. The sounds were caused by the eager burrowing of tiny, wood-eating insects known as Deathwatch Beetles. Hearing them was said to be an omen of death.

Womanly superstition, Black Elk scoffed. He moved closer to the purling river, a ghost figure adrift in the swirling fog.

Even before the birds could begin their sunrise songfest, Touch the Sky had prepared the sweat lodge.

It stood near the water's edge, a framework of bent saplings well covered with layers of hide. Huge rocks were ringed within, heated by fire until they glowed blood orange.

Touch the Sky stripped off his clout and moccasins. Then he dipped a rawhide bucket in the lazy current and carried the water inside the sweat lodge. Huge billows of hissing steam rose from the rocks.

At first the sudden heat irritated his ravaged face. But soon the air cooled tolerably and he felt his pores opening up, sweating him clean. His muscles were growing slack and heavy.

As a shaman must, he began the difficult job of quieting his mind; of crowding out the thoughts of the little day, trying to set his mind on the upward path known as the Vision Way.

Arrow Keeper had taught him that signs and visions can only be apprehended when the mind is ready. And it could not be ready until normal 'thought' had been quieted, allowing the shaman eye to open.

But even as his mind quieted, a very real sound drifted to him from outside: the sudden, fierce clicking noises of the Deathwatch Beetle.

Recognizing it, he felt a prickling in his skin.

Touch the Sky's survival, since his controversial arrival among this camp, had been assured only by paying close attention to the warnings of nature. The sudden flight of a jay, a fresh bend in the grass, a turned-over stone—any of these could signal death behind the next tree. But he had also learned to respect signs sometimes ignored as the fears of the weak and elderly.

The clicking sound echoed out over the river again. Touch the Sky rose and stepped outside into the cooler billows of fog.

Wolf Who Hunts Smiling frowned as he peered out from his position behind a tangled deadfall. He had welcomed this fog, at first. But so far Sister Sun was having little luck at burning it away. Even this close to the river, he risked missing his shot. He could barely make out the rough, dark shape of the sweat lodge. Would he even see Woman Face coming?

Yet . . . the thought of going any closer made even the fearless Wolf Who Hunts Smiling pause. This Touch the Sky was the last brave any sane warrior would trifle with. It was said he could hear the grass grow. If. . . .

There was a sudden rush of excited blood to his face as Wolf Who Hunts Smiling spotted it: a glimpse of bronzed flesh moving along the trail near the sweat lodge.

The cruel, thin-lipped smile that had earned him his name now divided his face. Wolf Who Hunts Smiling lay the long muzzle of the dragoon pistol on a log in front of him. His head fell forward, one cheek resting on the silvered grip as he sighted down the barrel.

All of his being was focused on that notch sight. The young warrior was only vaguely aware when the rapid clicking noise started.

Touch the Sky had taken only a few steps toward the camp. All of an instant, a human shape emerged from the fog and almost bumped into him.

"You!" Black Elk said, startled.

Touch the Sky stood, sweat-sheening, in the dim light. Neither brave carried a weapon.

Touch the Sky's eyes dropped to the thick hank of hair tied to Black Elk's clout.

"You have enjoyed strutting around with my locks for all to see. Anyone is welcome to look and laugh. But you would be wise not to taunt *my* eyes with your trophy. If you think one fight has left me quailing at sight of you, test your belief now and bridge the gap."

Touch the Sky braced for trouble. But a moment later, Black Elk untied the rawhide string holding the hair.

"Buck," he said, "we are enemies and will be unto death. My wife aches to fertilize your seed, and I cannot bury this thing in the ground as you did your white name. But I trained you in the warrior arts, and you are a credit to this tribe. No man on the plains can defeat you. Nor did I. *Here* is the 'fist' that knocked you Wendigo."

Black Elk removed the bent horseshoe nails from his pouch.

"Touch the Sky—and from this day I call you Touch the Sky and nothing else—know this. I blame no man for my weakness. But a blindfold has been lifted from my eyes. I can never be your friend. But I admit I did wrong by you, and I regret it.

"From where I stand now to the place where the sun sleeps, I swear this thing, and this spot hears me: Never again will I speak in a wolf bark against you or join those who do."

Touch the Sky could not have been more surprised if Black Elk had suddenly turned into a tree. Now his enemy held the hair out to him. He started to reach for it, then stopped.

Sweat broke out on his back.

The clicking began again, high-pitched, rapid, insistent. It seemed to emanate from everywhere in the damp fog that amplified the sound. Touch the Sky glanced all around them, his shaman sense at full alarm.

"Black Elk," he said uncertainly as he accepted the hair, "step off the path and take cover!"

Wolf Who Hunts Smiling squinted in the grainy fog, trying his best to hold his target. He breathed deep and slipped his finger inside the trigger guard. He relaxed. Took up the slack. Slowly sque-e-zed . . .

The gunshot shattered the peaceful stillness of the sleeping camp. Honey Eater sat upright, instantly wide awake. Her breath snagged in her throat.

One glance told her that Black Elk was not here.

Touch the Sky!

Her heart began pounding so hard it throbbed tight in her temples. She jumped up, quickly dressed, and joined the growing number of Cheyennes racing toward the river.

Chapter Seven

Black Elk had the honed reflexes of a seasoned warrior. The moment Touch the Sky finished speaking his warning, Black Elk leaped toward the side of the path. Touch the Sky leaped the opposite way. But at the same moment that both men reacted, the shot sounded.

Even now, as he crashed into the hawthorn thickets, Touch the Sky knew his time had not yet come. As Black Elk himself had taught him, you never hear the shot that kills you.

He landed hard and heard Black Elk crashing into the ground-cover on the other side. Touch the Sky rose quickly on one elbow and strained to see anyone in the swirling fog.

"Black Elk!" he said urgently, glimpsing a flicker of dark movement out ahead. "You wait here! I see our quarry! He ran up the bank to-

85

ward camp. I will take the escape trail and try to flush him back this way!"

At the sound of the shot, the outlying night sentries had raised the wolf howl of alarm. Already Touch the Sky could hear more shouts of alarm as the people woke up and flocked to the river. He sprang up and angled toward a narrow cutbank which had been dug deeper and wider by human effort. It started well behind camp and was part of the emergency escape route to the river—intended for use by noncombatants in case of a surprise attack.

But Touch the Sky encountered even thicker fog now. In the pounding rush of feet from camp, and the din of howling and barking dogs, he could not detect the steps of a lone attacker. He gave up in frustration and returned to the path near the river.

"Unless someone else saw something I did not," he said as he approached, "our mystery enemy has eluded us."

Spotted Tail saw him first. He was standing near a group of braves who were all kneeling over something.

"Spotted Tail," Touch the Sky said impatiently, "are you still asleep? Have your Bow String soldiers fan out through camp. It would be an easy matter to smell the guns and see which have just been fired. Whoever. . . ."

Touch the Sky trailed off. Not only Spotted Tail, but now many others, were staring hard at the front of his clout. He glanced down. His own dark hair protruded from the pouch, where he had carelessly stuffed it after Black Elk handed it over to him.

But this thing was awkward. Black Elk had done this privately, as a rare gesture of conciliation, and Touch the Sky had no desire to let others know their proud war leader had humbled himself. He had meant to discard the hair before he returned to camp.

Hastily, hoping to spare Black Elk needless embarrassment, he stuffed it further out of sight. But why were they all staring at him like this, their eyes so accusing? And look, he told himself. Even Little Horse, Two Twists, Tangle Hair—look how they, too, stood gawing at him as if he were some total stranger, and an unwelcome one, at that.

And Honey Eater. . . .

Suddenly one of the kneeling braves stood up, and Touch the Sky saw Black Elk lying face down beside the path—the entire back of his head now a pebbly clot of exposed brains and blood!

He met Honey Eater's shocked, unbelieving eyes. The meaning of her look—of all these accusing stares—was clear. Yes, she hated this dead man for what he had become, for the terrible wrong he had done to her. Perhaps, in her secret misery, she had even wished for his death and her release. But *this!* There he lay—a brave warrior dead from an unclean death. It was a coward's kill to the back, meaning he was not able to sing his death song and ensure his place in the Land of Ghosts. That meant spending eternity alone—the only hell an Indian could conceive of.

A true and honorable warrior could never inflict so horrible a death on anyone, not even a mortal enemy. And yet, she thinks *I* am the killer, Touch the Sky thought.

"Honey Eater," he said, and in that moment only the two of them existed, "do you believe I could do this thing? That I would kill any man from behind?"

"Believe it?" she replied miserably. "In my heart, no. Never. But how do I convince my senses?"

She was careful to say nothing more in front of his enemies. But her eyes, too, fell to the pouch and the concealed hair. Now Touch the Sky realized his mistake in trying to hide it. That simple movement went far toward condemning him as a murderer.

"Treachery!" shouted Lone Bear, leader of Black Elk's Bull Whip soldier society. "He has slain our war leader! He who guards the Arrows has now *stained* them!"

"He could not bear his humiliation!" a Bull Whip shouted. "Black Elk defeated him like a man, battered his face as you see it now. And now he has sought a coward's revenge!"

This caused a mad confusion of arguing voices even as Chief Gray Thunder arrived on the scene. It was Spotted Tail who shouted them down.

"Have ears for my words! Never mind appearances here. We are the *Shaiyena*, not the

88

barbaric Comanches. We do not determine guilt in a heartbeat. Certainly not when one of our own is the accused."

"One of our own is also *dead*!" Lone Bear retorted. There was no love lost between the Bull Whips and the Bow Strings. "Who else had better cause to kill him? That hair you saw Touch the Sky try to hide just now—everyone knows it *was* tied to a certain one's sash."

He avoided naming the dead. For everyone knew dead people could sometimes hear their name and might answer it.

"Touch the Sky," Spotted Tail said bluntly. "You have ears to hear the charge. Did you kill our war leader?"

"No," Touch the Sky replied forcefully. And now, glancing quickly around at the accusing faces, he added, "And I answer a question with another question. Where is Wolf Who Hunts Smiling?"

That question hung in the air, followed by a long silence.

"*Here* I am, cowardly murderer! First you shoot my cousin from behind. Then you blame me. And did *I* also push that hair into your pouch for you?"

Wolf Who Hunts Smiling boldly made his way forward from the rear of the throng. Touch the Sky saw that he was trying to hide the fact that he was short of breath—as if he'd been running. His words had caused a second explosion of shouts and confused arguing.

But now Little Horse began to gather his wits

about him, recovering from the shock of this murder. He immediately understood the drift of his friend's question.

"Look!" Little Horse shouted to the rest. "Remember this later, that Wolf Who Hunts Smiling is only now speaking up. He who is always first to make trouble with words is the last to arrive. See where he stands? Yet his clan circle is close to the river, the rest of the Panthers are here. Why not him? Because he murdered his cousin!"

"Not intentionally," Touch the Sky corrected his friend. "He *meant* to murder me. That is why his face was so surprised just now when he saw Black Elk lying there. But adept at wearing two faces, he has quickly recovered."

In a heartbeat Wolf Who Hunts Smiling unsheathed his knife. "White Man Runs Him works true to form. He covers his own guilt by shifting attention to others. But never mind his smokescreen! He has slain my cousin, now his blood will wash the Arrows clean!"

The two soldier troops squared off uneasily.

"Hold!" Chief Gray Thunder commanded. "Spotted Tail spoke straight. Never mind appearances. Would you shed more blood on top of this? This matter will be discussed in council.

"Our war leader lies murdered! The High Holy Ones who first made the days and gave them to men placed one crime above all others—the shedding of our own blood. Yes, this blood must be avenged. But not in the heat of passion, with more blood in our eyes.

"Headmen! Return to your tipis and don your battle finery. We will appease the four directions and council at once."

Never before, in the entire history of the tribe, had Touch the Sky seen a council so bitterly divided.

Women were not normally permitted at council. But murder of fellow Cheyennes was a rare and serious crime. The Medicine Arrows had been seriously tainted. All agreed that this matter directly touched the entire tribe. So instead of convening inside the council lodge, the Headmen gathered in the central clearing.

They passed the ceremonial calumet, smoking to the four directions of the wind. Usually Touch the Sky, as shaman, offered a brief prayer-chant meant to influence Maiyun, the Good Supernatural, in their favor.

But ominously, Chief Gray Thunder asked Medicine Flute to perform this honor. Nor did the lazy-lidded 'shaman' neglect any opportunity to catch Touch the Sky's eye, goading him with knowing smiles.

The tense and divisive atmosphere was felt by all. Touch the Sky knew he had many enemies. But by now, he could also count many hard-won friends. Unfortunately, many of his most loyal supporters—the tribe's women, children, and elders, whom he had once saved in a heroic stand against Kiowa and Comanche attackers—carried much less influence at council than the more vigorous younger warriors.

Also, Touch the Sky knew he was up against one of the most fiery and eloquent speakers in the tribe: Wolf Who Hunts Smiling. A brave who spoke well at council commanded many followers.

"Fathers! Brothers! Cheyenne people!" his enemy called out, leaping atop a flat stump. "Pick up my words and examine them closely! How long now have I, my murdered cousin, and others in this tribe attempted to warn our people? How long has this murdering white man's dog been welcomed by the traitors among us?

"Had the people listened, the one who was my cousin would still be among us. *This* one"—he pointed accusingly to the place where Touch the Sky stood—"first tried to steal Black Elk's squaw. Failing in this, he stole his *life!*"

A confused riot of voices broke out at these words. The sturdy, barrel-chested Little Horse overpowered them all.

"Have ears! This Wolf Who Hunts Smiling is a warrior second to none in battlefield courage! But he has never been one to grasp truth firmly by the tail. Have we forgotten *why* he was stripped of his coup feathers? Have we forgotten how he bribed an addled old grandmother into reporting a 'vision'? And what was the result of this lie? Touch the Sky hung from the pole, pointed hooks through his chest, for hours."

"Nor is this the worst of his sins," Tangle Hair put in. "He has conspired with the Comanche named Big Tree, with the Blackfoot called Sis-ki-dee, both sworn enemies of our tribe. He has even stolen our Sacred Arrows and delivered them up to Sis-ki-dee! And once again Touch the Sky faced death to rescue them."

"Just as he risked death to rescue this tribe from Pawnees, from Bluecoats, just as he has fought white land-grabbers and whiskey peddlers," Two Twists said. "And during all this, he has been forced to cover his back from attacks by his own people. So far the white-livered cowards have failed to kill him."

Another chaotic outburst. Touch the Sky could see that the camp was literally dividing itself. As emotions ran deeper, supporters gathered into two distinct groups.

All, that is, except for poor Honey Eater. She stood alone, forlorn, confused, and nearly forgotten. Touch the Sky felt his heart turn over when he realized that she was deliberately avoiding his eye. She had sworn her eternal love for him. Now her dilemma was cruel: She could not believe in his guilt, but neither could she be assured of his innocence. Nor could Touch the Sky resent her confusion. For indeed, appearances condemned him. As the daughter of a great chief, she must behave with impeccable decency and show this reserve until more was known.

Touch the Sky could see that Gray Thunder, too, was deeply troubled. Whatever opinion he held, he kept it to himself as a good chief must. It was his task to try to determine the collective will of the people.

But the worry lines etched deep into his face made it clear, Touch the Sky thought. The "collective voice" was close to being silenced. Indeed, perhaps it no longer existed. This was a tribe on the brink of anarchy and self-destruction.

"Cheyenne people!" Gray Thunder called out. "We have heard from everyone except Touch the Sky. Much has been said about the hair that was cut from his head. Whatever you think of him, he has more than earned his right to speak. Let *him* tell us how this hair came to be in his possession after all in camp saw it dangling from the clout of . . . of the one who will soon be washed and dressed for his final journey."

Now, as every face in camp turned to stare at him, Touch the Sky felt the cruel nature of his position. Black Elk's behavior at the end was atypical of this battle-hardened warrior—who would believe Touch the Sky now? But if truth was his only weapon, he resolved to aim it straight where it would do the most good. Let the rest think what they would.

"Honey Eater!" he called out. "Look at me!"

Startled, as were all in camp, Honey Eater did as told. Warm blood rushed into her face.

"I did not kill your husband. *Look* at me! See these eyes which refuse to run from yours? Neither will I play the hypocrite like Wolf Who Hunts Smiling and the rest. I do not pretend your husband's death is a tragedy for you.

"No. It is a long-deserved release! He never merited you and never treated you with the respect you deserve. In fact, he beat and tormented you."

"You pig's afterbirth!" Wolf Who Hunts Smiling exploded. "You sheep rutter! My brave, noble cousin lies slaughtered, and you who killed him now malign his ghost!"

"Your mouth is the hind end of a horse," Touch the Sky said calmly. "Nothing falls from it but dung."

He looked at Honey Eater again. "But though I cannot mourn his death, I can tell you this. Your husband died with a kind and noble gesture in his parfleche. Nothing spoke as well for his life as his conduct in the final moments of it."

Still talking only to Honey Eater, Touch the Sky quickly and concisely explained what had taken place: How Black Elk had struck a truce of honor with him. Further, how Black Elk had condemned the secret machinations of Wolf Who Hunts Smiling and his dishonorable comrades.

"The final act of his life," Touch the Sky assured Honey Eater, "was a repudiation of his behavior. He told me he had not truly earned this"—here Touch the Sky tugged the hair from his pouch—"because he cheated in the fight. He put these bent nails over his knuckles before he hit me. So he handed the hair back to me himself."

"This," Wolf Who Hunts Smiling protested, "is Woman Face's finest hour in deception. See? Look at the old grandmothers swiping at tears!

Only see how cleverly this ridiculous lie plays to our Cheyenne sense of honor.

"But all of you *know* my cousin! Honey Eater, I know you hate me, sister! But I, too, am looking you in the eye. And I ask you this thing because you know my cousin best. *Could* he have done this 'act of forgiveness' that Woman Fa— I mean, Touch the Sky describes? I say this would not be 'honor' to a warrior as hard as my cousin. This is womanly weakness he would never display. Am I right?"

Honey Eater looked him full in the eye. "Since you have pulled me into this, I will answer you directly. First, let me say this. Wolf Who Hunts Smiling, I despise you! Never until now have you called me 'sister' or spoken five friendly words to me. You are the greatest enemy of Gray Thunder's people, and I will not take an easy breath until you are dead and wrapped tight on your funeral scaffold."

A shocked gasp swept through the camp. But Wolf Who Hunts Smiling flinched only momentarily.

"Fine," he said archly, his furtive eyes mocking her. "Your feelings will be remembered. Now answer my question, woman, and show respect to this council! I say Touch the Sky's story is a lie. I say my cousin would never have displayed this womanly weakness. Am I right?"

"It is neither womanly nor weakness," she replied in a more subdued voice. "Nor do I think Touch the Sky lies. But I must confess, it is dif-

ficult to envision my husband being so conciliatory."

"Never would he! My point exactly."

"Never mind this useless speculation about
why he did it," Little Horse cut in. "Will you
drag dreams into it, too? No man can say for
certain what another *might* do or say. I ask this
instead. You have all seen the wound on the victim. Touch the Sky owns no weapon capable of
such a wound. His only weapon is his Sharps.
It fires a small, penetrating bullet, not a big and
destructive one."

Here Wolf Who Hunts Smiling looked at
Medicine Flute. The latter spoke up casually.
"What about his pistol?"

Little Horse whirled. "What pistol, bone
blower? He owns no pistol, and you know it."

"What? You would presume to tell a shaman
what he does or does not know?"

"If you are a shaman, I am a she-grizz. What
pistol, you mincing little squaw man?"

"The Bluecoat dragoon pistol he seized as a
trophy at the Tongue River Battle," spoke up the
Bull Whip named Lance Hurler.

"Have you broken fast by eating peyote?"
Touch the Sky demanded. "I own no such
weapon and never did."

"Bent words," Lone Bear said. "I, too, recall
this weapon. A shiny cap-and-ball pistol. I even
tried to trade for it. But Touch the Sky praised
it lavishly. He told me he would hold onto it
forever."

"This is their usual ploy," Little Horse said

scornfully. "Notice who speaks to 'verify' this pistol: All Whips! The story is concocted. Odd, is it not, that none of his close friends has seen this weapon—yet all his enemies have?"

"Not odd at all," Wolf Who Hunts Smiling said in a low, threatening voice. "Lying conspirators must stick together. Clearly, if we would kill the one traitor, we would need to kill them *all*."

These words marked the very air with menace. Both sides seemed poised to draw weapons. By order of the soldier troops, all firearms had been left behind for inspection. But other weapons had not been forbidden.

"Finally," Little Horse said, "you have spoken words with which I can agree. It *is* all or none, wolf barker. That tall warrior will someday lead the entire Cheyenne nation. If you go for him, you must also kill some of the best fighters in this tribe."

"Both of you," Gray Thunder said angrily, "remember that *I* am your chief. Save all these grand future predictions and show some respect in the present. Which of you is prepared to kill me now. Now, in front of the women and children?"

At this, all the hotheads looked away in shame.

"Good. Some humility at last! Now I say this. Tempers grow too short, fingers itch to draw weapons. I pronounce this council concluded. We have determined no one's guilt or innocence. There is no point in continuing at present. We will only end up staining the Arrows past all hope of renewal. *Then* how will we live?"

His question sobered the entire tribe. But before the huge gathering could begin to break up, two Bow String soldiers reported to the Headmen. They were named Scalp Cane and Blue Robe. They had been sent through camp to smell the muzzles of all the guns.

"Was any weapon fired?" Spotted Tail demanded.

The braves, admirers of Touch the Sky as were many others in the Bow String troop, cast their eyes down and were reluctant to speak.

"One was indeed fired," Blue Robe said.

He held up a silver-plated dragoon pistol. "So freshly fired the muzzle was still warm when we found it."

"Found it where?" Spotted Tail said.

"Hidden among the Medicine Arrows," Blue Robe answered reluctantly, "in Touch the Sky's tipi."

Chapter Eight

Kristen felt Stoney MacGruder's eyes watching her from across the parlor, as invasive as a pair of unwelcome hands. Nonetheless she continued to move around the room, filling the lamps from a bottle of coal oil.

Once again the drone of masculine voices leaked past the door of her father's library. But the thick slab oak muted the words so she couldn't make them out. Frustration made her mutter a mild oath under her breath.

"Mr. MacGruder," she said sweetly, for she had noticed that Stoney was less hostile when Fontaine wasn't around. "Do you *really* believe I'm so dangerous?"

The slow-witted gunsel lifted his head in surprise at being addressed. He had been about to doze off in one of the comfortable wing chairs.

"How's that?" he said.

"Dangerous. Do I really pose such a threat that you must watch me as if I were a hardened criminal?"

"Why . . . a course you ain't igzacly dangerous, Miz Steele. But your pa, well, he's the big nabob what pays my wages. And *he* says to watch you close. 'Stick to 'er like ugly on a buzzard,' was his very words. Either I do what the boss says, or I'm ridin' the grub line to earn three hots 'n' a cot."

"Well," she said petulantly, making a charming little moue for him, "I surely hope you're gentleman enough that there's *some* places a lady can go in private."

She moved toward the side door—the one which gave direct access to the outside privy.

MacGruder flushed. "You go right ahead, Miz Steele. Your tether ain't *that* short."

Gratefully, Kristen escaped into the cool darkness of early evening. The big, two-story frame house had been built on a wide and grassy ledge just above the floor of the Blackford Valley, cut by an ancient river long gone dry. It was thus a natural defensive bastion— the back was built close to the steep south wall of the valley. The only easy approach was from the open expanse of grass to the front.

Hunted men like her father, she thought bitterly, had to be more concerned with good gun emplacements than with the style of the house—after all, they required forts, not homes.

The blue-black dome of sky was aglitter with

fiery pinpoints of starlight. A steady breeze caressed her cheeks and wrapped her skirt around her hips. Cicadas sent up their eerie rhythm, and now and then an owl hooted from the trees beyond the grass.

It was all so peaceful. But Kristen had come outside neither to use the privy nor to commune with nature. Abbot Fontaine and her father were in the library with their heads together, plotting. And whatever scheme they were hatching was bound to bring new grief to the Cheyenne people—especially to Matthew. No matter the danger from her father's wrath, she *must* learn what she could.

First Kristen hurried to the privy and loudly banged the thin plank door closed. Then she doubled around to the west side of the house. A slanting shaft of yellow light marked the library window. And even as she watched, a flimsy white muslin curtain liner licked out at the night on a vagrant breeze—proving the window was open.

She glanced quickly back over her shoulder toward the side door, watching for MacGruder. Then Kristen swallowed the hard stone in her throat and crept closer to the window.

"One incident won't be enough," Hiram Steele said. "It will have to be a campaign of terror against white interests before this Colonel Thompson will serve urgent notice to the Indian Bureau. If we can get this malcontent Cheyenne buck to fly our colors, all well and good. If not, you and Stoney might have to paint your faces and learn how to mount a horse from the Indian side."

Abbot Fontaine grinned. "It's all one to me. Money spends the same no matter how a man earns it."

"You're game, Abbot, I'll give you that. It takes a . . . flexible man to survive out here."

Steele stood before the huge Mercator map of the Montana and Wyoming Territories. Fontaine was sprawled in the Boston rocker, sipping from a pony glass of whiskey. Steele glanced at his muddy, down-at-the-heels boots and frowned.

"Not only are you wearing four-point rowels, you've filed them down to make them sharper. It's your business if you're willing to cut your horse so bad for extra speed. But my daughter is right this time, you boys're also tearing up the house."

"Aww . . . no offense, Hiram. But that girl a yourn has got a little too much starch in her petticoats. She needs to meet the backside of your hand."

"Granted, she's high-minded and prideful just like her ma was. But she's got a point. That rug you're mucking up right now with your boots. It came by clipper ship all the way from the Orient."

"Do tell?" Fontaine said absently. His sawed-off shotgun hung at his right side, suspended in its jury-rigged sling. Abbot's right palm rested easy against the butt, almost caressing it.

"Yes, I *do* tell. Kristen tells me something else. She says that twice now she's found piles of cigarette ashes outside her bedroom door. Right under the keyhole. As if someone had stood there quite some time, smoking and spying on her."

"Hunh. I'll be jiggered. Twice, you say? You'd think a girl what was truly worried woulda covered that-air keyhole the first time. But then, I reckon a woman that'll cozy up with redskins needn't worry about white men peekin' at her. I mean, ain't that sorta like a whore yellin' rape?"

Hiram flushed. This was a sore point with him. "Abbot, I won't appeal to your decency. I confess I didn't hire you because I thought you were decent. We've always talked plain, haven't we?"

Abbot grinned even wider, enjoying this immensely. "Well now, we have, and that's a puredee fact, Hiram."

"I'll talk plain again now. Don't throw a good-paying job down a rathole. You and Stoney keep your hands off my daughter. I admit she has shamed me once. But I also admit she's a fine-looking woman with a good head on her shoulders. I'll marry her off yet, get some useful connections out of it. But no man wants to take delivery of damaged goods."

Fontaine threw his head back and laughed so hard he made himself cough. "By Godfrey, I like a plain talker, too! Don't you fret, Hiram. I agitate your girl some, but it's only funnin'. So long as you keep paying in good double-eagle gold, I won't shit where I eat."

Hiram accepted this and dropped the issue. "Nuff said on that. Now, about this Cheyenne who might work for us. Carlson is coming later with word from his scout, the Southern Cheyenne who's supposed to set up a parley with him.

"Even if I get him on the payroll, that doesn't mean we can trust him. I already got burned trying to trust in a Cherokee who I *thought* had a white man's cunning when it came to profits. The truth is, savages can't grasp the concept of gold being worth more than any other pretty trade item."

"Any red son bears watching. But when he's called Wolf Who Hunts Smiling, best keep your back to a tree."

"Mm. I'm told this one is on a vendetta to wipe out the palefaces. Only the hope of killing Matthew Hanchon will make him cooperate with us. He could turn on us at any time."

"Could," Abbot said, "and prob'ly will. No need to warn me about trusting Injins. 'Specially no Cheyenne. Them and the goddamn Apaches are the two tribes what invented most of the sneaky tricks. You won't read nothing but trouble in their faces."

Hiram's face wrinkled in disgust when Abbot lifted an index finger up to the musket-ball wound on his cheek, tracing the puckered edges of the deep impression.

But suddenly Abbot was all cold-eyed business. He said, "What's that?" and stood up, staring out the open window. In an eyeblink he swung the shotgun up to the ready. "The hell's that?" he said again.

"What?" Hiram's voice was tight with alarm. He slid open the top drawer of his desk and removed a Colt Navy revolver, checking the load. Abbot grabbed the lamp on Hiram's desk and turned down the wick. Then he crossed to the window and looked out.

"Ahh . . . I thought I saw something move, but now I ain't sure. Coulda been my reflection on the glass. Hey, Stoney!" Abbot shouted back over his shoulder toward the parlor.

"Yo!"

"Everything all right in there?"

"Hunky-dory. Why?"

"Just checking," Abbot said.

He turned the wick back up. "Prob'ly a dog or somethin'. Don't hurt to be careful."

"Hurt? Being careful is what you're paid to do! I didn't bring you two smelly buffalos into my house for companionship."

Again Fontaine laughed. "Hiram, I thought *I* was tough, but by God you're jerked leather! Did you even cry when your mama died?"

Steele was taken aback by this. "What kind of fool question is that? I don't recall, but I expect I did. Didn't you?"

"What, cry for Ma? I shorely did. Cried till my tears dried up," Fontaine replied as he pulled the makings for a cigarette from the fob pocket of his vest. "Tell you God's truth, some-times I wish I'd never killed her."

Crouching under the outside sill of the case-ment, Kristen barely escaped being caught when Abbot Fontaine suddenly appeared at the window. Heart leaping into her throat, she quickly jutted to one side and pressed flat against the clinker-built wall of the house. Ab-bot stood so close she could smell the stale sweat and tobacco stink of him. But thank God he couldn't see her in the darkness just to his right.

She had not overheard enough to understand much. But clearly they were hoping to enlist the help of a Cheyenne traitor. Wolf Who Hunts Smiling . . . the very name conjured an image that made her shiver. At least she had learned something potentially useful. Now she must somehow get word to Matthew.

The side door of the house slapped open.

"Miz Steele?" MacGruder's braying voice called out uncertainly. "You almost done in there?"

"I'm right here, Mr. MacGruder. I simply took a turn around the yard."

"There's somebody here to see you. That sol-jer boy from Fort Bates that knows your pa."

Kristen's brow wrinkled in a frown of annoy-ance. Seth Carlson was at least tenacious, if not very realistic. In his persistent quest for her hand, he employed whatever weapon fit his mood: flattery, threats, bribes. And despite the

107

Judd Cole

fact that she loathed him, avoiding him like a bad habit, the fool continued to press his case. By now "love" had nothing to do with it. She knew he was obsessed about her the same way her father was obsessed with power. Both men would stop at nothing to be winners.

But now she recalled her need to reach and warn Matthew. Her first choice of messengers would be her friend and Matthew's, Capt. Tom Riley. But he was presently back home in Illinois on a long-overdue leave. That left only one other reliable messenger: Matthew's former boyhood friend, Corey Robinson.

Carlson stood waiting for her in front of the fieldstone fireplace, his black-brimmed officer's hat in hand. "Miss Steele," he greeted her while Stoney reluctantly made himself scarce.

"Capt. Carlson," she said coolly. "You wish to speak with me?"

Clearly, something out of the ordinary had him upset. Like her father, Carlson was not one for social amenities. Now he simply blurted it out.

"I just heard some scuttlebutt that's going around the fort. At least, I hope it's scuttlebutt and not the truth. Some of the men in Tom Riley's platoon claim . . . well, that is, they say the reason he went home on leave is that he's bringing his parents out here for his wedding."

He stopped, looking at her expectantly.

"Yes?" she said impatiently. "Why should I be interested in this 'scuttlebutt,' as you call it?"

"Because they say he's getting married to you.

I came to see if that's true?"

This silly rumor took Kristen by surprise. She and Riley had certainly enjoyed each other's company in the past, all right. But they had never even come close to a kiss, much less matrimony. Thanks to her father's eagle eyes and his new gunsels, they'd hardly seen each other lately.

"No, it's *not* true," she replied firmly. "I suggest the fort open a subscription library so the men can read romances on paper instead of making them up out of whole cloth."

This answer clearly relieved Carlson. "Personally, I never believed it," he assured her hastily. "And of course, it's none of my business."

"No. It isn't, is it?"

Her haughty tone nettled him. Carlson's voice took on a brittle edge. "It's just . . . a man has a right to wonder when he's going to get *his* chance. Most men in my position wouldn't even. . . . "

Carlson lost courage and trailed off. But Kristen finished his thought for him. "Wouldn't even consider marrying a white woman who loved an Indian. I should feel fortunate that you would even touch me, right?"

He flushed, but didn't deny her charge. In fact, like her father, he did believe that. Kristen, however, was not interested right now in further angering him. She needed his help.

"Mr. Carlson? Would you do me a small favor?"

The abrupt change of tone and subject startled him. But it also got him off the hook. He nodded a bit too quickly. "Always my pleasure."

"I hear from my friend Laura that Corey Robinson is a carpenter now?"

Carlson's face immediately tightened with suspicion. "That's right. He just built the new addition to the Quartermaster's stores at the fort. Did some other work there too. Why?"

They both knew that Corey Robinson, son of an itinerant mining-camp preacher, had been Matthew Hanchon's good friend before Carlson drove Matthew out of Bighorn Falls.

"Would you ask him to ride out here? You see, Pa said I can have some cabinets built in the kitchen. Sakes and saints!" she added with false enthusiasm. "What good is a kitchen, Mr. Carlson, if a body has no place to put anything?"

Carlson didn't like this. He couldn't prove it certain-sure, but he suspected the Robinson youth had assisted Hanchon in eluding the Army.

"I'll tell him," he finally replied before he crossed toward the door of the library. His questioning eyes drilled into hers. "We can't let you be without cabinets, can we?"

Chapter Nine

Chief Gray Thunder had been wise to disband the council meeting before it degenerated into a bloody battle. But the dramatic note upon which it ended—the discovery of the recently fired dragoon pistol in Touch the Sky's tipi—ensured a dangerous and divisive tension throughout camp.

"There is no fresh sign here," Little Horse insisted to his friend. "This is the same old trail. Your followers know full well that weapon was planted and *which* sly wolf planted it."

Touch the Sky nodded, though he also reminded himself that having truth on your side meant little against Wolf Who Hunts Smiling. Ironically, Black Elk's defiant act of cutting off Touch the Sky's hair to set him apart now meant little—the rest of the men in the tribe, too, had cropped their hair off in honor of Black Elk, and all of them resembled Touch the Sky.

"There is nothing new here so far as treachery is concerned," Touch the Sky agreed. "Wolf Who Hunts Smiling has killed our own before this, we have proof of it. But look."

Touch the Sky pointed back toward camp. He and Little Horse stood near the treeline where the camp clearing met a thick stand of pine. They were hollowing out a log canoe, using a new adz recently acquired at the trading post.

Little Horse saw where his friend pointed— toward the tipi of Medicine Flute. At least thirty braves—mostly Bull Whips—were gathered around it.

"*This* is something new. True it is, Medicine Flute has had followers since he and Wolf Who Hunts Smiling first planned that 'miracle' with the comet. But recently? He has easily doubled his followers. Count upon it, they are massing for the final battle. Who wins it will claim the title of shaman and thus shape the future of the tribe."

Little Horse frowned. "Followers, indeed. Like any good herd, they will follow the most belligerent bulls."

"Even over a cliff."

"Yes, even that."

"Many of those misguided wretches," Touch the Sky said, "truly believe Medicine Flute is a vision-seeker with powers blessed by the Holy Ones. Arrow Keeper warned me about this. He told me that our people's strong belief in visions could too easily be abused.

"Wolf Who Hunts Smiling knows this well. Like Roman Nose who leads the Southern Cheyenne Dog Men, he believes in nothing but power."

"Spoken straight-arrow, brother," Little Horse said. "The Whips are not all bad men. They follow bad examples. Warriors are lost without good leaders."

Again Touch the Sky nodded. "Arrow Keeper asked me a thing once. 'If gold will rust, what then will iron do?' His meaning comes clearer each day."

Touch the Sky openly pronounced Arrow Keeper's name as he had since the old man's disappearance, refusing to declare him dead in the absence of proof. Most others in the tribe now refused to speak his name and made the cut-off sign when they heard it.

Little Horse said, "I fear, brother, that Gray Thunder's decision to end the council has only delayed—not prevented—a tragedy. I have heard a thing."

"I suspect I have heard it, too," Touch the Sky said grimly. His back and shoulder muscles leaped like logs tumbling over a sluice gate as he ran the adz back and forth, back and forth, producing a pile of fragrant pine shavings. "Gray Thunder has gone to the Star Chamber. *This* is the thing you mean."

Little Horse nodded, avoiding his friend's eye. If true, this was an emergency indeed. For all knew the Star Chamber was the Cheyenne court of last resort. Composed of headmen secretly chosen by the peace chief, their decisions were above challenges.

Little Horse said, "I do not believe Gray Thunder accepts your guilt. I suspect he did not go to the Star Chamber on that question. Rather, he is seeking advice about the tribe's future. About what to do when the true traitors make their bid for power."

Touch the Sky wiped sweat from his eyes and examined his work before he answered.

"I agree with you, stout buck. Gray Thunder does not accept my guilt. By now, no man of honor has that right."

Little Horse was alerted by something in his friend's pensive tone. "Neither does Honey Eater believe in your guilt," he said firmly. "She and I will be the last to turn against you, Bear Caller. That will happen when the mountains melt and birds nest in the rivers."

These words cheered Touch the Sky. "No," he admitted, "Honey Eater has not accepted my guilt. Nor have you. But appearances are damning. And truly, who among us can believe our fiery war leader acted as I say he did in the final moments of his life? My story has the smell of a lie to it."

"Truth does not always smell as we would have it, Brother. Who would believe that an eagle once refused to let you starve on the plains? That it led you to a food cache? Yet, these things happened.

"Who would believe a shaman's sacrifice and

powerful medicine could turn bullets to sand?
Yet, I stood shoulder to shoulder with you while
Seth Carlson's mountain soldiers missed us at
spitting range! Tell me, buck, that I may some
day tell my son. What *is* the smell of truth?"

Touch the Sky looked at his friend in open
admiration at such eloquence. The normally
taciturn Little Horse was not known for
speeches.

"Brother," Touch the Sky said, grinning, "admit it. You *welcome* this new trouble. You are
keen for sport."

Little Horse, too, rallied. "Life is too long anyway! I, for one, do not plan to die in my tipi.
Face it, buck. This next council will decide *our*
fate, not just yours. Let them come at us, I am
for them! Hi-ya, hiii-*ya!*"

His shrill war cry startled the entire camp.
The Whips gathered around Medicine Flute's
tipi fell silent and stared over at them.

Two Twists was working nearby. Now, as
Touch the Sky and Little Horse watched, he
shouted out, "Wolf Who Hunts Smiling! Bull
Whips! *Look!*"

A moment later, with most of the camp staring curiously, Two Twists lifted his clout at
Touch the Sky's enemies—a gesture of scorn
and contempt usually reserved for battlefield
enemies.

Many in the camp roared with laughter at this
brazen effrontery. That spirited gesture reminded Touch the Sky that no band in camp
had a finer fighting fettle than his.

"Let us go into this next council with our eyes and ears alert, Little Horse. For as you say, it will decide our fate. And I have heard another thing."

Little Horse looked at him, waiting.

"Did you notice that Wolf Who Hunts Smiling had a visitor recently?" Touch the Sky asked.

"The Hunkpapa on the handsome roan?"

Touch the Sky nodded. "That one. Do you know him?"

"No. Do you?"

"I do not. He wore leggings and a rawhide shirt in the proper style of his tribe. But his clothing was a ruse."

"A ruse? Brother, I have always been slow at hearing unspoken words. If you have more to speak, spit them out."

"Only this. I broke apart droppings left by his horse. They were rich with grain. He is an Indian spy from Fort Bates, and he came to see Wolf Who Hunts Smiling."

"Hey, Sugar Britches!" Abbot Fontaine yelled from the front yard. "There's a carrot-top carpenter out here asking for you. Says he come to build you some cabinets."

The young man holding the reins of the buckboard flushed at Fontaine's comment. His thick thatch of hair was indeed almost the color of carrots.

"Friend," Corey Robinson said, taking care not to move quickly, "you got no call to rowel me nor to level that weapon on me. I ain't even armed."

"No gun in sight, mebbe," Fontaine replied. "But I figure a little piss-pants like you for a hideout gun."

"I came here to do some work for Miss Hanchon. Not to listen to your chin music."

Fontaine wrapped his finger around the double triggers of his scattergun. "My daddy—may he rest in peace—was a carpenter, too, just like you, carrothead. Only, *he* had a set of oysters on him. He taught me a carpenter's rule that a man can live by. 'Measure it twice, then cut it once.' Don't push me, boy, 'cause I done took your measure and found you lacking."

Corey swallowed hard—those twin gun barrels stared back at him like unblinking eyes.

Kristen emerged into the bright sunshine.

"Mr. Fontaine! Really, your zeal is getting ridiculous. I told you Corey was coming."

Fontaine sneered. "You did, cuddle corset. But see, I was expectin' a man. This here freckled clothes dummy throwed me off."

"I wish some around here were half the man he is," Kristen said defiantly.

"An Injin' is just about half a man," Abbot said coolly. "And I hear you got a hankering for them red sons of the plains. I wunner if that's on account of you're too scairt to try a whole man like me?"

"Mr. Fontaine, I'd rather clean the filth out of a corral with my bare hands than listen to what comes out of your mouth. Come on, Corey."

"Hey, carrot top!" Fontaine called out as Corey wrapped the reins around the brake and swung down. "Didja know that an Injin ain't got no hair around his pecker? Smooth as a baby's butt down there, even when they're full-growed. Ain't that sumpin'?"

His face set tight, Corey swung down and grabbed his leather toolbag from the bed of the wagon. "Funny," he muttered evenly, "what some men choose to think about."

The barb got through, but it only made Fontaine meaner. " 'Course, Miz Steele could a told us that from experience on account of how she—"

"As you were, mister!" Corey slammed his toolbag down after pulling a hammer out. "Stranger, I'll tell you once and you best listen good. You keep that scummy talk up in front of this lady and you will *have* to shoot me. Otherwise, I'm smashing more holes in that goddamn mud-ugly face of yours!"

Kristen paled in fright. She had not been aware of this streak of temper in Corey. But violence was the currency of Fontaine's existence, and Corey's outburst made him roar with pleased laughter. This was treatment he could respect.

Fontaine grabbed his floppy hat and doffed it at Kristen. "Hoo—eee! By God, them redheads got a short fuse! Miz Steele, I beg your pardon all to hell and back for my range manners."

He winked at both of them. "Enjoy your visit," he added with another exaggerated smirk. He laughed again as he rode off.

Hiram Steele did not know Corey well, but he knew of him. Kristen, knowing her father was in the library, pressed her fingers to her lips, warning Corey.

Once inside the kitchen, Corey broke out his plumbline and began measuring and marking surfaces. Kristen, her eye constantly alert for her father, loudly gave directions and described the cabinets she had in mind.

But speaking quickly, in a whisper, she also managed to fill Corey in on the real reason she had Carlson send him: this new threat to Matthew and his tribe.

Despite the problems it would surely present, Corey never once debated whether or not he would ride to warn Matthew. Even though Corey was white, he, too, had grown up on the fringe of "decent frontier society." His preacher father practiced what he preached, so the Robinsons were decent but poor. He also unleashed a sharp tongue when it came to condemning the area's sinners. As a result, the Robinsons had no shortage of enemies around Bighorn Falls.

Corey knew he would have to dig through his poke at home—dig out the specially dyed blue feather presented to him by the late Cheyenne chief Yellow Bear. It was given to him to honor his part in defeating a Pawnee attack on the camp. It had been Matthew's desperate plan: Corey had stripped naked, painted his body, and capered right into the middle of a battlefield spouting Gospel like his fire-breathing old man. The Pawnee feared nothing more than they dreaded insane palefaces—and none paler than this one. Seasoned warriors dropped their weapons and fled, crying out like frightened children.

That blue feather forever assured Corey safe passage through Cheyenne country or through the country of any of their allies. Anyone carrying it was considered a friend of the red man and a warrior worthy of full honors. Of course, Corey reminded himself reluctantly, that same blue feather guaranteed a nasty death if he fell into the hands of Cheyenne enemies. No shortage of those, either.

"I'll go," he whispered to Kristen. "This whole territory owes Matthew for stopping your pa that first time. But God-in-whirlwinds! If that filthy hardcase outside is a hint of the weather that's coming, I sure wish Tom Riley was back from leave. Pretty soon all hell is gonna be a-poppin'!"

"Little Brother," Tangle Hair said to young Two Twists, "why the deep furrow between your brows? You look angry enough to knock a silvertip bear off the path."

The two braves were working their ponies in the common corral. Tangle Hair held a captured cavalry tunic in one hand. Repeatedly he stuffed it against his ginger mustang's nose. Then he pulled it away and swatted at her sensitive nostrils with a light sisal whip. He didn't hit hard enough to seriously hurt the ginger. But gradually he was teaching his mustang to hate the smell of whites.

"Never mind bears, buck!" Two Twists replied. "I would rather knock a skinny, lying, cowardly, pretend shaman off the path."

Tangle Hair nodded grimly. He had about 22 winters behind him, several more than Two Twists, although they had fought side by side many times. "You mean Medicine Flute, of course. What new lies is he spreading now about Touch the Sky?"

The two friends were quickly absorbed in discussing the troubles dividing their camp. They let their ponies frisk in the lush grass while they walked down toward the river.

"It is not only what he says. It is the insufferable way he speaks as if Maiyun Himself were speaking through him. Just now, as I passed that pack of worthless jays around his tipi, I heard slanders that should get the speaker expelled from his tribe."

Two Twists grabbed a stick from the ground and clutched it close to his chest the way Medicine Flute always held his leg-bone flute. He squinted, mocking the brave's drooping eyelids.

" 'Of course Touch the Sky killed our war leader so he could freely sate his loins on Honey Eater. Little Horse helped him plan it. Both are well-paid spies for the Long Knives. But this so far is nothing compared to the treachery in store for this entire village!' "

Quoting Medicine Flute's lies left a deep and

bitter disgust in Two Twists. He and Tangle Hair walked on in gloomy silence, each fearing that events were about to come to a bloody head.

Honey Eater had faced no dearth of trials and tribulations in her young life. But this new tragedy threatened to write a new chapter in the long saga of Cheyenne suffering.

How, she asked herself again as she wandered along a path near the river, had it come to *this*? The entire tribe in such turmoil that a fight now seemed inevitable. And Touch the Sky so thoroughly discredited that any who openly supported him risked death. This, so soon after Touch the Sky's bravery had saved her and many others from the deadly mountain fever— making him a hero to many in camp.

Black Elk now lay silent forever on a scaffold deep in the secret Cheyenne burial forest. But the legacy of his brutal murder would endure to ruin Gray Thunder's village.

She watched water bugs skimming the placid surface of the Powder. Cheyennes despised eating fish, so of course the river was alive with the loud splashing of bluegills and trout. The sun lay warm on her skin; the breeze was as gentle on her face as the loving fingers of a blind grandmother.

But abruptly, voices approached from the other side of the thickets: someone coming from the opposite direction.

Honey Eater quickly recognized the voice of

Two Twists, her most trusted confidant. A smile touched her lips. She was about to call out, but now his words drifted to her ear:

"Of course Touch the Sky killed our war leader so he could freely sate his loins on Honey Eater. Little Horse helped him plan it. Both are well-paid spies for the Long Knives. But this is nothing compared to the treachery in store for this entire village!"

A moment later they had passed. And if her heart could not believe her ears, her eyes certified this cruelty. She glimpsed Two Twists and Tangle Hair through the thickets.

Despite the laughing sunshine, a cold numbness seeped into her bone marrow. Honey Eater was far too gone with shock to cry or otherwise register her feelings.

"Touch the Sky," she said out loud. But the words fell dead from her lips like stones. One chance moment, a few chance words she was never meant to hear, had just destroyed the only waking dream of her hard life: her hope for a future with Touch the Sky.

She stared for a long time, silent and unmoving. Then, as if they had their own will, her hands lifted to her hair. In a moment she removed all the white columbine petals and tossed them into the river along with her dream.

Chapter Ten

"You are certain," Wolf Who Hunts Smiling said, "that White Man Runs Him knows? He *knows* this hair-face named Steele has returned?"

"He knows," replied the Southern Cheyenne called Lightfoot. "They traded insults recently."

Wolf Who Hunts Smiling liked what his ears were hearing. As they had agreed in their brief initial meeting, this time the two Indians met in the dense birch forest near Beaver Creek.

Lightfoot had taken an oath of enlistment under the Stars and Bars. Now he served as a private of scouts for Fort Bates. He wore his single braid wrapped tight around his head in the style of the clans who had settled south of the Platte River. His braid, his moccasins, and his bear-claw necklace were the only remaining signs of his own culture. For he also wore blue kersey Army trousers and one of the coarse gray pullovers issued to soldiers on work details.

"Cousin," Lightfoot said patiently, "this is the second time my soldier chief has sent me. The first time was merely a polite inquiry to sound the depths of your heart. Now Carlson wishes to sit and parley with you."

"*He* wishes it? And do you take me for a dog who leaps on cue for whiteskins? Do not mistake me, *cousin*, for the squaw-men in your clan."

While he spoke, Wolf Who Hunts Smiling automatically kept flicking his eyes to the surrounding terrain, watching for movement. He trusted no one, Bluecoats least of all. As a mere boy he had watched Bluecoat canister shot shred his father into stewmeat.

"This is indeed the second time we have met," he said, "and will be the last! Did you think you could ride into camp stinking of whites and ask for me without stirring up trouble? All of my authority to rule stems from my long hatred of whiteskins. I make no exception for you."

"I may stink of whites, buck, as you say. But then I also stink of choice coffee and fine tobacco and the purest sugar. For they are rich in these things and many more."

"Here you have said something I can pick up and examine. They have all these things and more. As for you, I will say this much. At least you have not adopted shoes like the turncoat Utes. But back to these goods you have named.

125

Tell me a thing. Are they worth the loss of your manhood?"

Lightfoot frowned. "How have I lost this?"

"Are you a warrior? Where is your lance, your shield, your coup stick? I was once a prisoner at a Bluecoat soldier house. I saw how the Indian scouts lived. You now answer the white man's roll call. When the Mah-ish-ta-shee-da are done with you, they will put you behind one of their plows. Or, if you are fortunate, kill you."

Lightfoot held his face impassive. But anger burned in his black eyes. However, everyone north *or* south of the Platte knew that Wolf Who Hunts Smiling was no brave to trifle with.

"I, too, despise the hair-faces," he said in a reasonable tone. "Most of them treat us worse than they treat dogs. And how can one truly respect men who stupidly wrap their feet in thick cowhide so they cannot even sneak up on an enemy? Who show their feelings in their faces like women and foolishly shout and pump each other's hands up and down when they make greetings? You know how they waste wood when they make a fire, waste buffalo when they hunt, how they break a horse's spirit forever with their stupid training."

"Straight words, buck!" Wolf Who Hunts Smiling said.

"But have you not eyes to see? Your 'war of extermination' against the paleface invasion is a chimera. You have no clear mind picture of their real numbers. It would be easier for one man to swat every fly in Creation with a quirt than to kill all the whites.

"You think they are only a large tribe. But Cousin! I have ridden east to the Great Waters which the whites call the Missouri. The white settlements there are so huge one cannot count their lodges. Our language has no words to describe what I saw. And even further east, where Sister Sun is born each day, there are so many palefaces they cover the land like prairie grass."

"Prairie grass, buck, will quickly burn. Enough of this womanly talk," Wolf Who Hunts Smiling scoffed. "When a Pawnee wrongs me, I do not ask how many more there are in his clan before I kill him. Why should I do less when my enemy is a paleface?

"Only tell me this, Lightfoot. Where and when shall I meet with your soldier chief?"

"In two sleeps. Ride to the big redrock canyon north of the valley the whites call Blackford Valley. I will meet you there and take you to him."

Wolf Who Hunts Smiling nodded, his slitted eyes thoughtful. Whatever the hair-faces had in mind did not trouble him: he had no plans to honor any promises to them unless he stood to gain from doing so.

Nonetheless, this was a golden opportunity. For one thing, Lightfoot had already hinted at enough of the whiteskin plan. Woman Face would surely get involved once his sworn enemies began framing the Cheyenne tribe and jeopardizing their homeland. He never missed an opportunity to play the big Indian.

And by conspiring with the whites, Wolf Who Hunts Smiling would thus be in an excellent position—this would afford opportunities for once again making Medicine Flute's magic look more powerful than Touch the Sky's. Armed with inside knowledge, Wolf Who Hunts Smiling could also more deeply implicate his enemy as a spy for the whites.

At first Wolf Who Hunts Smiling had bitterly regretted his mistake in murdering Black Elk instead of Touch the Sky. But it had quickly worked out in his favor—it threw serious suspicion on Woman Face. Even worse than death, to an Indian, was rejection by the tribe.

But clearly it had not been enough to destroy him. However, this new trouble with white men, arriving so soon after Black Elk's funeral, just might be enough to ensure the tall intruder's final downfall.

"Tell your white masters I will be there," he said. "It matters not that I consider all white men combined worth less than a handful of spider leavings. For any man who would command an empire must reason coolly and harness *every* breeze to his advantage.

"So tell them I want what they want. To see buzzards picking out Woman Face's eyeballs."

Corey's friendship with Matthew Hanchon had made him more naturally curious about Indians than were most town-dwellers. He had learned to notice the physical traits that differentiated the many Plains Indian tribes. Thirty miles east of Red Shale, in the sandhill country, that curiosity saved his life.

Corey, riding a healthy but slow Arabian mare, had just emerged from a narrow defile between two sand blights. Dismounting so he wouldn't be sky-lined, he studied a group of Indians riding at right angles to him across a low plain.

Even at this distance it was easy to see that all the men had full heads of long, beautiful hair, completely unrestrained.

Crows. Longtime enemies of the Cheyenne. His blue feather might get his scalp lifted, if they spotted him.

Chafing at the delay, he tugged the mare's reins and walked her back into the defile until the Crows had ridden out of sight. Corey glanced at the coppery tinge over the western horizon, gauging how much daylight was left.

His horse resented this hard use and nickered from time to time, demanding good forage. The animal was hungry—Corey reminded himself to steer around the big patch of Johnson grass near Headwater Bluff. The last thing he needed right about now was for his horse to gorge himself on that damn loco weed.

For a moment Corey saw a stark image of Fontaine's sawed-off shotgun dangling from that jury-rigged sling—a cold-blooded killer's rig, Corey told himself. No need to even aim—just lift it and blast.

But even more chilling than the gun were Fontaine's hard little snake eyes—like the button eyes of a child's doll, with no spark of human soul in them. Corey recalled those, too, and his mouth went dry with fear.

Wolf Who Hunts Smiling had just returned from his meeting with Lightfoot. Swift Canoe met him in the common corral.

"Brother! I know a thing!" Swift Canoe said.

Anger tightened his face as Wolf Who Hunts Smiling stared at his fawning lackey. "What, are we girls in their sewing lodge trading choice gossip? Either speak this thing or hold your silence. I will not press to hear about it."

Swift Canoe frowned at the rebuke. He, too, hated Touch the Sky with all his being. He was convinced that Touch the Sky had caused the death of his twin brother, True Son. Wolf Who Hunts Smiling knew better. It was he, not Touch the Sky, who disobeyed orders and tried to scalp a sleeping Pawnee, waking him up. True Son died in the resulting chaos.

Swift Canoe turned and started to leave.

"Brother!"

Swift Canoe turned around, feigning curiosity. "Yes, brother? What is it?"

By now Wolf Who Hunts Smiling was seething. *Look* at this soft-brained fool! If he were not such a loyal follower, Wolf Who Hunts Smiling would have murdered him long ago out of sheer exasperation.

"You rabbit brain! Do not play the coy maiden with me! 'Yes, brother, what is it?' Spit your words out before I tear them from your throat!"

"But you called it gossip. You said—"

"Buck! My last warning, have ears!" Fire blazed in his dark eyes. "Have done with this womanly indirection at once. Say what you know, and say it simple and plain. Or by Mai-yun, I will spill your guts onto the ground."

"Touch the Sky's white friend is here," Swift Canoe answered sullenly but quickly. "The one with hair the color of embers. The one they call Firetop. The one—"

"I *know* who he is, stone-skull!" Wolf Who Hunts Smiling snapped impatiently. "Crack the shell and expose the meat. Why did he come?"

"Who knows this thing? You know he has the medicine feather, none can question him. Even now, as we speak, he and Woman Face are huddling together. Clearly, some mischief is afoot."

Wolf Who Hunts Smiling knew precisely why Corey Robinson was here. And the timing could not be worse for Touch the Sky. In fact, it played right into Wolf Who Hunts Smiling's plans. By now many in the tribe had only dim memories of the young Corey Robinson who had saved the tribe. With Black Elk's ghost now pointing an accusing finger at Touch the Sky, a visit from a whiteskin could only hurt.

This good news softened Wolf Who Hunts Smiling's anger toward Swift Canoe.

"Buck!" he called out. "I heartily thank you for this good news. Never mind my harsh words. You are a stout warrior, and you will sit behind few men in council once I am chief."

A wide smile divided Swift Canoe's face.

"Know this," Wolf Who Hunts Smiling added as they began walking toward camp. "The trap is closing on White Man Runs Him. If we red men do not soon send him under, his white masters will."

By the time Corey fell silent, Touch the Sky knew he was trapped between a rock and a hard place.

Outside the tipi, the camp was unusually silent. And he knew why: All were awaiting the outcome of this suspicious meeting between their shaman and his white friend.

Burning wood snapped in the firepit. Their shadows stretched long on the sloping sides of the tipi. The English words felt odd in his mouth when Touch the Sky spoke.

"It's bad enough to face Hiram Steele on his own. If he joins forces with Wolf Who Hunts Smiling, it will be the bloodiest marriage since the Kiowas took a loaded pipe to the Comanches."

"I don't like how Kristen gets sucked into all this," Corey said. "Steele couldn't've hired no worse pond scums than them 'bodyguards' of his, not even if he tried. I'm wondering, who will protect Kristen's body from *them*?"

"This isn't the first time," Touch the Sky said quietly, "that she's suffered on my account."

Touch the Sky stood up, his lips set in a straight, determined line. "Wait here, Firetop.

That blue feather carries some weight. But after I announce what I'm about to announce, I can't guarantee your safety."

Touch the Sky unfolded the red Hudson's Bay blanket that protected his Sharps from dew at night. He verified that the bore was charged, that a bullet was seated behind the gate.

He stepped outside and signalled the camp crier. Touch the Sky instructed him to gather the people in the common square. By the time Uncle Moon had traveled the length of a lodge pole, Gray Thunder's Cheyennes were listening as their shaman spoke from the center of the clearing.

No one missed the rare fact that Touch the Sky—never one to condone belligerence within the camp—held his rifle in the crook of his elbow as he spoke. Nor did Little Horse, Two Twists, and Tangle Hair need any urging to assume their usual protective formation around him.

"Cheyenne people! Firetop brings us disturbing news of more whiteskin treachery! A paleface plan has been launched to steal our homeland and give it to paleface dust scatterers. I and several warriors must return with Firetop to fight it."

An excited buzzing erupted among the people. Here Touch the Sky leveled accusing eyes on Wolf Who Hunts Smiling. He knew it was useless to also report on the secret machinations of *this* one. Why bother? Such treason could not be believed by most, so the accusation would only hurt Touch the Sky.

Wolf Who Hunts Smiling coolly met that stare. Now he, too, spoke out.

"Cheyenne people, have ears for my words! Notice how convenient for Woman Face the timing is. Now, with the charge of murder hanging over him, he tells us how he must ride out. Now, when he knows the Star Chamber is deciding his fate. And why? Oh, how noble this red man! He is off to 'save our land' from whiteskin thieves!"

"This has a foul stench to it," threw in Medicine Flute. "It is clearly an attempt to avoid punishment. And this visit from whites in our very camp. Yet one more tie to the hair-face masters *this* one serves!"

"Give over with this familiar litany," Touch the Sky said finally. "I fully expected it. That is why this matter is not before council."

Just then Touch the Sky inadvertently caught sight of Honey Eater. He frowned, then felt his stomach sink when he realized what troubled him. For the first time in his memory, she wore no columbine petals in her hair.

He met Honey Eater's eyes. What he saw in her glance shocked him speechless for a moment. Could this be, he wondered. Could it? For those eyes clearly *hated* him!

Why? Of course she was upset. That had been clear when Black Elk was discovered. But this now was not suspicion—this woman he loved with all his heart now hated and despised him.

As if to confirm it, she abruptly turned her

back on him and walked away.

For a moment the strength drained from his limbs, and Touch the Sky wanted to sit down. But the unjustness of her behavior stirred a deep pride and resentment in him and only hardened his resolve.

His final remarks were delivered with a fiery eloquence and determination that momentarily cowered his enemies.

"It matters not who would like my guts for new tipi ropes. *I* am shaman and Arrow Keeper. It is my task to protect my tribe however I must. I will brook no debate on this matter. I have spoken, and this place knows what I said.

"My band and I will ride out, Firetop with us, at sunrise. Let any man who plans to stop us sing his death song first!"

Chapter Eleven

"Honey Eater," Sharp Nosed Woman scolded, "you have never been one to sulk and pine. Now *eat* this."

Honey Eater turned away from the succulent elk steak that her aunt had carried across camp to her.

"Aunt, thank you. But I cannot eat. I am *not* sulking or pining. I promise this thing. Only. . . ."

Her voice broke as a sob hitched in her throat. Embarrassed to lose control like this in front of her aunt, she stared mournfully into the fire and said nothing.

"Only," Sharp Nosed Woman finished quietly for her, "that you have been caught in a love as tragic as the very fate of our people! Oh, child, I am covered with hard bark and not easily moved to pity. But I wish I could sit upon the ground and keen as I did when my brave husband died fighting the Pawnees! You are such a good girl, and your lot has been so hard."

Those who knew Honey Eater best would not have been surprised by her response to this. Even now, with her heart broken past all repair, she could not bear to see a loved one in such grief. As her aunt began to shake with sobs, Honey Eater bravely dried her eyes. How could the daughter of Yellow Bear wallow in self-pity? She cut a piece off the meat and poked it into her mouth.

This gesture immediately cheered Sharp Nosed Woman.

"Honey Eater, you are an adult now. As a widow, our law-ways do not prohibit you from living here alone if you wish."

"As they did when my father died," she said quietly, automatically making the cut-off sign as one did when speaking of the dead. She didn't need to add: *Thus ensuring my fate by forcing me to accept Black Elk's bride-price.*

"But though you are permitted to live alone," her aunt went on, "please do not! You visit at my tipi constantly anyway. Come live with me. Now that we are both widows, it is only natural."

The steak was tender, but Honey Eater struggled to chew it. Nausea fluttered in her stomach, but she willed it away.

"For now, Aunt," she said, "I will stay in my own tipi. But thank you for suggesting it."

"Well, at least you are eating again. Here, cut another piece, and try a bite of that wild onion. I know you like them. I will make us some nice tea, and—"

"Aunt?"

"What is it, child?"

"You have not told me. Do you believe Touch the Sky killed the one who was my husband?"

Sharp Nosed Woman was suddenly terribly uncomfortable. She wrapped her blanket around herself tighter.

"Honey Eater, you are sweet but your honesty often inspires some bitter questions. I cannot say that I believe he did this thing. Yet, neither can I say he did not. Maiyun knows that, whether he did it or not, no man had greater cause.

"Granted, he is the bravest warrior I have known. But even the best can fall, and when they do, they fall hardest of all. Appearances damn him. That pistol, this sudden arrival of a white man even as the Star Chamber deliberates. Yes, Wolf Who Hunts Smiling is a dog off his leash. An ambitious dog! But I cannot believe he would kill Black—"

Sharp Nosed Woman caught herself in the nick of time. She quickly made the cut-off sign. "Would kill his own cousin," she amended. "But little one, never mind what *I* think! I would love you no matter what."

Sharp Nosed Woman lowered her voice in urgency. "Have you thought how these secret events make you look? This love between you

138

and Touch the Sky. You know the unmarried girls used to sing of it in the sewing lodge.

"Now? Now they are silent. What was once romantic and sweet is now filth. Ugly rumors abound. Rumors about a young couple so overcome with lust they resorted to murder to satisfy it."

"Aunt, I am a Cheyenne woman. Of course I value what others think and say. How could I not and be a good Cheyenne? But for my part, I can swear they are all wrong about one point. I, too, could of course succumb to desire and be unfaithful. I admit it. Other good women have done it for love, and though our tribe frowns, we have always forgiven and worked it out.

"But *never* could I resort to murder for the base purpose of satisfying animal lust. By Mai-yun, I could never be a party to such treachery."

"Child, I never doubted this thing. But tell me. Why did you say'for my part?' Do you know of some treachery by Touch the Sky?"

Even in the grainy light, her aunt's intense stare made Honey Eater flush. Now a knife twisted deep inside her as she recalled the horrible words she had heard Two Twists speak. Two Twists! The one friend she trusted most. And he had stated it baldly, all unadorned: Touch the Sky murdered Black Elk!

"Aunt," she finally replied, her misery complete. "I know of nothing but talk. And I know what I can see. My little troubles are hardly the end of this. Look, over there."

She pointed clear across the common square to Medicine Flute's tipi. At least half the Bull Whips were gathered there.

"You see treachery there," Honey Eater said with firm conviction. "Whatever Touch the Sky has done, Wolf Who Hunts Smiling has surpassed it. Or soon will."

Indeed, this was the greatest misery of her young life. Not only did Honey Eater feel forced by honor to reject the only man she loved—she was also forced to watch his enemies rally around Medicine Flute. Once he was declared 'shaman,' they would make their final bid to take over the tribe.

Her aunt's voice jarred her back to awareness. "Well, never mind those wild bucks. We are women, our will has never mattered to them! We are not welcome at their councils. When they wish to insult one another, they call other men women. I have heard some Whips say a girl child should be killed to save food for a warrior! Let these men play at war and kill one another. Good riddance.

"But child, *you* must be better than they. Your father was the greatest peace chief in *Shaiyena* history. How many times has our winter-count recorded his deeds, yet was he a hard man with no soft place left in him? No. Even after burying two wives he loved with all his life, he retained great compassion for suffering. *This* is a virtue only the best warriors exhibit.

"And so it is that you must stay above their level. Never mind how tongues wag against you now. You must hold your head high and not fail this hard test of your goodness. So long as the stink of the murderer clings to Touch the Sky, *you must avoid him.*"

"Brother," Wolf Who Hunts Smiling said quietly to Medicine Flute, "did you watch Woman Face and his band ride out earlier?"

Medicine Flute had long ago realized that his eerie music not only annoyed the people—it also intimidated them and made them nervous. So, as usual, he was busy piping the few off-key, monotonous notes he had mastered. He nodded without taking the leg-bone flute from his lips.

"And did he not ride his favorite pony, the chestnut with the brown mane?"

Again Medicine Flute nodded. His eyelids drooped lazily in the flickering firelight.

"Little Horse and the rest were mounted, too. So tell me a thing. Where is the new dugout I watched them make?"

This question was interesting enough to cause Medicine Flute to finally pause in his playing.

"Hidden?" he suggested.

"Perhaps." Wolf Who Hunts Smiling's quick-as-minnow eyes darted about the camp. "But where? I know the best places, and I have searched well. I think they sneaked it out before they left."

"Why, buck?"

Wolf Who Hunts Smiling grinned. "*You* are the shaman. You tell me this thing."

Medicine Flute matched his grin. "Soon I will indeed be the shaman, officially. So best hide your scorn well. You and I know the only 'god' is the gun. The others who worship the High Holy Ones are fools. We will build our monuments on their bones."

"We will, buck, we will. But one world at a time! First we must find out about this canoe. As Woman Face will learn, it is a dangerous game, trying to fox a wolf!"

"What the hell is it?" Hiram Steele demanded.

They sat their horses in a well-sheltered jumble of boulders on the northern rim of Blackford Valley: Hiram, Seth Carlson, Abbot Fontaine, Stoney MacGruder, and an Assiniboin scout named Sinew. Overhead to the north, black smoke traced a lingering parabola across the sky.

"Sioux smoking-arrow," Sinew replied tersely. He rode a tough little calico mustang. The other Indian scout, Lightfoot, was due to be arriving anytime now with the Cheyenne renegade.

"It's part of the moccasin telegraph," Carlson explained to the older man. "It's a system the savages have in place to spread news amongst themselves. Smoke signals, mirror flashes, runners. That arrow was wetted and then dipped in gunpowder. They lit it before it was shot. That black smoke is visible for fifty miles. We've also spotted Indian runners."

"What are they saying?" Steele asked.

Carlson looked at Sinew.

"Trouble. Gray Thunder's Cheyenne camp," the scout said.

"What kind of trouble?" Steele demanded.

Sinew's face remained as still as a leather death mask. He shook his head. "Trouble. Plenty trouble, you bet."

"You've made that clear. Now spell it out better. What kind of trouble, John?" Steele persisted. He used the name commonly employed by frontier whites in direct address to any Indian. "You can't say or *won't* say?"

The scout cast him a long, inscrutable look before turning his pony and edging a few more feet away.

"By Godfrey!" Abbot said. "Mrs. Fontaine's favorite son don't brook no high-hat treatment from no red Arab. Hiram, you want I should put some buckshot in his sitter, teach him some respect?"

"Put it away from your mind," Steele said. "We—"

"Behold this, Lightfoot!" a voice above them said in rusty but discernible English. "A horse with a load of stinking dung on its back. Dung that speaks like a he-bear and threatens red men!"

"Jesus hell!" Fontaine said.

As one, the five men sitting their horses had glanced straight up. The meanest-looking wild savage they'd ever seen peered at them over the edge of a traprock shelf a few feet above them. He held a Colt Model 1855 percussion rifle

143

Judd Cole

trained on Fontaine. It was badly nicked and battered, and a buckskin patch reinforced the cracked wooden stock. But at this range, no one below cared to challenge its accuracy.

Another Cheyenne, this one skinny but as wily looking as the other, held a British trade rifle aimed at Steele. The scout named Lightfoot, gagged with a strip of chamois, was with them. He shrugged helplessly.

Wolf Who Hunts Smiling had learned some English while a prisoner at the Bluecoat fort. "You, pig!" he said to Fontaine. "Did your brain leak through that hole in your face? Truly, brother," he said to Medicine Flute, though his companion understood very little English, "a blue-bloused soldier rutted on a sheep and *that* dungheap was the issue."

A purple rage flowed up out of his neck and into Fontaine's face, darkening it above his grizzled beard. But though his right index finger itched, the Colt above—and the hardcase Cheyenne aiming it at him—kept his hand off his scattergun.

"You'll swallow back them words yet," was all he said now.

"I take it," Hiram Steele said coldly, "that you're the buck they call Wolf Who Hunts Smiling?"

"Whiteskin, place these words close to your heart. If I hear you pronounce my name again, I will kill you."

Steele was too startled by all this to feel his famous temper flaring up. Like most mean

144

men, he respected a brutal tyrant.

"Don't say their names," Carlson said quietly to Steele. "These ignorant savages are convinced their names have power, and that they will lose power if whites speak them out loud."

Wolf Who Hunts Smiling was enjoying himself immensely. The next few sleeps should prove an interesting diversion. Lone Bear, leader of the Bull Whips, had cleverly covered for him and Medicine Flute. Lone Bear had used his powers as a soldier chief to send the two braves on an "extended scout" for sign of buffalo herds. Some in camp would not be fooled, of course. But this excuse officially covered their absence.

Wolf Who Hunts Smiling directed his remarks at Steele.

"Have ears, flint-eyed one! You are a whiteskin and I hate you as surely as I hate the yellow vomit or the red-speckled cough. But I confess, I admire the hard-edged look to you. If any other man hates this pretend Cheyenne as much as I do, you are he!

"So let it be straight between us now and always. I hate you, you hate me. Our hearts are stone toward each other. But though the Pawnee hate the Mandan, they made common cause to destroy their common enemies."

"Jesus, he ain't exactly as sweet as scrubbed angels, is he?" Fontaine remarked in a low tone.

"Rough as a badger out of his hole," Steele agreed with an approving glint in his eyes.

"Maybe this benighted savage is just the man we need."

Steele thought about everything the bold Cheyenne had said. Then he looked at Carlson. "What's your gut tell you, soldier blue?"

"Well, Hiram, you wanted a killer. Up there stands one now, or I'll eat my forage cap."

"He's about half rough," Fontaine conceded. "He'll kill this here Hanchon for you, right enough. Kill him deader 'n a Paiute grave. But I don't expect he plans to stop there."

Steele's eyes puckered in disgust. "You don't 'expect' he'll stop? Of course he won't, you fool. You and Stoney are being paid to make sure he does."

Fontaine winked at MacGruder. "Oh, I figure we can powder his butt and tuck him in, hey, Stoney?"

"Are you women?" Wolf Who Hunts Smiling taunted. "You huddle and whisper down there like young girls getting their first blood. If you wish to destroy a boil, you must first draw it out. Only tell me what you require me to do."

"All right," Steele agreed. "I like a man who doesn't sugarcoat his words. We need to draw Matthew Hanchon out, all right. Draw him into more danger than he's ever had to face. With your help, we can guarantee more trouble than ten men could handle. We can get the U.S. Army, the territorial militia, the miners' vigilante committee after him. We can get so many men peddling lead at him that he won't stand a chance."

"All this just to send one mere brave under?"

"From what I hear, buck, you of all people know he's not so 'mere.' "

Wolf Who Hunts Smiling conceded this with a single nod. "I also know that white wrath will not end with his death. *All* Indians in this area will be attacked. And I, for one, welcome it! We will kill this tall one, whiteskins! Then we will kill one another!"

"Count on it, John," Fontaine said, his voice low with menace.

"Stow it," Hiram ordered. He looked up toward the Indians. "All right, then. In a minute I'll tell you what I need you to do first. But right now I got a question."

"Speak it or bury it, paleface! Only women waste words."

Stoney MacGruder guffawed at this, but the big man shut up quick at a glower from Steele.

"Just this. What's the big trouble at your camp? How come all the mirror signals and smoke?"

Wolf Who Hunts Smiling truly savored the irony of this. "You do not know? You of all white fools?"

"Know what?"

"Know that our enemy's paleface friend has arrived to warn my people about you. About your plan to steal our land and sell it to white dust scatterers."

Both Steele and Carlson flushed deep. "What friend?" Steele said coldly. "You mean Corey Robinson?"

"Your foolish names mean nothing to me. We call him Firetop because his hair has caught flame."

"There's her goddamn 'cabinets,'" Steele said in a low, murderous tone to Carlson. "That goddamn Indian-loving daughter of mine is a *spy* for the blanket asses!"

Carlson was equally enraged. She played him for a fool to help the very enemy he was sworn to kill!

A few moments later, Hiram got his breathing under control. "All right. First things first. We'll end up controlling this territory yet. But for now let's tell this buck what we need him to do. Then we'll have a little talk with Kristen and her carpenter friend."

Chapter Twelve

Even as Wolf Who Hunts Smiling parleyed with Hiram Steele, Touch the Sky slipped into Blackford Valley literally beneath his enemies' noses.

The valley was bisected by a small, seasonal river. It was known to the Cheyenne as Salt Lick Creek because of the numerous saline springs dotting its length, which attracted animals to its banks. A tributary of the Powder, it flowed only when the spring thaw arrived and the high-country snowpack was as deep as it had been this winter.

Instead of trusting the familiar Indian trails, Touch the Sky listened to the new warnings of his shaman sense. He devised a plan and divided his small band into two sets.

Tangle Hair and Two Twists, leading their friends' ponies, rode to the valley by the usual route. But Touch the Sky and Little Horse, Corey with them, slipped back into camp after they rode out. They dragged their new dugout to the river and set out on a lively current toward the confluence at Salt Lick Creek.

And once again Touch the Sky's 'third eye' proved accurate. Twice, as they neared the valley under shelter of gathering darkness and overhead branches, they had spotted Seth Carlson himself watching the trail above them.

"I only hope, brother," Little Horse said, "that you are right. I hope Carlson and his blue-blouses ignored Tangle Hair and Two Twists."

"They did," Touch the Sky said confidently. "Count upon the white man's disdain, it will save our comrades. For truly, all Indians look alike to a hair face. Carlson knows you well by now. But he will not recognize these two as our band. He has no interest in them. Killing them will only risk warning our tribe they are after us."

Little Horse considered this, then nodded. "Straight words, buck. Besides, that trail also points to the trading post at Red Shale. He will think they are taking extra ponies there to trade."

"I wish you'd jabber in English now and again," Corey groused. "Or else learn me some Cheyenne talk. I'm gettin' lonely."

"Believe me, when trouble comes one language is enough," Touch the Sky assured him. "Right now I'm doing some serious worrying in two."

He looked closer at Corey in the dim light. "Tell me. Is there direct communication between Steele and Wolf Who Hunts Smiling?"

Corey hesitated as his friend's meaning sank home. "I don't know," he admitted. "I didn't think about it in my hurry. Neither did Kristen, I don't reckon. But I catch your drift. If them two are in communication, Steele might find out I was in the Cheyenne camp to warn you."

"And if that happens, he'll know who sent you," Touch the Sky finished. "Or anyway, he'll as good as know."

"Shit-oh-dear," Corey said quietly. "Poor Kristen. Neither one of us thought it out careful. There just wasn't time."

"Well, we were all careless," Touch the Sky said. "Anyway, the fat is in the fire now."

"Brother," Little Horse complained, "you speak too many words in the tongue of the *Mah-ish-ta-schee-da*. You should teach me their language."

Despite the serious trouble they were heading into, these words prodded a wry smile from Touch the Sky. This same complaint from both of his friends symbolized the competing demands of the two worlds he moved back and forth between.

A three-quarter moon laid a ghostly, silver-white glow over the water. The dugout, built for two travelling light, was overloaded by three men lugging weapons and equipment. Nonetheless, it had proven worthy of the task. Its shallow draw meant they seldom scraped on sand bars, and its light weight made it easy to maneuver around dangerous sawyers—places in the river where large branches got caught just beneath the surface and formed hazardous traps.

"We'll hafta keep our eyes peeled good now," Corey warned them. "The mill comes up fast, and it's easy to miss among all them willow trees. Just hope the wrong party ain't waiting there to welcome us with lead."

Touch the Sky translated this for Little Horse.

"What is this mill?" his friend demanded.

"A place where the hair faces crush grain to make flour. They use the river's power to turn huge stones which crush the grain. It is much more efficient than the pestles our women use. But Firetop says this mill was abandoned many winters ago when a drought left the river empty."

Corey and Kristen had agreed that Padgett's Mill, although risky, would be the only possible staging area for this battle that was shaping up. Wildly overgrown, located in a remote spot thick with trees, it was virtually ignored by the few whites in the area. Corey had already sneaked in forage and oats for the horses. The animals could be kept inside the spacious mill by day—watered from a bucket—and tethered near the river after dark.

Touch the Sky knew they were up against another hard fight. And truly there was fate behind these events; the hand of Maiyun was in it. For only look how so many forces and events were now conspiring against him. Steele's greedy plan, Wolf Who Hunts Smiling's murderous ambition, the death of Black Elk . . . all of it would daunt him, force him to waver and perhaps lose the never-ending fight, if not for the power of his epic vision at Medicine Lake.

How he had suffered, following Arrow Keeper's urging, to achieve that vision! And now, in spite of all he faced, he must believe in its ultimate promise: That all this suffering would eventually be justified. That the day was coming when he would defeat his tribal enemies and rally the entire Cheyenne Nation to its greatest victory.

Oddly, that epic vision had promised nothing about his private happiness as a man—only his public role as a warrior. No man, himself included, knew whether his life would ever merge with Honey Eater's. And now, recalling the accusing hatred he had seen recently in her eyes, Touch the Sky's misery was acute.

"Brother!" the keen-eared Little Horse suddenly cut into these unwelcome thoughts. "What was that?"

All three men held silent. Now Touch the Sky heard the bubbling chuckle of the current, the monotonous chorus of frogs and insects. Out ahead in the darkness an owl hooted. The sound echoed loudly over the water, ghostly and menacing.

Then Touch the Sky heard it: a fast clicking like the sound of a gecko lizard. A moment later he turned his stretched-hide paddle wide, steering them into the bank.

Hands reached out, grabbed the dugout and pulled it up onto the bank. Now Touch the Sky could make out the looming mass of a building almost flush with the water's edge.

"Brothers," Two Twists greeted them, "we are all here despite the bluecoat traps. Our smallest Cheyenne children could cut sign on these pale warriors."

"Getting here is not the battle," Touch the Sky reminded them. "And white soldiers are not our only enemies."

Even before he inspected the interior of Padgett's Mill, Touch the Sky removed a stick of charcoal from his parfleche. In the luminous moonlight he solemnly marked his comrades's faces black—the Cheyenne warrior's symbol of joy at the death of an enemy.

"Brothers," he told them, "I admire Two Twists' fighting spirit. But do not take these blue-blouses lightly. True it is, man-for-man out on the plains they cannot match a Comanche, an Apache, a Sioux, a Cheyenne.

"But we are not out on the plains, nor is it man-for-man. They, too, have their own strengths, just as we red men do. They are highly organized and methodical. They have rigid battle discipline, and they use the new carbines which even the Cheyenne Dog Men respect.

"And perhaps most destructive for us, they are like diseased men in their thirst to kill redskins. It is sometimes called, by honorable white men, 'Indian fever.' In a battle where surrendered Mexicans are taken prisoner, Indians who surrendered would be killed every time. Some of them are fanatical in their need to exterminate us."

"As Wolf Who Hunts Smiling is fanatical to exterminate *them*," Little Horse said. "But as you said, brother. We face more than blue soldiers. We face Hiram Steele and Wolf Who Hunts Smiling, also."

"We do. Either one of them could frighten the Wendigo. Both of them together make even a brave man quail to think on it."

"Good thing we are not merely brave, but also crazy!" Little Horse made a tight fist and thumped his chest with it. "As for me, I did not come here to ensure a long life! I will ride my pony in the Land of Ghosts, too."

Touch the Sky grinned at Little Horse's typical show of fighting spirit. It was a style openly emulated by the younger Two Twists. Indians admired a boaster so long as he lived up to his brags. And no Indian melded brag with deed better than the highly respected warrior, Little Horse.

"Buck," Touch the Sky said, "I have marked you, and the color that is on you is death. Only one thing will wash it off: our enemy's blood!"

Even before her father entered the house, Kristen knew she was in serious trouble.

She had suspected, of course, what her father

was up to when he rode out earlier that day with Carlson—she had overheard enough to know they were meeting with one of Matthew's tribal enemies.

But in her desperation to help Matthew, she knew she had been careless. What if this renegade mentioned Corey? True, there was no proof she had teamed up with Corey to warn Matthew. But it was a logical conclusion. And in any event, her father was not one to require proof before he cocked the hammer.

Now, hearing the clink of bit rings, the snuffling of horses in the yard below, she knew her father and his gunsels had returned. And she knew *he* knew about her. She could sense it.

Cold blood prickled the nape of her neck and raised the fine hairs. It was well after dark, and she was up in her room, trying to read a leatherbound copy of *Pride and Prejudice* by candlelight. But in fact she had been fretting all evening as she wondered what was happening, wondered if Matthew was again fighting for his life. She could not forget what Pastor West had said last Sunday in a sermon about American Indians: "They are not blameless. But God knows they have been forced to fight too hard for the mere right to exist."

Matthew had told her once that Indians believed all men of all colors were part of a circle, all connected to one another. All were linked, and no one could deny that link, ever. She believed it, too. But men like her father and Fontaine and MacGruder denied their link to the rest of humanity.

Now, hearing her father ride in, all her courage and conviction seemed like paltry help. Cold dread replaced her stomach as she heard the door bang open below, heard boots scraping the stairs, heavy footsteps moving purposefully down the hallway toward her room.

The steps ceased right outside her door. Kristen, hands trembling, pulled her dressing sacque tighter around her. She sat up straighter in the spindleback chair, clutching her book to her breast.

"You know I'm out here, girl. Them ears of yours hear too damn much. Now open this door."

The voice, ominous as a hangman's wake-up call, struck terror to her very marrow. She was unable to budge from the chair.

An abrupt crash, then wood splintered to the floor as her father suddenly stomped the locked door open.

"By Godfrey, Hiram!" Fontaine said admiringly. "You got a kick on you like a Mex mule! You see that-air kick, Stoney? *One* kick! Old son, I'll be go to hell!"

All three men stood in the doorway staring at her. Fontaine tapped his shotgun, making it wiggle in its sling. MacGruder lifted his hat, leering like a woman-hungry mountain man.

Kristen tried to muster up a show of indignation to mask her fear. "What is the meaning of this?" she demanded.

"Don't you play the quality miss with me," Steele said in that low, slow voice that always turned her limbs to water. "We've already twigged your little game with Corey Robinson and that redskin criminal, Matthew Hanchon."

"What . . . what game?"

"Shut your goddamn, filthy, Injun-kissing mouth and mark me, girl. My own flesh, spying on me and ruining my business ventures—that don't set well with me."

Despite the fear freezing her to the chair, these words sent angry blood into her cheeks. The bottomless blue eyes sparkled with indignation. " 'Business ventures!' Conspiring to steal Indian land, to sell their homes right out from under them, isn't business. It's thievery."

"Whoa there, Hiram!" Abbot Fontaine said, placing a restraining hand on Steele's shoulder as the big man started to lunge at his daughter. "If you kill l'il sweet britches, what are me and Stoney spozed to do for a little fun around here?"

"By God," Steele fumed, agitated breath whistling in his nostrils, "she pokes her Injun-loving nose into white men's affairs one more time, and I *will* let you boys have her. I'll throw her in that room with both of you, like meat to dogs, and lock the door."

"Well now," Abbot said, "that'd be more lively than a Green River ronnyvoo, eh, Stoney?"

Kristen watched MacGruder swallow the tight lump of lust in his throat. The big man's dull, leering stare felt like slugs squirming against her skin. "I'd like that real good," he said, his voice oddly husky. Kristen shivered.

Seeing Kristen humbled like this began to calm Hiram down somewhat. Now a tight smile compressed his lips as he watched his haughty and rebellious daughter actually squirm. "Abbot?"

"Yo?"

"You remember those directions I gave you to Corey Robinson's place?"

"That I do, boss. Mrs Fontaine's boy Abbot has got a memory like a steel trap."

Hiram watched Kristen turn noticeably paler. His smile widened. "All right, then. You and Stoney put some chuck in your belly, then fork fresh horses and pay that redhead a little visit. Wake him up, give him my regards."

This order left ice water in Kristen's veins. But she had enough presence of mind to rise quickly after the trio finally, and mercifully, filed away from her broken door. She peeked cautiously past the doorjamb and saw them conferring in quiet voices at the head of the stairs.

"You want we should watch her even closer now, Hiram?"

"Don't bother. Right now she's too damned scared to spit, she'll stay out of it. I can't spare you boys, there's bigger fish to fry. You heard what that Cheyenne buck said about the missing canoe. First, go take care of Corey Robinson. But first thing tomorrow, I want you and Stoney to start searching the entire length of the river, the part that cuts through this valley. Find out where those damn redskins are holed up.

"It'll take a few days to search all of it, but Stoney is good with sign. I want 'er done right. I know this redskin devil Matthew Hanchon. It ain't safe having him anywhere near this place."

Corey was bone-weary from his courier mission into Cheyenne country and the cramped canoe trip back into Blackford Valley. It was a good night for travelling, the bright moon combining with a dome of glittering stars. So he retrieved his horse from Matthew's Cheyenne friends and returned to the cabin he shared with his father near the river-bend settlement of Bighorn Falls.

Queasy apprehension tickled his stomach as he rode up to the Robinson place well after sundown. The cabin was dark and graveyard silent. He noticed that his old man's mule was missing from the pole corral, but that wasn't unusual. The itinerant preacher often pitched his dog tent at the outlying miners' camps.

His absence was fine by Corey. His old man constantly harped after the rebellious boy to beg the lord's forgiveness. Corey, in turn, told his father he respected the lord just fine. But he figured he hadn't done anything near so black that he had to beg anybody for forgiveness. A quiet apology was enough, he figured. His old man wanted a show to wake up the angels.

Corey relaxed when their old bloodhound crawled out from under the sloped-off kitchen and started howling until he recognized the smell of Corey's horse. Corey grinned in the generous moonwash, watching the arthritic old dog limp toward him with his tail sweeping the yard.

"Hey, Zebulon! C'mere, old campaigner! C'mere, boy!"

He scratched the old mutt behind the ears, then went inside and lit the lamp hanging from a crosstree of the low ceiling. Despite his exhaustion, hunger gnawed at Corey's belly. He built up a fire in the iron cookstove, pulled the skillet down from its nail on the wall, and sliced some slab bacon into it.

Now and then a noise from outside the cabin caught his attention: a stick snapping, the croak of a bullfrog changing slightly in pitch. Corey knew by now that news of his ride to Gray Thunder's camp might well get back to Hiram Steele. But certainly Steele's retribution would not be so swift as to come this very evening? Besides, old or no, Zebulon still had good hearing and was a loyal watchdog.

Corey sat down at the split-slab table, using an old nail keg for a chair and eating his bacon right from the skillet with a clasp knife. He used an old heel of pan bread to soak up the tasty drippings.

Abruptly, he heard Zebulon growl—a low, menacing growl from deep in his chest.

Moving carefully, Corey laid his knife down and reached for the lamp. He had just turned the wick completely down when a tremendous blast split the silence of the night. The lamp flew from Corey's hands, the chimney shattering on the plank floor.

Buckshot slammed into the cabin like tornado-driven hail. Corey stiffened, then rose and took his rifle from its wall pegs. He crossed to a small Judas hole in the door. He opened the cover and placed one eye to the hole, peeking outside.

Zebulon—or rather the once-vital parts that had been Zebulon—lay strewn about the yard, a glistening mess in the cruel moonlight.

Hot fury warred with cold fear in Corey's blood. Now he heard the rapid drumbeat of retreating hooves. Whoever the cowardly, scum-sucking bastard was, he must be escaping. Corey lifted the latchstring, quietly nudged open the door. He cautiously poked his head outside. He saw a lone rider disappearing in the hazy moonlight.

"Hey, there, Carrot Top!" a familiar voice greeted him out of the nearby darkness. "You shoulda allowed for a second rider. And you damn sure shoulda stuck to building them cabinets."

Before Corey could react, a bright orange light exploded inside his skull and then his world shut down to darkness.

Chapter Thirteen

Wolf Who Hunts Smiling had his instructions for the first 'Indian attack' on white interests. Two sleeps after Touch the Sky's band rode out, Wolf Who Hunts Smiling and Medicine Flute rode back into camp. This surprised many, as they were supposed to be on a scouting mission, preparing for the annual buffalo hunt. The mystery, however, was soon explained.

"Fathers and brothers!" Wolf Who Hunts Smiling said to the assembled Headmen. "Medicine Flute and I will indeed complete our scouting mission as Lone Bear commanded us. However, never forget my pony flies the streamer of the Bull Whip soldiers! I am one of our tribe's policemen.

"A more important temporary mission has been charged to us. One that overrides the authority of my Bull Whip leader—of our peace chief, even!"

Wolf Who Hunts Smiling was in his element when he was thus holding listeners spellbound with such dramatic speech. Some, who wisely held silence, could not help comparing his speech and gesturing to the white politicians, who jumped on stumps to scatter their lies like seeds in the wind. Now the Councillors all watched him with tense expectation.

"Fathers and brothers! Medicine Flute has had an important vision. As it touches on the welfare of the entire tribe, we have ridden back, as duty demands, to report it."

Even among his enemies this announcement triggered a deep, respectful silence. With his hair cropped short to honor his dead cousin Black Elk, Wolf Who Hunts Smiling looked especially fierce. More important than this, however, was the strong Cheyenne belief in medicine visions. Even many of those who supported Touch the Sky freely admitted that Medicine Flute had impressively demonstrated his powers of prediction and divination. How else but with powerful medicine could he have predicted that a star would catch on fire and shoot across the sky? Did he not do this very thing?

"What manner of vision?" Chief Gray Thunder demanded. Though he kept his tone and face neutral, ever the impartial leader, Gray Thunder's eyes revealed a glint of suspicion.

"Let Medicine Flute, the source of this supernatural revelation from Maiyun, speak it himself," Wolf Who Hunts Smiling said. "As our shaman, he—"

"This wolf here often barks in presumptuous error," cut in Spotted Tail, leader of the Bow String soldiers. "Our shaman bears the name of Touch the Sky. He was chosen by a warrior whose medicine was bigger than the Plains—I say 'was' only if indeed he is even gone from this world. Now, only an act of Council can snatch that title from his parfleche."

"An act of Council," Lone Bear corrected him, his eyes meeting Gray Thunder's, "or a decision of the Star Chamber. Touch the Sky stands accused of tribal murder. Those who bloody the Arrows are hardly fit to guard them!"

An awkward silence followed this. For all assembled knew that the Star Chamber would soon make known to Gray Thunder its secret decision about Touch the Sky. Wolf Who Hunts Smiling sent Spotted Tail a cunning glance, a glance that promised him a hard death as reward for his loyalty to Touch the Sky.

"Fathers and brothers!" he continued. "Let us cease this present dissension! We need not fight among ourselves. Events will soon enough prove the treacherous depths of that Woman Face's soul! For now, Medicine Flute! Speak the vision that was placed over your eyes for all loyal Cheyennes to know."

Medicine Flute had spent years perfecting his deceptive arts. Shrewd, intelligent, and observant as a hungry hawk, he had carefully noticed how childish the people could be about 'visions.' He had also closely studied the behavior of white men who went insane. Such wandering wretches dotted the Plains, often driven crazy by the sheer, treeless immensity of a land they had not been prepared to encounter. They were considered powerful bad medicine, to be both respected and avoided. He learned their quirks and mannerisms, adding them to his 'holy performance.'

Now, as they all turned to stare at him, he slowly rose and brought his leg-bone flute to his lips.

He widened his eyes dramatically and put what he called the "trance glaze" over them. The slow, eerie, monotonous notes soon took hold of all assembled and held them in reluctant thrall.

Medicine Flute lowered his crude instrument. He began chanting the minor-key chant the old people always sounded when the warriors rode out to battle.

Then, in an "other world" voice that impressed even Wolf Who Hunts Smiling, Medicine Flute spoke.

"A wild pony ran past my father's tipi while my mother was having me! Now I see with the shaman eye. Those who worship a false medicine man and mock me now will rue their destiny! Just as those who follow the wrong war leader will pay with their lives."

These words were not wasted on the Councillors. With Black Elk gone, the tribe was without an official war leader. No one disputed that

Touch the Sky and Wolf Who Hunts Smiling were the warriors most deserving of the honor, in terms of raw courage and fighting skill. But Medicine Flute's words subtly reminded them that one of these two stood accused of bloodying the Sacred Arrows.

"Even the fall of a pine cone is the shadow of a deeper meaning! Even when Uncle Pte, the buffalo, sniffs the air, he smells the red man's destiny! Even the—"

"Even the wind from a pony's ass will blow a campfire out," Spotted Tail cut in scornfully. "Yet this breeze from your mouth could not flutter a dead leaf. Less chatter, more matter!"

"You mock sacred things, traitor?" Wolf Who Hunts Smiling demanded.

"That they are 'sacred,' I am not so sure."

But despite his defiant words, Spotted Tail now came to his senses as he looked around. Every Bull Whip present looked murder at him. He bit back any further comment, already in enough danger. However, he knew that any Indian's safety lay in numbers. So he quickly and quietly announced to his troop:

"Bow Strings! They have called *me* a traitor, who once counted coup on a sleeping Pawnee in his lodge! This strong language proves that serious treachery is afoot. I now openly declare my allegiance to Touch the Sky. And I charge you, Bow Strings, with this order. From here on, watch your backs and sleep with your weapons to hand. Know where your brothers are, and never forget that all Cheyennes serve the

Sacred Arrows and the High Holy Ones!"

"The same High Holy Ones, *brother*," Wolf Who Hunts Smiling said, "who sent us this sacred vision. Now let Medicine Flute speak it."

To prevent any more outbursts, Wolf Who Hunts Smiling shot a warning glance at Medicine Flute: *Womanly fool! Hurry to the essence.*

"The High Holy Ones, who first made the days and gave them to men, are unhappy. Everyone here knows the Law-ways are clear on this thing, that we are sworn to protect with our lives the land they gave us.

"But I have seen a thing. I have seen this Touch the Sky, this White Man Runs Him, in a vision. I saw him dressed as a whiteskin pony warrior, wearing their boots, pouring blood from the Medicine Hat onto a talking paper which the palefaces call treaties. These symbols can mean all things, but to a shaman can mean only one thing.

"Soon will come the first sign that I speak straight-arrow. But for now, know this. This White Man Runs Him left to join hair-face soldiers in the final destruction of our homeland!"

Honey Eater and the other women had not been permitted at this council. But even caught deep in the grief and pain of Touch the Sky's apparent betrayal of honor, she was furious at the duplicity of his tribal enemies.

"Aunt," she said to Sharp Nosed Woman soon after the council was over, "did you see the faces of the men as they filed from the council lodge?"

Sharp Nosed Woman was busy shelling wild peas into a stew simmering over her cooking tripod. She frowned deeply and nodded.

"I have eyes, pretty one, I have eyes. The Whips and the Strings were almost at each other's jugulars. Child, this tribe is balanced on the feather edge of its own destiny. Fall one way, and we succumb to the shame and barbarism of the heathen Comanches who abandoned their laws. Fall the other way, we may end in tragedy but it will be a tragedy with honor."

This was an unusually perceptive insight, coming from her deadly practical aunt. Honey Eater stared at her in open wonder.

"Aunt! *You* are a vision seeker, and a good one."

"*Ipewa*. Good. Then perhaps I can predict when you will finish peeling those turnips, idle one?"

But Honey Eater was not in a playful mood. "Aunt, you saw the trouble in their faces. I know that—that Touch the Sky is at the center of a hurting thing, a thing so ugly I cannot see the possibility of his innocence. And yet. . . ."

"And yet what, child?"

"And yet, I wish he were here now to fight for his tribe."

"Honey Eater, I understand this. Even *if* he did kill the one who may not be mentioned, he has not been proven a traitor. But this is a dangerous direction in which your thoughts wander. Remember who you are!

"From this present level of thinking, you will

169

leap to other ledges, until you have climbed high enough to forgive him everything. Again I say, who are you? The daughter of our greatest chief ever. Yes, you love him. But if you weaken now, you are saying that the murder of a fellow Cheyenne counts for nothing at all."

Honey Eater met this remark in miserable silence. For indeed, what was there to say? Her aunt was blunt but candid. Honey Eater's actions counted more than those of most other Cheyenne women. This was indeed the interpretation that would be given to any softening on her part toward Touch the Sky.

"Honey Eater," her aunt said now. She stopped shelling peas to stare at her niece. "What is different about you?"

But now a sob caught in her throat, and Honey Eater only shook her head, unable to speak. Suddenly, though, Sharp Nosed Woman fell silent and went to work again, visibly upset. For she had just realized what was different—and why.

For the first time in her memory, Honey Eater's beautiful long hair was devoid of the pretty white columbine petals.

Chief Gray Thunder felt trapped between the sap and the bark.

He sat alone in his tipi, the lines of his face etched deep in worried thought. Though well past his fortieth winter, Gray Thunder was still a stout, vigorous warrior. However, recent events had aged him spiritually.

And now—this.

He glanced down at a square of buckskin which had been neatly tied shut with a rawhide whang. It contained six stones, any combination of either black agates or white moonstones. It had just arrived by secret courier from the six elder warriors who served as the Star Chamber, the Cheyenne court of last resort.

He had put the crucial question to them. And now, when he untied that buckskin, it would be decided: More white stones than black, Touch the Sky remained unpunished; more black ones than white ones, he would be punished. And knowing his enemies as Gray Thunder did, they would press for execution.

So Gray Thunder dreaded untying that bundle. As a chief, he was allowed even less say than a common warrior. For it was the chief's solemn duty to determine the will of the tribe, not to dictate to them.

And yet—privately, as a man and not a chief, he believed in Touch the Sky. He believed old Arrow Keeper was right in his conviction that the tall youth was marked out for a great destiny. Gray Thunder was completely baffled by the murder of Black Elk. But damning appearances aside, he could not truly suspect Touch the Sky. Especially not when the shot was fired from behind. Had Touch the Sky killed Black Elk, it would have been another bloody contest—face to face—as their fistfight in front of the entire camp had been.

As for Wolf Who Hunts Smiling. . . .

171

Gray Thunder frowned, picked up the buckskin-wrapped stones, hefted them a few times in his hand. As for Wolf Who Hunts Smiling, here was serious trouble. An overweening ambition burned in his young eyes. Yet Gray Thunder was powerless to prevent his machinations. That wily young brave worked like Maiyun in the universe, everywhere felt but nowhere seen. One could not pick up his treachery and examine it.

Truly, a chief's lot was a hard one! Well, now the hard decision was about to be taken out of his hands—literally.

He sighed, untied the rawhide whang, spilled the six stones out onto the buffalo robes that covered the ground under his tipi.

Gray Thunder stared, his heart turning over for a moment at the cruel irony of it.

So the hard decision would be his, after all. Because of the six stones scattered before him, three were black and three were white.

Chapter Fourteen

"Brothers," Touch the Sky said, "we are Plains warriors. Trained to fight in skirmishes from our ponies. And here we are, forced to fort up like white men. Like you, I prefer to take the fight into their very teeth and be done with it. But there will be no trance-fasting or war dances this time. *This* place hints at the foreign and difficult fight to come."

Touch the Sky glanced around the mostly deserted interior of Padgett's Mill. The huge single room had been divided by a buffalo hair rope, turning one half into a makeshift corral. Corey had brought in hay and oats. He had also scrounged up old nosebags from their friend Knobby, the hostler in Bighorn Falls. Now the delighted ponies, hardly used to such pampering, were quite effectively silenced as they stood contentedly munching oats.

The dugout canoe leaned against the back wall. At one time a huge paddle wheel, connected to a vertical axle, had turned the heavy millstones. The wheel, though in bad repair, still went round. But an intricate series of iron gears, which once connected it to the millstones inside, had long since been melted for bullets.

Someone had evidently tried to remove one of the heavy stones, then given up. Taller than a big man, it was propped up at a dangerous angle near the west wall. Only one small edge of a sturdy support beam kept the huge stone from falling the rest of the way down.

"This big stone lodge is sturdy enough. But to me it is a huge death wickiup," Tangle Hair complained. "I will hide here, if we must, during the day. But, brothers, I will not sleep in this place. At least my tipi has a smokehole at the top, I can see the sky. I will spread my robes near the horses when we take them out for the night."

"You, double-braid," Little Horse called out to young Two Twists, "come over here, buck! Help me block this odd, small entrance which was stupidly built off the floor."

Touch the Sky could not help a brief grin. His friend meant one of the mill's three windows. They had once been covered with oilcloth, but it too had succumbed to the elements. Bright sunlight filtered through these openings in slanting shafts. But one of the windows, especially, allowed a dangerous view inside from without, and it faced the river. Little Horse and Two Twists dragged in an old and dilapidated wagon bed from outside and propped it up sideways over the window.

"By now," Touch the Sky reminded his companions, "Wolf Who Hunts Smiling is preparing to help these same white enemies he has sworn to exterminate. And Seth Carlson's men will surely be thick in this area, combing the brush for us. But I feel certain they believe we *rode* in. They will not expect us to be hidden so near the river. This should be the last place they look. By that time, if Maiyun wills it, we will have made their world a hurting place."

"Where is Firetop, brother?" Tangle Hair asked. "He was to have returned by now."

Touch the Sky nodded thoughtfully, his lips set in their grim, determined line that meant he was deeply worried. "I have been wondering this thing, too."

During all this, no one paid much attention to Little Horse. When things looked most grim for Touch the Sky's band, Little Horse was apt to be at his most playful. No one watched when he moved into the bright sunlight right behind Two Twists. All of a sudden Touch the Sky's jaw fell open in amazement—Two Twists' clan feather had just burst into flame!

"Brothers!" Tangle Hair shouted. "Look at Two Twists! Have I eaten peyote, or did lightning just strike him?"

Two Twists whirled, saw them all gaping, and

reached up to feel searing flames lick at his finger.

"The Wendigo lives in this place!" he shouted. "He has me! Run, brothers!"

As he clawed his headband off, face draining almost white with fear, Little Horse fell to the ground, convulsed with laughter.

"Two Twists," he managed between violent spasms of mirth, "*here* is your Wendigo."

Little Horse held out the magnifying glass he'd been given at the trading post. Despite the danger they all faced, the other three joined Little Horse in laughter. For Indians truly loved a good practical joke, and it relieved the tension of this unfamiliar mission.

"Come then, Death," Touch the Sky said fondly. "We will not be cheated out of *that* laugh."

Thus distracted, no one had paid attention to the obvious sounds of a rider approaching—until a horse nickered just outside.

All four young braves, caught unprepared, froze for a moment, glancing at one another. Then, first to recover his wits, Touch the Sky snatched up his Sharps and moved quickly toward the open door. The others fanned out at Touch the Sky's signal, covering down behind old wooden flour barrels.

Touch the Sky slipped his finger inside the trigger guard and curled it around the trigger. Then, cautiously, he peered past the slanted-open door into the bright sunlight.

Just in time to watch a frightened-looking

Kristen Steele dismount from her side-saddle. She wore a leather riding skirt and soft calfskin boots with a pretty yellow shirtwaist tucked into the skirt.

"Matthew!" she greeted him desperately when he stepped outside. "Oh, Matthew! I was afraid—that is, my father and his hired guns are gone, so I took a crazy chance coming here because I *have* to warn you!"

In her nervousness she was short of breath. Touch the Sky watched brilliant flashes of gold in her hair as the sun backlit the thick, wheat-colored mass. Even now, when clearly she had not come to pay a social call, they were acutely aware of each other's nearness. Time may have altered the old feelings, Touch the Sky realized. But they had not gone away.

"Warn me of what?" he said when she finally had her breath.

"My father and his men know you came into the valley by canoe, not horse. Abbot Fontaine and Stoney MacGruder have been systematically searching every foot along the river. I don't know how close they are to this place. They started at the east end, I think, so this spot should be near the end of their search."

"How do they know about the canoe?"

"From that brave who's helping them."

"Wolf Who Hunts Smiling?"

She shuddered. "Yes, that's his name. Does he live up to it?"

"Do bears love honey?" The furrow between his eyes deepened as Touch the Sky frowned.

By now his companions had crowded close, curious about this sun-haired beauty and her urgent news.

Touch the Sky translated for them. "At least," he finished up, "we have been warned."

"But what can we do, brother?" Little Horse said. "This close to the soldiertown, we cannot make a camp in the open. Yet without a camp, how do we fight? Our ponies must have a place to rest, and so must we."

Touch the Sky nodded. "Straight words, buck. So we will stay right here. You know the secret place Firetop showed us."

Little Horse nodded, though dubiously. These paleface tricks were not to his liking. Beneath the straw in the makeshift corral was a tiny crawl space under the floor. A cramped tunnel led to a nearby thicket behind the mill. Such emergency tunnels had been common on the frontier before the Indians began signing treaties.

"When we are here, we will post a sentry outside night and day. We will have to kill anyone who discovers us. Or rely on the tunnel if too many attack us."

"But, brother," Little Horse objected. "What if our ponies are here? And the straw . . . if enemies do come in here, we will lose this place as well as our mounts."

"We cannot have the ponies in here," Touch the Sky agreed, "unless we are with them. Leave *no* equipment or weapons to view. The hay and straw will tell them nothing, nor will the dugout. White squatters and other Indians have used this place. Red men commonly stash dugouts for others who are following behind them."

He turned back to Kristen and switched to English again. "If your father talked to Wolf Who Hunts Smiling, then he must know?"

"You mean . . . that I sent you a message?"

He nodded.

Kristen turned pale and looked away. "Oh, does he *ever* know. But, Matthew, don't feel sorry for me! I hate him, and I hate what he's doing to your people. Even if I didn't—if I didn't—"

She faltered, blushed, glanced away. "Even if I didn't feel the way I do about you I would defy him. Pastor West says that a person who sees evil and doesn't try to stop it is *part* of that evil."

"Sounds like a good man, Kristen. But I don't think he means for you to take on your father."

Distress was clear in her pleading eyes. "Matthew, it's not just me. He sent Fontaine and MacGruder to Corey's place!"

"When?" Touch the Sky demanded.

"Night before last."

Touch the Sky's jaw muscles formed a tight bunch. He turned to the others and quickly translated this. Then he looked at Kristen again. "Get on back home now. You can't risk this again, Kristen. Understand?"

She nodded. "But Matthew? Please be careful! My father and Carlson, they don't just intend to get rich off Indian land. What's really behind all this is their hatred of you. More than anything else, they want to kill you. And if they can't do it, they mean to make sure your own people do."

Seth Carlson's commanding officer, Col. Jedediah Thompson, was a ramrod-straight, God-fearing soldier who mixed harsh discipline with Christian decency. He was ruthless on deserters and thieves within the ranks. He ordered their heads shaved, and the letter of their offense branded into their skin forever.

However, he did not believe, as did Phil Sheridan and other famous generals of the day, in the deliberate extermination of the red aboriginals. He was a devout Methodist who subscribed to local Pastor Jim West's unpopular view: the Bible and the plow would tame the Indian.

But neither would he tolerate any nonsense from the Indians in his jurisdiction. Knowing this, Seth Carlson now appealed to his C.O.'s pragmatic sense of duty.

"That's just about it, sir," he said, wrapping up his latest reconnaissance report. "We definitely have signs of increased hostile activity lately, particularly among the Northern Cheyenne. The moccasin telegraph has been active lately. They're organizing for something."

Thompson frowned. He leaned back in his chair and folded his hands over the new blotter on his desk. "War path?"

"Could be, sir."

"Why would the Cheyenne paint their faces

against the settlers around here, Captain? Granted, all the miners swarming into the Black Hills in violation of the treaty have got them riled, especially the Sioux. But that's farther east. Things have been quiet around here lately."

"Yes, sir. It's a stumper. But Lightfoot, one of my scouts, says there's a new malcontent. A young Northern Cheyenne buck who's looking to set himself up as another Dog Soldier like Roman Nose."

"That's all we need. What's he call himself?"

Carlson's lips tightened around the words. "Touch the Sky."

"Hmm. That *is* an ambitious name," Colonel Thompson agreed thoughtfully. "You keeping an eye on him?"

"He's my top priority right now, sir."

Thompson nodded. "Very good, Captain. I wish Tom Riley were back from leave to give you a hand in the field. All right, keep me informed."

Carlson, standing at ease before his commander's desk, came smartly to attention and saluted. "Yes, sir."

"Carlson?" the colonel called out when his subordinate was about to exit the headquarters office. Carlson turned back around.

"Sir?"

"Carlson, I've reviewed your record. You're a sound officer. Graduated fifth in your class at West Point, and twice decorated for combat bravery. But I also noticed a certain pattern emerging in your conduct-and-proficiency reports."

"A pattern, sir?"

"Yes. A pattern of comments by superiors, and minor disciplinary actions, which point up one fact. You have a certain . . . zeal for persecuting Indians. Just a reminder, soldier. A professional military man fights from a cool sense of detachment and devotion to duty. *Not* from emotion. I do not want my officers motivated by a personal vendetta against Indians. Remember, they are not all automatically enemies. Only the ones who break the law and fight us are. *Watch* this renegade, yes. But don't goad him into a fight."

Carlson nodded. "Yes, sir. But I assume I have the right to intercede if we catch him red-handed in a treaty violation?"

"Of course. The current rules of engagement permit that. And I want a full report on every violation. I won't go belly-aching to Congress over the theft of an occasional cow. Indians get hungry too, and God wouldn't have made them if they weren't meant to serve His purpose. But there's an old saying. 'Enough butterflies can kill a man.' If the Cheyenne push this too far, they're going to deeply regret it."

Shortly after Kristen left, Touch the Sky prepared to ride out. He knew it was risky approaching Bighorn Falls by daylight. But Corey must be in trouble—assuming he was still alive. He sent Two Twists further down the river on sentry duty. Then, sticking to the timbered ridges, relying on his old childhood memory map of the area, he set out for the Robinson place.

Long ago, during Touch the Sky's apprenticeship, Arrow Keeper had taught him a valuable wilderness survival lesson: Spend less time thinking and more time attending to the language of the senses. But Touch the Sky could not shake loose the image of Honey Eater's accusing eyes—or, since her visit earlier, of Kristen's blue ones. Those two conflicting images symbolized his life's worst dilemma: He lived in two worlds, the white man's and the red man's, but he was welcome in neither.

He forced these thoughts out and concentrated on the foothill country surrounding him. Fort Bates lay nearby, and twice he spotted small patrols of pony soldiers. He took cover until they were out of sight. But the way they studied the terrain carefully through field-glasses made him nervous. These were not work details or men on maneuvers. They were roving sentries.

Touch the Sky was still north of the big bend in the river where the town was built, following a long defile that divided two ranges of hills. Now he spotted a lone rider, cutting across the face of the nearest hills.

The Cheyenne spoke to his chestnut and coaxed her into deeper cover, watching the rider draw near. He recognized the mount first: a distinguished Arabian, small but well-formed.

Then Corey Robinson's red-orange hair reflected in the afternoon sunlight.

Even when his friend was still some distance off, Touch the Sky noticed the dark discoloration of his face. The Cheyenne's lips showed a hard, tight anger when Corey drew abreast. His face was bruised the color of purple grapes, battered beyond recognition. One eye was swollen almost shut.

"Hey, pard," the game little redhead greeted him through lips still swollen twice their normal size. "You think I look bad? You oughta see the grizz I skinned alive."

"I see Steele's 'bodyguards' paid you a visit. Anything else hurt besides what I can see?"

Gingerly, Corey touched his lower ribs. "I'm a mite stove up in the cage, I reckon. One or two ribs might be cracked. The old man taped them for me. Course, he had to give me a lecture on how I'm going to hell in a haywagon unless I reform my sinning ways and get religion quick."

"Religion won't hurt," Touch the Sky conceded. "But sometimes it's best to go straight after the Devil himself. And the Devil's name this time is Hiram Steele."

"Ahuh. Devil? Hell, he's meaner than Satan with a sunburn! And there's more devils where *he* come from," Corey said. "He's got two of 'em on his payroll."

"Three, if you count Seth Carlson."

"Oh, I count him, believe me."

While the two friends spoke, hidden in the

trees just off the trail, a group of bull-whackers was winding its meandering way into the valley below them, following the long switchback turns of the federal freight road. Watching them, Touch the Sky abruptly felt it: invisible ants biting at the back of his neck—the familiar warning of his shaman sense.

Feeling it, he quickly scanned the length of the freight road. Ahead of the lead teamster, in a cutbank further along the trail, a slight movement caught Touch the Sky's attention.

He stared, saw the motion again: a rider nudging his pony nearer to the trail. Now a second rider, a third, moved up beside the first.

Riders . . . Indian riders!

And suddenly he recognized the leader by his leather shirt: Wolf Who Hunts Smiling.

"Corey! You too bunged up to use that Winchester in your scabbard?"

Corey looked surprised. "Why . . . if I can jack a round into the chamber, by God I can pull the trigger."

Sky whirled his mount and pointed her bridle into the valley. "Good. Cover me. That's our friend Wolf Who Hunts Smiling down there, and he's getting set to frame my tribe for murder!"

Chapter Fifteen

Touch the Sky's chestnut was from quick, strong mountain blood, as sure-footed as a mountain man's mule and trained as sharp as a circus pony. But Wolf Who Hunts Smiling had less than half the distance he himself had to cover.

Nor, despite Touch the Sky's shouted instructions to Corey, would covering fire be of much use to him—Corey seldom shot more than the occasional squirrel, anyway. And at this distance even a sharpshooter would be lucky if he could hit a horse, much less a man.

But Touch the Sky urged his mount on down the ridge. Clearly, a single bullet would be worthless. He left his Sharps in its boot and quickly pulled a handful of fire-hardened arrows from their foxskin quiver.

Like many frontier survivors, Touch the Sky sometimes copied the battle styles of his enemies. And from watching Big Tree and other fierce Comanches fight from horseback he had learned how to grip as many as fifteen arrows in his hand. He could string them one after another with less than an eyeblink's time between them. In this way a flurry of arrows could be shot almost simultaneously to overwhelm the target.

Even as he plucked his new osage-wood bow from its rope rigging, he saw two more riders move out behind Wolf Who Hunts Smiling: Swift Canoe and Medicine Flute. The cowardly Medicine Flute was no serious challenge. But Swift Canoe, though stupid, was a stout warrior who would carry out any order Wolf Who Hunts Smiling gave him.

"Hii-ya!" Touch the Sky yipped, nerving his pony for more speed with the Cheyenne battle cry. "Hii-ya, hii-*ya!*"

The lead bull-whacker was about to debouch from a long switchback. The second he did, he would be square in Wolf Who Hunts Smiling's sights. Then it occurred to Touch the Sky: From here he could aim at *either* party, Indian or white. Maybe this time it was better to stop the river than to catch the fish.

Fwip! Fwip! Fwip!

Again and again, his buffalo-sinew string twanging hard, Touch the Sky sent his first flurry of arrows down on the unsuspecting freighters. Each shot also produced a sharp *thwap* as the bowstring slapped the leather band protecting his left wrist. More faintly, he heard his arrows solidly embedding in the wooden sideboards of the lead wagon.

Elation sang in Touch the Sky's blood when the freighter, battle savvy from experience, immediately reined in his team of oxen. He rolled into the bed of his wagon and came up with a long Henry rifle in his hands.

By now Wolf Who Hunts Smiling had spotted his worst enemy in the tribe, flying down the ridge toward him. Their eyes met across the narrowing distance. Even this far back, Touch the Sky felt the hatred and defiance his adversary nurtured against him.

That same defiance made Wolf Who Hunts Smiling predictably do the unpredictable. Buttplate of his Colt resting against his thigh, he urged his black forward into the turn, determined to go after the kill that Woman Face had tried to deny him.

Above and behind Touch the Sky, Corey's rifle spoke its piece. Touch the Sky grabbed another handful of arrows. He was forced to lean back hard to counterbalance his pony's wild downward rush. He could feel the chestnut's powerful muscles heaving beneath him as he strung his first arrow. A heartbeat later, the chestnut's right foreleg suddenly slipped on a hidden patch of loose shale.

At this headlong speed, the fall was incredibly violent and fast for both animal and rider. The pony flew one way, Touch the Sky another, both smashing into the ground hard. The impact stomped the wind out of the Cheyenne. But even as he tumbled, Touch the Sky retained a desperate and protective grip on his bow and arrows.

He was aware when his pony, dazed and scared but apparently uninjured beyond a few scratches, scrambled to her feet down the slope from him. Dizzy, still struggling for wind, Touch the Sky nonetheless kept himself intensely focused on the warrior's task, closing for combat—the winner could lick his wounds later. He immediately rose to his feet and again lifted his bow.

Below, Wolf Who Hunts Smiling's Colt spat muzzle smoke. Touch the Sky felt his face go cold when the lead freighter folded over the side of his wagon and sprawled in an ungainly heap in the middle of the road.

The freighters behind him had broken out their long guns and covered down when the attack commenced. Now Touch the Sky saw all of them excitedly point in his direction: The next moment, slugs started buzzing past Touch the Sky's ear with an angry-hornet sound, forcing him to retreat. Clearly, they assumed he was one of the attackers.

Just as clear was the blood-soaked hair of the bullwhacker who lay sprawled in the road. Wolf Who Hunts Smiling's shot had been fatal.

"You murdering, savage bastard!" one of the freighters shouted behind Touch the Sky. "Put at 'em, boys!"

Desperately he whistled for his pony. There's the first 'treaty violation,' Touch the Sky told himself even as bullets nipped at his heels. He grabbed handfuls of mane and swung up, then urged the chestnut back up the ridge toward Corey's position in the trees. He had almost gained safety, when there was a sudden, sharp tug just above his left hip.

The tug was followed by a bursting flash of white-hot pain. Touch the Sky called on all his reserves of strength to hang on.

Not only was he seriously wounded—he had failed to stop Wolf Who Hunts Smiling in time. Those sage-freighters were bound for Fort Bates. Now it would go in the official post log: a record of this deadly 'attack' by Northern Cheyennes.

This failure today, he told himself grimly even through the hot, red welling of pain—it meant he must survive to fight again. And next time, he must *not* fail.

The Northern Arapaho word-bringer named High Road always made a point of swinging wide past the paleface settlement at Bighorn Falls.

It was his job to run messages between the Northern Arapaho camp at the Yellowstone River and their Southern Arapaho clan near the place whites called the Solomon Hills. The Northern chief named Battle Sash had recently died of Mountain Fever. Now High Road was headed south carrying news of a special Chief

Renewal ceremony coming up during the Moon When the Cherries Ripen.

His pony picked her way along an old game trace, out of sight of any soldier patrols in the valley below. So far his journey had been uneventful, and High Road fervently hoped it remained that way.

A shrill Cheyenne battle cry, just below him, announced that his hopes had just been scattered to the wind.

High Road heard the rapid pounding of hooves. He swung down from his mount, hobbled her foreleg to rear with a loop of rawhide. As he cautiously leap-frogged from pine tree to juniper, making for the treeline below, a rifle shot rang out from above and behind him; moments later, another shot sounded from below, near the freight road.

He reached the treeline and cautiously peeked out.

Now more shots rang out, and High Road was just in time to see a lone Cheyenne racing uphill, dodging bullets. Below, a paleface lay in the road.

The Cheyenne's hair was cropped close and ragged. But the *Shaiyena* tribe were longtime allies of the Arapahos, having made common cause against the blood-thirsty Pawnees. High Road had danced with Gray Thunder's people during the recent Animal Dance. So he easily recognized that extraordinarily tall, broad-shouldered brave. He was the young shaman from Chief Gray Thunder's Powder River camp.

The formidable warrior named Touch the Sky.

But why, High Road wondered now with growing anger, would a lone Cheyenne attack and kill a white freighter? Such an irresponsible act would not just mean trouble for the Cheyennes. *All* Indians suffered for the criminal acts of a few. Whites were implacable in their thirst for revenge.

He made up his mind. There was no critical hurry to deliver his news to their Southern cousins. He would make an important detour first.

What had just taken place was serious. High Road would first take a report to the Headmen at Gray Thunder's camp.

Kristen almost regretted this new privacy she enjoyed, this freedom from the prying and lusting eyes of Fontaine and MacGruder. After all, she knew the price of this new privacy—they were busy searching out Matthew.

The sun had just gone down in a blaze of glory over the mountains. She sat alone in the front parlor, reading *Pride and Prejudice*. But despite Jane Austen's wonderful story, Kristen could not concentrate on the words. The real world kept intruding itself. It wasn't Matthew alone she worried about. How was Corey?

Thinking of Corey made her glance toward the closed door of the library. As always, her father sat in there alone, scheming great schemes of wealth and power. She supposed he had always been a hard, hidebound man. But the sudden death of Kristen's mother left him bitter—in part because she died before he could have the son he wanted. And then that bitterness just cankered, the man's soul went sour, and a hard man became a criminal. If only—

"Kristen! Kristen! Help me, are you here?"

Laura Bishop's voice—pitched high in fright—brought Kristen immediately to her feet. Laura banged on the front door, hard enough to bring Hiram out of the library.

"Oh, Kristen! Mr. Steele!" Laura greeted them. "It's so terrible! I'm on my way to my cousin Rebecca's house. She—she's—well, *you* know, Kristen, she's in the family way, of course. She, well, she—"

Hiram, despite his nature, liked Laura and considered her the only decent friend his errant daughter had. Now he raised his hand to quiet her.

"Whoa, girl! What the hell's got you so upset? Spit it out clear."

"Yessir, Mr. Steele. Rebecca's time is here. But it's going hard—real hard, Mr. Steele. The midwife has been there for hours, I—Mr. Steele, Rebecca might not make it! Pastor West has called all of us family, but—I—oh, Mr. Steele, can Kristen go with me to give me strength? I'm *so* frightened. It's a moonlit night and I've got the landau outside."

This was woman's business and very remote from Hiram's experience. "She'll go with you," he replied, not even asking his daughter. But Kristen's curiosity was piqued—Rebecca had

193

delivered her baby a week ago, a healthy baby boy! What had put Laura up to such a wild tale?

Kristen grabbed a shawl for protection against the damp chill of the river valley. The moment they were outside, Laura gripped her arm tight just above the elbow.

"La! I can't believe I lied to *your* father! He frightens me. Kristen, Corey told me he can't come around here any more. So he sent me with this cock-and-bull story to get you out. He said to tell you your friend Matthew has been shot, and it looks like it might be serious."

"Brother," Little Horse said quietly to Tangle Hair, "we have done what little we can. But truly, that bullet went deep. He lost much blood when I cut it out. Nor dare I cauterize such a deep wound without first packing it with something to fight infection. There is moss by the river, but no balsam or yarrow root in this area."

Tangle Hair nodded quickly. Touch the Sky lay atop a heap of buffalo robes, semiconscious.

"We cannot leave that wound open much longer," Tangle Hair said. "We may have to take a chance and pack it with gun powder."

Little Horse winced, but knew this was true. "We may, buck. But when we light it, in a wound that deep, we may do more than clean the wound. We may kill our comrade."

An owl hoot from outside. Two Twists, on sentry duty, telling them a friend approached.

"Firetop again?" Little Horse said.

The two friends crossed the moonlit, but otherwise dark, interior of the mill. When they reached the door and stepped outside, their curiosity gave way to deep surprise at sight of the two pretty young paleface girls. They approached on foot, and Little Horse recognized only Kristen Steele.

Kristen carried a cloth poke into which Laura had hastily shoved some emergency medical supplies. The area hereabouts was too overgrown for even the light, two-wheeled landau. So they'd left it back near the trail.

The two women and the two Cheyennes shared a long moment of awkward silence as they confronted the language barrier. But the moment Kristen lifted the poke, then pointed inside the mill, the Indians understood. Wordlessly, they led the women inside.

Kristen had to force back a gasp when she saw Matthew lying there in the stark moonlight. He was conscious, his eyes open; but the glaze over them told her what a battle his body was waging.

"Here, Laura," she said, her voice all business now as she opened the poke. "Never mind all the fretting. Light these candles so we can see better."

But Kristen had to flinch when she saw the ugly, puckered flesh of the wound over Matthew's hip. First she poured plenty of alcohol disinfectant into it, the pain causing the brave's muscular body to arc like a bow. Laura had also

195

included gauze dressing soaked in gentian and oil of camphene.

However, with the wound disinfected, one very rough step remained.

Little Horse quickly built a small fire and heated up the blade of his knife in it. Then, motioning for the women to turn away, he slipped a strip of rawhide between Touch the Sky's teeth. A moment later there was a sizzling sound like bacon frying as Little Horse lay the red-hot blade against the puckered wound.

Touch the Sky flexed taut and bit down hard on the rawhide. Both women wrinkled their noses at the sickly-sweet stink of scorched flesh. The wounded Cheyenne passed out briefly. When he floated to the surface of consciousness again, the others had discreetly drifted away, leaving him and Kristen alone.

"Looks like you've added one more scar to the collection," she greeted him with a smile.

"Better a scar than new moccasins for my funeral." He smiled at her weakly. "And looks like I can thank you for that."

Kristen reached one hand out and laid it on his cheek. "Oh, Matthew, it's so unfair. Ever since I've known you, white men have persecuted you. *Look* at you! Burns, knife cuts, bullet wounds, lord knows what else."

"Don't forget. Red men made their share of those."

"Yes, I know. Because you grew up among whites! It's not at all unlike my father's sick logic. If the Indians run wild, they must be hunted down and killed as savages. If they live peacefully on the reservations, they're scorned as 'praying Indians' and swindled out of their allotments. Same with you. You're guilty no matter what you try to do. What do they want of you?"

"My scalp. But I'm not about to hand it over on a platter. They'll have to earn the right to dance on my bones."

But his humor was lost on Kristen. Hot tears welled from her eyelids and dropped onto him. Her hand felt cool and soft against his cheek— the softest thing lately in a very hard life. Touch the Sky reached up and pulled the hand to his lips, kissing it. He felt a shudder move through Kristen.

"Matthew," she implored him, "do you have to fight this battle?"

He nodded. Already he was sleepy again. "Got to," he assured her, waves of weak exhaustion washing over him. "But it's *my* battle, not yours. You . . . you get on . . . home."

The brave, weak from blood loss, slipped off into unconsciousness.

Despite the dread heavy in her bones, Kristen shook her head at the sleeping warrior. Thinking of her father's cruelty, she recalled something else Pastor West had once said. " 'And the children's meek goodness shall cleanse the stains of their fathers' violent dishonor.' "

She spoke softly to the unconscious Cheyenne. "It's *our* battle, Matthew. He'll have to kill both of us."

Chapter Sixteen

The Arapaho runner named High Road spoke his words clearly, simply, and truthfully, demonstrating good sense in the details he chose to remember. These qualities had ensured his place as a valued messenger and scout among his own people. And they now impressed his Northern Cheyenne allies gathered in their central camp clearing.

"Cheyenne cousins! My father stood beside your chief Gray Thunder during the battle at Medicine Creek. There, our two tribes painted their bodies in Crow and Pawnee blood! When the Arapaho needed pemmican to survive the short white days, the *Shaiyena* shared the little they had. No red men love their ponies more than Cheyennes. Yet when game was scarce you slew several to feed our starving babes and elders!

"For these good reasons, I could never speak bent words to any Cheyenne. What I have told you is the truth that I have seen. However, I am no god, nor even blessed with the eyes of an eagle. I may not have seen the things I believe I saw. Indeed, I admire this Touch the Sky, and I would give much to be wrong. For if not, I fear the entire Plains Nation will atone for his bloody deed!"

These words impressed Honey Eater, too, if indeed sad news could be called impressive. However, even though she trusted High Road, she did *not* trust certain others in this very tribe. Unfortunately, having already overheard Two Twists himself admit that Touch the Sky murdered Black Elk, High Road's report counted for little with her. A bullet in the heart left little concern for a thorn in the side.

But she saw it clearly now—this was perhaps the most damning report against Touch the Sky. And his tribal enemies were glorying in their triumph.

"Fathers and brothers! Mark this moment!" Wolf Who Hunts Smiling called out, quieting the excited discussions among the listeners. "Mark it well, Spotted Tail and the rest of you Bow Strings who dare to mock Medicine Flute's shaman skills!"

Wolf Who Hunts Smiling had only just ridden back to camp himself, Honey Eater reminded herself. Of course, now he had the open excuse that he was a Bull Whip "policeman" monitoring Touch the Sky's activities. She had never seen him look so smugly sure of himself as he did now, his furtive eyes gleaming in the lurid glow of the sawing fires.

"Medicine Flute's vision has been vindicated. He told us this traitorous event was coming to pass, and so it has. Have ears, those of you who are reluctant to condemn Touch the Sky. I do not resent your loyalty, for it is understandable. Truly, this tall buck is a warrior second to none.

"But only think. Who trained him? My cousin, whose name may not be mentioned thanks to this traitor. Now he makes the final move to sell off our homeland to the hair-faced fence builders!

"I understand your loyalty. But know this. Sentiment cannot be allowed to disguise a murdering traitor. The time rapidly approaches when your 'sentiment' will become sedition!"

This indictment hung in the air—stark, loud, as unavoidable as the gunshot that felled Black Elk. Once again Honey Eater felt a chill at the awesome power of Wolf Who Hunts Smiling's speaking ability. It was a common belief among the men that Maiyun chose to express His wishes through the most eloquent male speaker.

"My best Bull Whip speaks straight-arrow," Lone Bear said. "This attack is clearly intended to endanger our treaty rights. However, I see Touch the Sky's deluded minions frowning. High Road?"

"I have ears," the Arapaho said.

"Indeed, red brother, and eyes, too, as well as a stout and honest heart. Tell us this thing now. Did you see *this* one"—here Lone Bear nodded toward Wolf Who Hunts Smiling—"anywhere close to this trouble?"

High Road shook his head. "I know Wolf Who Hunts Smiling. And I tell you now: He has a gleam to his eye that makes me eager always for a tree at my back." This caused a ripple of laughter. "But I did not see him. Only the tall shaman. And the dead whiteskin in the trail, the other palefaces shooting at Touch the Sky."

For Honey Eater, the silence following this remark was physically painful. She felt many of those around her sneaking slanted peeks in her direction. By now everyone had noticed that she no longer wore white columbine petals in her hair. Some interpreted this as an outright repudiation of Touch the Sky, and they approved of her loyalty to the tribe.

Others, of a more romantic bent, saw it as something akin to an act of mourning. Those gay petals had symbolized for Honey Eater the joy and beauty and vibrant vitality of life—feelings that had fled from her as the result of these recent and tragic events.

"Gray Thunder!" Wolf Who Hunts Smiling called out. "You are our chief. You have sworn to express the will of the people. You tell us the Star Chamber vote was tied. You tell us you refuse to settle this tie. But this is your duty! Speak now, justify this denial of your obligations."

Honey Eater could see that Gray Thunder had clearly aged greatly during the last few sleeps. The seams of his face were etched even deeper from the weight of this unwelcome responsibility.

"You are a bold one, Wolf Who Hunts Smiling," the Chief replied, "to remind me of my duty. Trust me, no man here feels it more keenly than I. But you have a right to question my refusal to act. Therefore, place these words in your sash.

"I will not act, for I fear that action will destroy my tribe! Only think. By letting this matter go to the Star Chamber, which I was forced to do, I am also forced to choose one of two extreme choices.

"Assume that I decide yes, Touch the Sky must have killed our war leader. Banishment, which is the normal punishment for murder of a fellow Cheyenne, would never satisfy his enemies. They have also accused him as a spy—the only crime for which our law-ways demand the execution of a Cheyenne. Truly, Touch the Sky *already* exists in banishment and always has, his enemies are so numerous. And I refuse to order this brave's execution because I am not certain of his guilt.

"Nor can I believe in his innocence. Our war leader lies on his scaffold, cruelly murdered. Squirrels did not do this bloody deed! But until I am sure in my heart who did, I will order no man's death."

This, too, was well-spoken, and Honey Eater

saw that Wolf Who Hunts Smiling was wisely holding silent. Gray Thunder was under great pressure now, but he was greatly respected.

And his fear about the tribe being on the verge of a tragic and bloody split—she, too, sensed the nearness of this impending trouble. These were the blackest days for her tribe since the surprise Pawnee attack that had killed her mother.

Now this new trouble. What was Touch the Sky's true part in it? She had always defended him in the face of every charge. Had she been wrong all those times? Had the daughter of Chief Yellow Bear all this time loved a scheming traitor?

But if so, other good Cheyennes made the same mistake in supporting him. She glanced toward Spotted Tail. He had courageously spoken up in favor of Touch the Sky at the last council. And since that time, a brave named River of Winds had become his constant companion. Considered the fairest man in the tribe, no man would hurt River of Winds with impunity.

But how had things come to such a dangerous head? Just as she turned to return to her tipi, Wolf Who Hunts Smiling caught her eye. The knowing grin he sent her promised that, soon, *he* would raise high the leader's lance— and then her life would be a hard and hurting place.

*   *   *

Even with the window wide open, Hiram Steele's library was thick with tobacco smoke.

"The buck performed like a well-oiled Henry," Steele boasted with admiration. "A sage-freighter killed and the rest stirred up. An editorial in the *Bighorn Ledger* exaggerated the hell out of it and called for a gold bounty on Indian scalps."

Seth Carlson scooched his chair a little further from Fontaine and MacGruder. Both men had a smell coming off them that could raise blood blisters on leather.

"He did damn good," Carlson agreed. "But he's an arrogant bastard. And I don't swallow his story about how he *thinks* he wounded Hanchon."

Hiram raised one hand from his desk and waved it carelessly. "Hell, neither do I. It's a stretcher, Indians like to color things up to impress us whites. But don't forget, he didn't say he did it. He said one of the freighters might have winged him. That makes it a little more possible."

"I see your point. Well, anyway, a few more strikes like that, Hanchon will be as good as shot. And Gray Thunder's blanket asses will be marching off to the Indian territory in Kansas while we start issuing land warrants."

"We?" Hiram, in a fine mood now, threw back his head and laughed. "Hell, Soldier Blue! I'm proud to have you as a business partner, but I'm thinking the U.S. Army might frown on it."

"I can resign my commission if the profits

look fat. My father will smooth all that for me."

Hiram nodded. Abbot Fontaine stood up, sawed-off shotgun swinging in its sling, and crossed to the door that opened on the parlor. "Just checking, sugar britches," he called in to the adjoining room before shutting the door again.

Carlson frowned. "These men work for you, Hiram. You let them be so free with your girl?"

"Why, Christ sakes, soljer!" Abbot smeared his grizzle-bearded face with both hands, highly amused. "She's been topped by Innuns! Laddie-buck, you best face it plain and call it Jane! You got a powerful hankering to eat off a red man's plate."

Stoney MacGruder found this so funny he laughed until phlegm rattled in his barrel chest. But Carlson flushed red to his very ear lobes.

"Friend," he warned Fontaine, "you better learn some respect for your betters."

"Last 'better' man I tangled with got his teeth shot out the back of his skull."

"The front, you mean."

Fontaine registered the insult, then shrugged. "Either way. He don't need his teeth now."

"Now, simmer down, boys," Hiram inter-rupted. "The money we all stand to make is more important than this stupid, hot-headed quarrel. Abbot?"

"Yo!"

"Seth is right. That mouth of yours gets ahead of your brain."

"Why, Hiram! Just the other night, when you

205

busted her door in, you promised me and Stoney that—"

"Never mind that," Steele cut in quickly. "A man says a lot of things when he's got blood in his eyes." He looked at Carlson and spoke in a mollifying tone. "If you're still marriage-minded, it could be that Kristen is finally learning to make herself useful on the frontier."

"How so?" Carlson asked.

"You should've seen her on Tuesday night. Evidently Laura Bishop's cousin had a rough time dropping her first foal. Kristen must have pitched right into it. My little high-hatting princess, coming home with blood on her clothes."

But by now Carlson was frowning. "Hiram, that can't be. You talking about Rebecca Sanford?"

"I am if she's the Bishop girl's cousin."

"She is. But the thing of it is, I personally assigned a man from my platoon to escort the fort's contract surgeon to the Sanford place. He delivered that baby with no problems, and it was well over a week ago."

A long, awkward silence ensued. Abruptly, Abbot Fontaine's shotgun was jiggling in its sling as the gunman shook with laughter.

"By God! Your girl is slicker than cat shit on oilcloth. I'll lay odds she sneaked off for a little foofaraw with that Cheyenne buck."

This time Steele and Carlson were both too outraged to take offense at Fontaine. Steele scraped his chair back to rise. But now Fontaine lost his foolish grin and spoke up quickly.

"Now, snub your rope, Hiram, and listen to me! That girl of yours is a sneak, that's clear as tits on a boar hog. So? Then let her sneak. Every time you lock horns with her over it, she warns the damn Indian. With me 'n' Stoney about to finish our river search, she don't matter anyhow. Besides—tell Hiram what you done, Stoney."

Stoney MacGruder was so stupid the Army had rejected him for enlistment. But it was their loss because he was an excellent tracker and a good shot who held up well when lead thickened the air.

"I notched the back right shoe on her hoss," MacGruder said. "There's been lots of rain lately. A notched shoe'll leave a clear sign."

Steele had slowly calmed down as he listened to Fontaine. Hireling or no, the man was right. Matthew Hanchon had to be holed up somewhere in the thick growth near the river. The rest of the valley was mostly open fields and meadows.

"This time your brain *did* get ahead of your words, Abbot," Steele conceded. "Instead of wasting so many man-hours watching her night and day, I'll just give her her head. Maybe she'll lead us right where we need to go. One thing is for damn sure. We don't stop Hanchon and his bunch, they'll do their damndest to stop this renegade, Wolf Who Hunts Smiling."

Abbot's hand caressed the linseed-oiled stock of his scattergun, his touch gentle as a lover's.

"They'll be stopped," he assured his employers.

Hiram nodded. "Good. And if Kristen happens to be with him when his time is up, kill her graveyard dead right along with him!"

Chapter Seventeen

"Shaman, you are still shy of your fighting fettle," Little Horse said. "But once again you have won the battle with Brother Ball."

Touch the Sky was propped up in his buffalo robes, eating a nourishing concoction made from mashed rosehips and the liver and bone marrow of a recently killed elk. Tangle Hair had waited near one of the many salt licks near the river and killed it silently with an arrow.

"Once again, brother, as you say. Here we are gloating again. Yet, if *he* ever wins the battle, Brother Ball can only claim me once."

Little Horse grinned. "Some men return humbled from the brink of death. You always come back sassy and eager for more sport."

Bright, early morning sunshine illuminated

the interior of Padgett's Mill. Now Touch the Sky noticed something. "Brother," he said, "where are the ponies?"

Little Horse looked at him askance. "Then you do not remember?"

"Remember what, buck? The day I was born, or which dug I first took in my mouth? Speak plain, remember what?"

"Never mind the day of your birth. I mean just lately, while you lay in a fever delirium from your wound. You spoke things."

Touch the Sky frowned. "What manner of things?"

"Yours was the ghost-wind voice of a vision trance. You said that soon—very soon now—the ponies must be moved or we would lose this spot and thus the battle. It was the shaman speaking, and we listened. You even commanded us to hide the canoe and the straw and to remove all the fresh pony droppings."

"Then where are the ponies?"

"As safe as we can get them—in a sheltered copse by the water. Tangle Hair is with them."

"But enough of vision voices. What about the hair-faces Steele hired," Touch the Sky said, "the ones searching the river?"

"We have had some good news on that score, at least. They started at the opposite end of the valley. Two Twists has been mounting scouting patrols. He now knows where they are and will ride out regularly to check their progress. They should not catch us unawares."

Touch the Sky managed a weak grin. "It would seem my warriors hardly need me. I lay sleeping, useless as a sick grandmother, while they carry on without me. But tell me a thing, brother."

"Ask it, Bear Caller."

"While I lay in this fever delirium, what other things did I say?"

Little Horse, never one for dissembling, looked uncomfortable and glanced away. "One says many things when in the grip of a fever. I cannot recall all of them."

"Buck, *you* can recall how many ants were dancing on a log you passed five winters ago in the heat of battle! Tell me what other things I said?"

Forced to it, Little Horse refused to mince words. "You spoke as if Honey Eater were present. You asked her how she could justify the heartless eyes she turned on you at camp. Yes, you told her, the one who was her husband is dead, and events appear to damn you. But Honey Eater never believed damning appearances so completely before. Why now, you demanded."

Touch the Sky regretted asking. He made no reply to these feelings which lay so close to his heart. Warriors could not discuss such things, for indeed, what good was talking? And thinking of Honey Eater's cold rejection, Touch the Sky could not help recalling how comforting Kristen's hands had felt.

He brought their talk around to more imme-

211

diate matters. "Little Horse, I failed to stop Wolf Who Hunts Smiling. Whatever the cost, we cannot let the next attack succeed. Once the white wrath is heated up past the boiling place, our people will pay and pay dearly."

Just then they heard an owl hoot—Two Twists telling them a friend approached. A few moments later Corey stood in the doorway, grinning at them through his lopsided face.

"Well, God-in-whirlwinds! Look who's still strutting between Heaven and Earth!"

"Sorry to disappoint you, paleface," Touch the Sky shot back. "What's on the spit?"

"Tasty fixens, for a change. That's why I rode out. To tell you that Tom Riley is due back any time from leave. I got a telegram through to him. He's coming back early."

Touch the Sky agreed—this was indeed good news. He and Tom Riley had faced some rough weather together. The young officer had not hesitated to put his life, and his military career, on the line to help Touch the Sky save his white parents' mustang ranch when Steele tried to force them out. Likewise, Touch the Sky faced death time and again, as well as the enmity of his own people, when Tom Riley's kid brother Caleb came up against the dreaded Blackfoot killer, Sis-ki-dee.

Corey's face, though on the mend, still showed the savagery of Abbot Fontaine's beating. It also reminded Touch the Sky, yet again, of the danger Kristen faced because of him.

Two Twists suddenly appeared in the door, limping painfully. His face had drained white.

"Brothers, look sharp! In my hurry to return with my warning, I turned my ankle on a root. I fear I am almost too late. Seth Carlson and a patrol of perhaps ten blue-blouses must have followed Firetop. Quickly, they are almost upon us!"

Even as Two Twists finished speaking this warning, Touch the Sky felt the floor vibrating through his thin moccasins—the big Cavalry horses pounding closer.

"What the hell's going on?" Corey demanded, baffled once again by the language barrier.

"Carlson," Touch the Sky replied tersely.

Two Twists limped further into the big stone building. "The trees will slow them down, but not for long. Quickly, help Touch the Sky!"

Every one of the Cheyennes was acutely aware that they were trapped white-man style in a fixed, closed-in position on foot. This was one of the worst ways an Indian could possibly die, short of drowning, for everyone knew that a drowned Indian's spirit remained trapped in water forever and could not fly up to the Land of Ghosts. The thought of an unclean death unnerved even the bravest warriors, and Touch the Sky knew they faced one now.

Corey followed Little Horse's example and

grabbed one of Touch the Sky's arms, helping him to his feet.

"Brothers," he told them, "the tunnel! I think I can walk by myself. But I cannot crawl through it hurt like I am. It is too cramped. You take it, quickly. Take your weapons, but leave them in the tunnel. When you emerge, break off some reeds to breathe with and roll out into the river. Grab rocks to hold you down. I will go out that far window and hide as best I can in the bushes."

Already they could hear bit rings clinking and horses snuffling. Touch the Sky's order was the best possible plan, under the circumstances. Little Horse threw back the planks over the narrow crawl space. But the red man's natural aversion to cramped spaces was even stronger now, and fear disturbed the normally stoic calm of his face.

"You, Grierson!" Carlson's voice called out. "Take Webber, Johnson, and O'Flaherty, check out the inside of the mill. Corporal Waites! Take four troopers from your squad down to look around near the river. The rest of you stay here, and look lively—if they're around here, they might try to break for it. These aren't blanket Indians who've jumped from the rez, these are renegade killers. Kill anything that moves, and identify it after."

"Katy Christ," Corey said, pushing the reluctant Little Horse into the tunnel. Corey wasn't surprised, he'd once seen a formidable Sioux warrior reduced to sobs of fear in Bighorn Falls when he negotiated his first flight of stairs. "*Move* your red ass, buck! This way to the white man's hell."

"Two Twists," Touch the Sky said, "what are you doing?"

"Helping you. You cannot climb out without help."

The stubborn youth was right. Even with his help, Touch the Sky was slow clearing the high window.

"Quick, Two Twists!" Touch the Sky whispered. "Never mind the tunnel now, there's no time. Come out the window with me and hide down in the water."

Two Twists, too, was somewhat slowed by his swollen ankle. But he managed to swing over the wide stone sill just before the first soldier cautiously poked his head into the mill.

Touch the Sky, unable to move quickly or assume cramped positions, took his chances standing stone-still in a thick willow bower. From where he stood, he could see through the window into the mill. Behind him Two Twists descended the sharp bank toward the river. He rounded the corner, gaining the side built flush with the water. Touch the Sky could just make out the dilapidated old wheel, flimsy and broken paddles slapping the water. Two Twists leaped into the churning foam.

More soldiers—including Seth Carlson—fanned out down near the water. Touch the Sky winced when they began randomly firing rounds into the river, obviously wise to the ancient Indian trick of hiding underwater. He also kept his eye on the soldiers inside. He could see several forage caps moving about.

One of the soldiers crossed to the window opening. He stood so close that Touch the Sky could count the smallpox scars ravaging his face. The Cheyenne tried to will himself invisible behind the curtain of willow branches.

"Cap'n Carlson! All secure in here."

"Take another look," Carlson ordered. He turned to the man closest to him. "Afraid to get your feet wet, trooper? Put some energy into it. If they were inside when we rode up, they have to be hiding close by. Jab your bayonet into those cattails."

Nervous sweat broke out on Touch the Sky's back as the soldiers neared the spot where he had seen Little Horse and Corey hide underwater.

The next moment Touch the Sky's jaw dropped in pure astonishment, even as his heart leaped into his throat. He simply couldn't believe what he was seeing: one splintered paddle of the mill wheel surged up out of the water with Two Twists squirming on it like a gut-hooked fish!

In a heartbeat Touch the Sky saw that he was desperately trying to wrench his breechclout free of a jagged point which had snagged him. Any other time, the sight would have been hilarious. But not now, when the area was crawling with blue soldiers, rifles capped and at the ready.

Incredibly, not one of the preoccupied soldiers had yet spotted this young brave come rising out of the river like a comic water god, drenched and squirming.

"*Hsssst!*"

Desperate, Touch the Sky waved his knife to catch Two Twists' attention. The struggling youth looked his way, eyes wide with panic. Touch the Sky flipped his obsidian knife in a wide arc, trying to time his throw to mesh with the revolving wheel. For several heart-stopping moments Two Twists bobbled the knife. He still hadn't gained a firm purchase on it as the wheel plunged him out of sight into the river again.

Touch the Sky had no idea if his young friend had that knife or not. But suddenly Seth Carlson, perhaps having glimpsed some movement in the corner of one eye, was staring hard at the paddle wheel. In a moment Two Twists might come rising out to a sure death.

Touch the Sky forgot to breathe. The groaning wheel turned, groaned, turned, groaned, and then relief flooded through the Cheyenne when the broken paddle emerged—nothing on it but a tatter of doeskin. Two Twists had cut himself free!

Carlson looked keenly disappointed. "All right, men! Return to the horses. If they're holed up here, they're gone now. We'll try again."

217

*   *   *

"I knew trouble was in the wind when Hiram Steele came back," Tom Riley said. "But I can see from your face, Corey, that the trouble is blowing in lots quicker than I expected."

"It's a twister full of trouble," Corey agreed. He lowered his voice even though the two men were safe in Riley's quarters. "Seth Carlson's men damn near cooked our hash yesterday. Atop of them, we're up against renegade Cheyennes and that cold-blooded, hardscrabble white trash hired by Steele."

Riley frowned. He was a ruddy-complexioned towhead in his mid-twenties. "I've heard of Abbot Fontaine. He killed one man too many back in Missouri with that sawed-off stove-pipe of his, had to dust his hocks west. Stoney MacGruder is dumb as a post. But they say he's crazy-dangerous when he gets riled, used to wrestle declawed bears up in Montana."

"That's the kind of pond scum Steele brings into the same house with Kristen," Corey said. "And no finer girl than her in Creation."

"None," Riley agreed, his face softening at mention of Kristen. Riley wouldn't admit it, even to himself—but fear for her safety was one of the main reasons he had cut short a badly needed furlough. What sane man would hurry back to this cramped room with its scant eight-foot high ceiling, to a narrow iron bedstead set in bowls of kerosene to keep the bedbugs off?

Capt. Tom Riley was a former enlisted man whose superior service resulted in a rare honor. He was breveted to the officer ranks without benefit of West Point. Such "mustang officers" were extremely popular with the enlisted men—and cruelly snubbed by the West Point men like Seth Carlson.

"Steele's got a solid plan," Riley had to acknowledge reluctantly. "It was a damned unpopular move when Congress set aside that Powder River tract for the Cheyennes. The Expansionists have been chomping at the bit to get it back. They'll leap on any 'violation' they can find or manufacture as proof the Indians are subhuman criminals who can't keep their word."

"Bosh," Corey said angrily. "There's Indian trash, but nobody values his word more than the red man. The Indian despises a liar even more than he does a killer because a liar is more cowardly."

Riley nodded. "That rings right in my experience. Never had one lie to me yet. They've stolen my grub and tried to boost my horse, and they've thrown lead and arrows at me. But I never knew one to lie or break his word to me. We need a few of *them* in Congress. Well, anyhow, that's all philosophy."

Riley stood and began pacing, even though a few steps took him across the room. "I've got a cavalry platoon now. If Carlson's using *his* troops to abet Steele, then I can by-God use mine to abet Touch the Sky."

"That's the gait!" Corey grinned. "You got the best pony soldiers in the territory."

"No," Riley corrected him, "that honor goes to the Sioux and the Cheyenne around here. But my lads are stout enough. Most have held the line under fire before. If we just—"

Three solid raps at the door startled both men.

"Capt. Riley? Private Meadows, sir, with a message from company headquarters."

Riley opened the door and accepted a sheaf of papers from Trooper Meadows. The runner took two steps backwards, saluted smartly, then performed an about-face and left.

Riley glanced at the papers. "Orders," he said wonderingly.

Corey glanced at them. "What's that TAD across the top mean?"

"Temporary Additional Duty. Means I keep my old job but take on a new one for now."

Corey watched his friend scan the first page, a frown wrinkling his sunburned face. "What is it?" Corey demanded.

"Tarnal hell!" Riley slapped the orders, tearing one of the pages in his anger. "That low-crawling son of a sage skunk!"

"Who?"

"Carlson, that's who. *He's* the one behind this, not Col. Thompson."

Corey's frustration had him almost hopping. "Damn you, Tom, you sure like to take the long way around the barn. Behind *what*?"

"These new orders that've been cut for me."

Riley met his eye. "I've been assigned from Cavalry to Quartermaster duty, effective at 0800 tomorrow. That's a desk job."

Corey was stunned. "That means no troopers to command in the field?"

"That's exactly what it means. Carlson and Steele are getting me out of the way."

"What can you do?"

Misery clear in his face, Riley stared at his new orders. "I can't do squat about these. I'm cut off from my men. But you tell Touch the Sky this for me. You tell him, orders or no, I promise to help on my own."

Chapter Eighteen

Wolf Who Hunts Smiling left Medicine Flute and Swift Canoe in their limestone cave hideout. He didn't want these clumsy companions with him because he had no intention of ever letting the dog-faced white soldiers get him in their sights.

According to Seth Carlson's latest message, they were to meet at the sandstone formation overlooking the trading post at Red Shale. But Wolf Who Hunts Smiling had back-trailed from this point and taken up an excellent position in a jumble of granite boulders.

When Carlson, riding alone, cantered past below, Wolf Who Hunts Smiling snapped off a round from his Colt rifle. Carlson's black-brimmed officer's hat flew from his head.

Carlson's big cavalry horse bolted, but the

strong officer managed to hold on long enough to gentle her. Wolf Who Hunts Smiling's mocking laughter echoed from ridge to ridge.

"Paleface, what good are those hats which fly off at the wind from a bullet? But why ask this, for truly, men who wear boots have no sense to answer."

"Sense? We whites had enough sense to harness the wheel while your people were dragging travois. You're *still* dragging travois. We've harnessed steam to the wheels."

"Wheels! I have seen how well your wheels worked on the Jornada del Muerto to the south! Broken wheels, broken wagons, the white-bleached bones of palefaces—all litter the deep sand there, which *wheels* could not defeat. All your 'superior' knowledge has not made men of you. Only squaw men who let their wives run them."

"You got a mouth on you, John. I thought all you noble savages were the strong, silent type."

"Nothing is more silent than death. Call me 'John' one more time, blue warrior, and you sleep silently with the worms!"

Hot rage flooded his face. But Carlson quietly sat his mount until his heart quit racing. He reminded himself that he needed this wily renegade. He had already proven his usefulness— Col. Thompson had shown a tight-lipped anger upon hearing the report from the sage-freighters who'd been ambushed.

"All right, never mind the threats. I've got the instructions for your next attack."

223

"Well? Do you expect me to beg for them?"

Carlson bit back his harsh retort. "Do you know the yellow pine country north of Beaver Creek?"

"Know it? Better than you know your mother's face. Long before soldiers stole it, Cheyennes trapped fur there."

"That right?" Carlson enjoyed a grin. "I guess the Red Nation has fallen on rough times since then. Anyway, there's a log-cutting detail heading out there soon. I want you to attack it."

Wolf Who Hunts Smiling had a good view from amidst the boulders. Now it was his turn again to offer a cynical grin. "So loyal to his own."

"Just like you, Jo—I mean, buck."

"This game goes nowhere and now tires me. We both hate this Touch the Sky, whom you call Matthew Hanchon. Until we kill him, neither of us gets what he wants. First him. *Then* we Indians and soldiers will have at it."

Carlson nodded. "As I was saying, the log-cutting detail. You'll have to make your strike quick because there'll be armed sentries posted."

"A kill?"

Carlson nodded. "At least one. More if you want."

Wolf Who Hunts Smiling enjoyed this. His grin stretched into a wide smile. "Perhaps, after all, I have been harsh in judging you, soldier chief. You do not shy back from hard deeds. This is the sign of a true leader."

Carlson thought of something else. "You say you've scouted Blackford Valley?"

The Cheyenne nodded.

"Do you know where Hanchon is holed up?"

"If I knew this thing, he would be carrion bait by now."

"How 'bout the girl? Steele's daughter. Have you spotted her?"

"Hair-face, unless one has a weapon aimed at me, I do not concern myself with women's business anymore than with children's."

"You should. She'll lead you to Hanchon."

Wolf Who Hunts Smiling narrowed his eyes. "The pony soldier is jealous! I see it in his face."

Carlson was helpless to vent his rage at this arrogant buck. But he reminded himself that Kristen Steele *must* be helping Hanchon. She knew damn good and well where he was holed up. Carlson hated her now. He would gladly kill this Indian-loving whore who had the audacity to spurn him.

"Never mind," Carlson said. "That's none of your business. You just high-tail it over to Beaver Creek. I'll have more instructions for you when I meet you there."

Capt. Tom Riley was chafing.

Never, in six years of good service wearing Uncle Sam's blue, had he ever held a desk job. Now here he was, the best platoon commander in the Department of Wyoming, turned into a damned coffee cooler for the Quartermaster!

He glanced around the drab cubbyhole where

he now spent his days reviewing invoices and monitoring the arithmetic of others. *Who wouldn't be a soldier?* some bored soul before him had carved into the desk—a popular cynicism of the day among disgruntled troopers and officers alike.

But at least his little prison had a small window. Thus it was that Riley spotted Cpl. Jim Mattson crossing the parade square, aiming for the Headquarters Office.

Riley scraped back his chair and hurried to the open window. "Mattson!"

The startled trooper looked around until he spotted his platoon commander. Then he crossed toward the window, halted, saluted.

"Morning, sir. *There* you are. The boys're wondering when you'll be coming back."

"Yeah, I'm wondering the same thing. Next thing you know, they'll have me in a paper collar and green eyeshades. Mattson, I saw on the company roster this morning that you're duty NCO this week at the company office?"

Mattson frowned. "There it is, sir. They know I taught school and can read and write. They call it duty NCO, but it means boring clerical work. Both of us are gettin' splinters in our hinders instead of saddle sores."

"Mattson, do you trust me?"

The young corporal looked startled. "Trust you, sir?"

"Yes, trust me. F'rinstance, if I asked you to do something that's against regulations—something that could get you drummed out of the

Army and into a military prison if you were caught—would you do it?"

"Cap'n, I've never once seen you take a bite until all us men are fed. If you said there was a reason behind it, I'd accept that as a gentleman's word."

"There's a damn good reason behind it."

"I figured that. Let's get 'er done, sir."

Riley nodded, feeling a quick glow of pride in the trooper's loyalty. Riley adhered to a consistent policy: Avoid chicken-shit discipline, never berate a man publicly, never give an enlisted man any order you wouldn't be willing to carry out yourself. As a result, although the desertion rate elsewhere at Fort Bates was nearly one-third, Riley hadn't lost one man to "French leave."

"All right, then. I need an important favor. Check the company record for me. I need to know what troop movements are scheduled in the next few days. Which units will be going where, how many days' rations they're packing, all that. Think you can do that?"

Mattson was clearly puzzled. But he nodded without hesitation. "Hell yes I can, sir. The logs are in the top drawer where the duty NCO sits."

"Good man. I don't like keeping you boys in the dark about a mission, you know that. But you'll have to trust me for a bit. Then, when I get off this Company Q slacker duty, I'll tell all of you the name of the game."

"Yessir."

"Bring me that information as soon as you can."

"That's an affirmative, sir."

Mattson saluted again, then resumed his trip across the heat-cracked parade ground. Riley fretted for the next few hours, wondering what Hiram Steele and Seth Carlson were up to now. There was plenty of time to worry, too: about Kristen and Corey and Touch the Sky. But for now, he was forced to work quietly behind the scenes. He could only hope to assemble enough clues to get a handle on trouble before it was too late.

Riley tried to concentrate on a column of figures. But the numbers kept swimming away on a red sea of anger. Seth Carlson! That traitorous sonofabitch was pushing it one time too many. This wasn't the first time he had abused his military authority for personal profit—and personal revenge.

Though he disapproved of it, Riley could overlook petty graft. He did not consider any man—himself least of all—capable of perfection. But it was one thing to merely profit. It was another altogether to steal a people's homeland right out from under them. And Carlson, like Steele, was personally on the warpath against *all* Indians simply because he couldn't kill the one he hated most: Matthew Hanchon, now known to every red warrior on the far-flung Plains as Touch the Sky of the Northern Cheyenne.

And Kristen. Caught up in all of it like an innocent child swept up in a war she never started and couldn't understand. Tom had carefully kept his deeper feelings for her his own secret. But it was his firm belief that God did His best work when he made Kristen Steele. That such a pretty, noble, brave, and decent girl could spring from the loins of Hiram Steele was no great surprise. Tom figured she was the light God sent to cancel the darkness of Hiram's soul.

But a light could be put out. Touch the Sky *and* Kristen were both surrounded by dangerous enemies. In his frustration, Riley knuckled a bottle of ink over and ruined the account sheets on his desk.

"C'mon, Mattson," he muttered in a low, urgent voice. "Bring me something useful."

"Hold up there, Stoney!" Abbot Fontaine called out. "I gotta drain my snake."

Fontaine reined in his big claybank. Sawed-off shotgun jiggling in its sling, he swung down from his mount to urinate into the river.

"This search ain't goin' so slick," Fontaine complained. "We got a lot of river left. You're a good tracker, Stoney, but you're slow."

"Got to be. Go fast, you miss sign."

"I expect that's so. But you've cut damn little sign so far. How 'bout that mark you made, the one you filed on the shoe of the girl's horse? Any sign of that?"

"Nothing yet. But it'll show."

Abbot nodded, glancing at the thick growth surrounding them. "I reckon it will, at that."

Stoney had climbed his massive bulk down to squat beside the outline of an old print. He tested the dirt inside the depression. It was dried to a flaky dust. The print was not recent enough to worry about.

"You know," Abbot said, buttoning his fly, "I like Hiram's decision to just let his wild little filly run where she will. Who knows what we'll catch her up to?"

Fontaine grinned, fingering the big dent in his cheek. "You know. It sorter gets a fella all excited. Like drinkin' cheap whiskey by choice. I mean, thinking on a girl that pretty and quality-acting, yet knowing she'll put her ankles behind her ears for a savage Injin. Makes you wonder what else she's willing to do."

Fontaine finished and stepped up into leather. "Well, me 'n' you are gonna find out, Stoney. How's that sound? That pop your corn for you, thinkin' on her?"

Stoney, too, mounted. The half-wit's face was concentrated as if on some great problem. His voice went husky when he answered. "I got her on my mind, Abbot. I got her on my mind powerful strong, so's I get . . ." Fontaine watched Stoney working his hands into tight fists, frustrated by his lack of vocabulary to describe this. "I get these feelings, sorta."

Abbot cocked his head, amused. "Feelings? Well, I reckon! She gives you a pup tent in your long-johns, you simple shit. Stoney, you do beat all, old son, you do.

"Well, you just keep a tight rein on them *feelings* a little bit longer. First we got to kill us some red Arabs. Then before too much longer we'll see about them *feelings* of yours."

Chapter Nineteen

Though Touch the Sky complained mightily, his friends forced him to spend one more full sleep resting and recuperating. Two Twists' excellent scouting abilities kept them informed of the progress of Fontaine and MacGruder. He also reported strong troop movements lately and two glimpses of Wolf Who Hunts Smiling.

Touch the Sky felt a new surge of optimism when Corey next visited, for this time Tom Riley accompanied him. However, joy at seeing his old friend soon gave way to the grim reality of the news they brought.

"I can't be sure about this," Tom explained.

They all sat in a council circle inside the mill: Riley, Touch the Sky, Little Horse, and Two Twists. Tangle Hair was ensconced high in a cottonwood outside, on sentry duty. Touch the

Sky tried to remember to translate all the main points.

"Understand, I'm putting it together second-hand. But a log-cutting detail under Lt. Martin has been sent to Beaver Creek to bring back yellow pine. New enlisted barracks are going up to replace the squad tents, and all the good timber close to the fort has been exhausted. Now, Carlson and his troop are reported to be on 'extended scouting duty.' And according to my Papago scout, they just happen to have headed toward Beaver Creek."

"As if Carlson intends to use Wolf Who Hunts Smiling as bait." Touch the Sky said, speculating out loud.

"My thoughts exactly. I figure, first off, that he's hoping you'll show up. And by being on hand himself, Carlson, as ranking officer, will file the report. It'll be colored up and calculated to rile Col. Thompson. The first step, for Congressional certification of treaty violations, is up to Thompson. His recommendation starts the ball rolling."

Touch the Sky turned to his Cheyenne companions and explained these things.

"Brother," Little Horse said, and clearly even this boaster was daunted by events. "I only wish you had all your sap in you. Only four of us. Yet, not only must we stop a wily wolf, but a swarm of Bluecoats."

"We four climbed Wendigo Mountain," Two Twists scoffed. "We got our Sacred Arrows back

233

from no less than the Contrary Warrior, Sis-ki-dee!"

"God-in-whirlwinds!" Corey exploded. "You all keep gibbering in Cheyenne. Tell a man what's in the wind."

Despite this good-natured grousing, Corey followed Tom Riley's respectful behavior. He avoided looking the Indians directly in the eye, for red men believed whites could thus steal their souls.

"It's *not* going to be just you four," Riley said when Touch the Sky had translated. "Corey and I are dealing ourselves in. This is going to require a two-strike plan. One force to handle Seth Carlson. The other to head off this Wolf Who Hunts Smiling before he completes his attack.

"Now, I figure white men should handle white criminals, red men handle red criminals. That's how the treaties spell it out."

Touch the Sky looked skeptical. "You and Corey mean to take on Carlson and his entire platoon?"

"Well, not exactly take them on. But don't worry, I'm smarter than that West Point stuffed shirt. Me and Corey will figure out some way to rain on his parade."

"This gets old, buck," Little Horse complained. "You jabber on in English and your own red brothers miss the meat in the meal."

Touch the Sky shook his head in resigned frustration. Even among friends he was accused of always favoring the wrong side!

"Whatever we do," Touch the Sky told Riley, "we *must* make sure Wolf Who Hunts Smiling never reaches those log-cutters. We can't allow another 'Indian attack' so soon after that freighter was killed."

Riley nodded. "I see we're both grazing the same path. If Martin and his men see nothing, if they sustain no damage, then Carlson *has* no report—and no witnesses. Everyone knows about Carlson's vendetta against Indians. His word isn't worth much unless someone else backs it."

"When would we have to leave?"

"I'd recommend tonight, after sunset. It's only a few hours' ride. But I'd guess, from Carlson's timing, the attack is set for as soon as tomorrow morning."

Touch the Sky nodded. He looked at Corey's still-ravaged face. "I thank both of you. This isn't your fight."

"The hell it's not," the fiery-tempered redhead retorted. "You think I'm gonna let those raggedy-assed, yellow-bellied sapsuckers whomp on my face and do the sheepherder's stomp on my ribs? My old man can preach 'turn the other cheek' all he wants. I don't let nobody lay a hand on me and get away with it."

"As for me," Riley quipped, his tone reminding Touch the Sky of Little Horse, "I'm in it for the glory. Meet you in hell, pards!"

Stoney MacGruder had not slept well lately. Images of Kristen Steele clung to his mind like burrs to wool, pricking at him. What he called his "feelings" for her had begun to disturb him night and day.

Working by himself now, Stoney slowly followed the meandering bank of Salt Lick Creek. He let his big, 17-hand sorrel move at his own pace, grazing the lush grass at will. Stoney watched for tracks, broken twigs, bent grass, droppings still fresh on the inside.

Stoney's mind held little. But when it caught hold of something, it seized onto it like a steel trap. And right now the jaws of his mind had ahold of Kristen Steele. Stoney wanted to touch her, to smell her, to crush her clean, fragrant, delicate beauty close, as he might crush a flower.

And Stoney knew something. He knew that Kristen rode out alone hereabouts. It wasn't safe to be with her at the house—Hiram and Abbot were always there. They would laugh, or even stop him, when he held Kristen in his powerful arms.

But out here—out here a man could lay a pretty girl right down on that soft bank, and sort of pet her. . . .

Slowly, Stoney's meandering mind focused on the damp ground beside him—focused on the fresh horseshoe prints.

Focused especially on the V-shaped mark in the dirt. The same mark he had filed on one shoe of Kristen's mare.

The prints had been made quite recently. Stoney knew because the edges were still damp, and the edges always dried up first. Stoney just stared at the prints, his breath beginning to whistle in his nostrils. A warm flush moved into his face. He was forced to swallow hard to clear his throat.

He calculated. This was the furthest east he had taken the search. If she were still in Blackford Valley, riding due east, she could not be more than 30 minutes ride away. Any further, she would be out of the valley.

Sweat broke out on his upper lip. Abbot's words came back to him now, goading him like the sight of naked flesh: *It sorter gets a fellow all excited . . . who knows what we'll catch her up to?*

Distracted from fear, but determined to deliver her news, Kristen urged her mount to a trot.

She had no way of knowing that Tom Riley was back and helping Matthew. Now she kept a sharp eye out for soldiers or her father's hirelings.

Kristen knew she was pushing her luck. But the night before she had sneaked around to the library window to eavesdrop on her father and Seth Carlson. She knew about the planned attack on the log-cutting detail.

She also understood now just how important it was to prevent that attack. Her father had expanded on his grandiose plans to dam the Powder River for farmland irrigation. The Cheyennes would end up the same way the

237

proud Cherokees had—following their own "trail of tears" to a godforsaken reservation on worthless land no white man would spit on. The Cheyennes would never submit to such relocation. If Matthew wasn't murdered in this present struggle, he would die in the inevitable fight to resist relocation.

So despite Matthew's order to stay away, she *must* deliver this warning.

Her mare began to fight her, thirsty for some cool river water. Kristen reined her in long enough to let her dip her sleek nose into the water.

Just then, while her horse drank, Kristen thought she heard a noise behind her.

She glanced back, and met the stupid, staring eyes of Stoney MacGruder.

For a moment her blood seemed to go slushy in her veins. He sat his saddle about 20 feet away, just staring at her.

"Mr. MacGruder," she said uncertainly, one hand flying to her throat. She injected a note of false gaiety into her voice. "It's a lovely afternoon for a ride, isn't it? I just *love* it when the sunshine is all coppery the way it is now. Have you noticed how pretty the yellow crocuses are, so shiny and bright against the green grass?"

"Pretty," he agreed, his voice gravelly with wanting her. It was clear, from the way his eyes held her pinned, that he didn't mean flowers.

He flicked his horse's neck with a rein. The sorrel began walking closer. Desperate, Kristen jerked her mare's head back from the water. By the time she had the reluctant animal turned away from the river, Stoney had plucked the braided leather *reata* from his saddle horn.

Kristen bent close to the mare's ear and urged her to bolt. The plucky animal finally sensed deep trouble. She surged up the bank, hooves tearing out thick divots of dirt and grass. But Kristen had just managed to point her bridle away from MacGruder when there was a hard tug at her middle, the tug turning to a tight grip.

A heartbeat later the *reata* lifted her from the saddle, and the green grass of the bank rushed up to claim her.

Knowing he would soon need all the strength he could summon, Touch the Sky had settled into his buffalo robe and drifted into an uneasy sleep.

It was not unusual, lately, for his sleep to be rife with disturbing images. Arrow Keeper had taught him how to decipher the various symbols that come to a shaman in quiet moments. Blood on the moon meant great danger for the tribe; dreaming of buffalo meant good luck; seeing the sun and a full moon in the sky simultaneously portended momentous change.

But now he did not dream in symbols. The vision that shocked him awake, leaving his back clammy with sweat, was as stark and real as some cruel painting in a white man's gallery of nightmares: Kristen lying in deep grass, her head twisted at an impossible angle from a broken neck!

Little Horse, busy cleaning his four-barreled flintlock shotgun, almost dropped his weapon in surprise when his friend sat up. Touch the Sky was wide-eyed with urgent fear.

"Brother, have you seen the face of the Wendigo?" Little Horse demanded.

"Worse, buck."

Touch the Sky tried to fight down his desperation, to think clearly. He must seize a clue from this momentary vision. The dream was a warning that he must act quickly, but how? That grass, he told himself—it was thick bunch grass. And the only place where that type of grass grew around here was along the banks of the river.

"Quickly, buck," he told Little Horse. "Bring your bow and arrows. And we need the dugout. Two Twists, stay here."

"But brother, what is it? You are not ready for—"

Touch the Sky raised one hand to silence his friends. Dizziness washed over him as he rose and grabbed several arrows from Two Twists' quiver. "Never mind, stout bucks! I have no time to tell it. You will see soon enough, so why waste words? Now turn your feet to wings, Little Horse, and hope the current is swift!"

For a long time—each second an agonizing eternity for Kristen—Stoney MacGruder did absolutely nothing, after first snubbing the braided lariat around a tree and, thus, tethering the girl.

Stoney was like a child with a new Christmas toy. At first, not believing his good fortune, he wanted to leave it in the box and merely look at it.

Then, eventually, he wanted to touch it.

"Mr. MacGruder," Kristen pleaded as the huge man slowly drew nearer, breath still whistling in his nostrils. "Stoney? Please, you've always been different from Mr. Fontaine, better than he."

Kristen was forced by the *reata* to move in an arc like a pendulum. Her only hope would be to circle the tree a few times to loosen the *reata*. But that hope was dashed when MacGruder grabbed the leather lariat and held her as easily as he might a puppy on a leash.

She smelled the stink of him as he drew nearer, shrank inside of herself at sight of the fleas leaping off his scalp. Now his breath blasted her full in the face; damp as an animal's breath, as foul as old bilge water.

"Please, Mr. MacGruder. *Please*! Let's talk about something, let's—

"I got feelings," he breathed in a husky voice like a bear woofing. "I got powerful feelings."

One thick, callused hand came out and stroked her hair—hesitantly, at first, then more forcefully.

"Soft," he whispered, his eyes glazed like a child's. "So soft and purdy. . . . "

241

"Mr. MacGruder, stop, please, you're hurting me!"

His rough hands moved down to her neck, felt the pulse in her carotid arteries—like the rapid heartbeat of a baby bird trapped in his hands.

"Soft," he moaned again, his fingers tightening, "so soft and purdy. . . . "

Kristen was beyond begging now, beyond words. It was a life-and-death struggle to force air past the tightening band of iron around her neck. The pressure increased, the light went out of the sky, and all she could see was Mac-Gruder's crazy face, eyes protruding like wet marbles only inches above her.

And then—had she gone insane?—an arrow suddenly pierced his left ear so hard it drove its flint tip out of the right temple. The dead man toppled onto her, even as Kristen's mind shut down to a long, dark scream.

Chapter Twenty

"Here comes yet another word-bringer," Sharp Nosed Woman said. "And are you surprised to see whose tipi he stops at?"

Honey Eater and her aunt sat before wooden frames upon which were stretched beadwork shawls and shirts. They were decorating these leather garments to exchange for more delicate manufactured cloths at the trading post in Red Shale, such as linsey-woolsey. The renown of Cheyenne bead artistry, already great on the Plains, was beginning to spread to the white-skin settlements. Demand was great for Cheyenne beadwork, the secrets of which were jealously protected by Cheyenne women.

Honey Eater watched the Bull Whip runner speaking with Medicine Flute.

"So many," she said. "No doubt sent by our

trusty 'policeman,' Wolf Who Hunts Smiling. They must coordinate their treachery."

"This Wolf Who Hunts Smiling is trouble," Sharp Nosed Woman agreed. "He has always hated Touch the Sky. But I fear a monster was created when the Headmen revoked his coup feathers as punishment for his tricks against Touch the Sky. For this, his hatred of Touch the Sky became the campaign of his life."

"You have eyes, Aunt. Sharp ones. And Medicine Flute hates Touch the Sky almost as much as does Wolf Who Hunts Smiling. He is lazy and a coward. He does not want to hunt or fight or break wild ponies. He knows a shaman need not do any of these things. He only has to get rid of Touch the Sky, then he can play the big Indian."

"Niece," Sharp Nosed Woman said firmly, "as usual, you speak true words. But beyond those words, I detect a dangerous tone. A tone which tells me Touch the Sky is much on your mind. Have you forgotten your resolve?

"He stands charged of killing your husband! I will not lie and say I am sorry that a certain person is dead. But Honey Eater, no man deserves to be taken from behind—certainly not a brave warrior whose war bonnet hung from head to heels. And now look! A trusted Arapaho friend of our tribe has seen Touch the Sky attack and kill white freighters!"

Honey Eater was silent in her misery.

"You must not give in, Honey Eater. So many of the younger ones look up to you. Many are saying that Touch the Sky killed a certain per-

son only so you two could be married. I told you
before, *I* do not believe this. But you are in a
critical place, with all eyes on you. The feeling
in your heart must not rule the decisions in
your brain."

All of it was true, and *oh* how Honey Eater
resented this stupid responsibility! If only she
had not overheard a brave so reliable as Two
Twists, brazenly declaring Touch the Sky's guilt
in a conversation.

"All these messages," she said now, watching
Medicine Flute confer with the runner. "What
can it mean?"

"Niece, I know not. But have you noticed a
thing? Have you noticed how Medicine Flute's
popularity has lately surged?"

Miserable, Honey Eater nodded. Her eyes
flicked back and forth between her unfolding
geometric patterns of beadwork and Medicine
Flute's tipi. "I have noticed. High Road's report
of Touch the Sky's attack has confirmed Medicine Flute's 'vision.' Or so his supporters say."

Sharp Nosed Woman frowned slightly. "Do
you mark how often Medicine Flute glances our
way? Good chance it is not *I* he gazes on so
longingly."

Honey Eater shuddered. Her aunt's words
forced her to confront a very unpleasant truth—
one that had only recently begun to reveal itself.
Medicine Flute, who hitherto had shown no interest in women, was suddenly far too interested in her—if a naked, disgusting lust could
be called "interest."

"Look!" Sharp Nosed Woman's fingers fell idle. "Maiyun protect us, he is crossing this way! Did that male witch hear me talking of him?"

Both women were fully absorbed in their work by the time Medicine Flute stopped, about ten paces from where they sat in front of Sharp Nosed Woman's tipi. Honey Eater felt the weight of his stare like a clammy hand on her cheek.

"This is amusing," he announced. "Both of you, so full of thoughts of me, both just now talking about me. Now look how you pretend to ignore me. Truly our women are a coy and devious lot. And truly, some of them are fine to look on. Especially the haughty ones who are not satisfied by one buck."

Honey Eater felt the heat moving up into her face. Her fingers trembled with anger, causing her to drop several beads. Medicine Flute laughed. "Indeed, the pretty and haughty ones make my blood sing. And perhaps, after Wolf Who Hunts Smiling is selected as our war leader and I as our shaman, the haughty ones will show me more respect."

That did it for Honey Eater. She looked him full in the face, repulsed by his soft, cunning, feminine features and drooping eyelids. As always, he clutched the disgusting leg-bone flute against his scrawny chest.

"I cannot speak for any woman but myself. As for me, I will *never* show you anything but what I feel. And what I feel is a pure and cold contempt, for you embody everything that is false and cowardly."

This unexpected barb struck deep. Rage flared in his eyes for a few heartbeats. Then he got his mocking composure back.

"Snake Eater has just ridden in with some interesting news. Your tall, randy buck has been spotted holding a sun-haired white girl in his blanket for love talk."

Honey Eater knew that Medicine Flute was an inveterate liar. And yet, was it not true that Touch the Sky had returned to the area near Bighorn Falls? And was it not true that once he had loved a sun-haired woman who lived there? *Why,* she thought desperately.

Why was there always so much damning evidence against Touch the Sky?

"Yes, indeed," Medicine Flute went on, "his white squaw was—"

Honey Eater suddenly threw down her materials and stared at her unwelcome visitor. "You," she spat out with undisguised contempt, "are a coward and a liar. You are not worthy to look a true man in the eye. And you have no more 'medicine' than a stump has brains. Such as you make a mockery of Cheyenne manhood."

"Truly," threw in Sharp Nosed Woman, glancing at his slat-ribbed torso. Although Medicine Flute intimidated her, she would not let him insult her favorite niece. "Boys with only twelve winters behind them have a bigger chest on them than you do."

"Perhaps," he replied, anger coloring his

cheeks, "Honey Eater will soon know full well how *big* I am. For things are the way they are. I am winning over the people. I and Wolf Who Hunts Smiling. After we have secured the reins of leadership, the tribe's care will be guided differently. As concerns our women, perhaps we will emulate our Comanche enemies."

Both women knew full well what this sinister remark meant. To the Comanches, women were worth less than horses. Not only were Comanche men permitted more than one wife, but their most influential leaders took any woman who was for the taking. And Comanche men were permitted to kill their women for cause.

Honey Eater felt invisible slugs squirming on her skin as Medicine Flute moved in closer. He lowered his voice to a husky whisper. His words made her stomach turn.

"Your tall buck will soon be smoke behind you. And *you* are a powerless widow surrounded by enemies. Either you will be my woman, haughty one, or you will be the woman of *many* braves, all Bull Whips. And when we are done topping you, we will leave you out on the prairie with a knife so you can fall on it and end your shame."

Wolf Who Hunts Smiling laid low behind a pine-timbered ridge, watching the bluecoats working below.

Two-man teams worked with long cross-cut saws, felling stacks of yellow pine trees. Finishing crews stripped off the larger branches and planed off most of the bark. Then the rough logs were stacked in long wagons drawn by mule teams. Sawyers back at Fort Bates would turn them into sturdy new planks.

In spite of his hatred for these stinking *Mah-ish-ta-shee-da*, Wolf Who Hunts Smiling was impressed by their industry and organization. How efficiently they worked, like busy ants driven by unerring instinct. No wonder, he thought, that the red men were having such a rough time of it against this odd enemy. Few tribes were as efficient as that, nor were the red men organized to fight as one nation.

But Wolf Who Hunts Smiling planned to change all that. So far his scheme was working: first he must kill Touch the Sky and wrest full control of the tribe. Then, through his crucial secret alliances with the Comanche Big Tree and the Blackfoot Sis-ki-dee, he must form one giant, warring red nation. And they would hold tight to one goal: a war of total destruction against the whiteskin invaders.

They had left their ponies tethered in a nearby coulee, handy for the charge. Medicine Flute held a position downridge to his right, Swift Canoe to his left. Luckily this attack would be easy. For Medicine Flute was virtually useless as a warrior, so concerned was he to stay hidden from hostile fire. But Wolf Who Hunts Smiling would hold off the attack, as planned, until Carlson's unit signaled they were near enough.

Actually, the wily brave was far more concerned about Touch the Sky's whereabouts. He had no doubt the tall Cheyenne would show up—Wolf Who Hunts Smiling did not mind playing the bait in any trap that snared White Man Runs Him, the pretend Cheyenne. This would be, ironically, a classic Bluecoat trap: the pincers. If Carlson's men couldn't send him under, Wolf Who Hunts Smiling would.

Tom Riley and Corey had worked out their strategy in a hurried conference. Riley could not risk much time away from his new desk job, nor did his new TAD orders authorize him to be in the field under arms.

So they agreed Corey would take care of the donkey work. Riley dug the old coarse gray sock out of his mattress and took out three double-eagle gold coins worth $20 apiece. It was a month's pay, with combat bonus, and he sighed at the loss. But he promptly turned them over to Corey.

Corey, pushing his mount hard, the gold tucked into his fob pocket, headed for the mining camp near Beaver Creek.

Hot pain pulsating hard in his still tender wound, Touch the Sky used isolated boulders as cover. He leap-frogged closer and closer to the three ponies tethered in the middle of the coulee.

A wide grin divided his face when he saw the rifles protruding from the ponies' riggings. Clearly, Wolf Who Hunts Smiling's little band was currently spying on their enemy and wanted to move swiftly and silently. But this had been a costly mistake.

The ponies knew Touch the Sky and his Cheyenne smell. It was easy to run a lead line through all three of their halters and lead them back out of the coulee. Easy—assuming Corey and Riley succeeded somehow at stopping Carlson's approaching unit. If not, Touch the Sky was about to debouch from the coulee onto open ground before the pine trees started—excellent country for drawing a tight bead on a target.

Despite his own danger, for a moment his mind ran to thoughts of Kristen's safety. His arrow had skewered Stoney MacGruder's head just in time to save her. But Abbot Fontaine was still on the loose—and his crazy eyes hinted at a mind far sicker than MacGruder's.

One battle at a time, Touch the Sky reminded himself. For now was the moment to outfox a wily wolf.

After Carlson's unit forded Beaver Creek, he had his men run their weapons and equipment through one final check.

Each man had been instructed to crimp 30 rounds for his Spencer carbine. Carlson had little faith in the average soldier's ability to shoot. The Army expended little money on training, figuring it was cheaper to replace a man than to train him well. Many of the men at Fort Bates had never fired their weapons, and would not until their first combat.

Not so with his crack regiment.

His platoon was a special Indian-hunting unit, each man a battle-hardened sharp-shooter from the Dragoons. They were taught to shoot plumb and follow the famous Sioux battle cry, adopted by their bullet-hoarding Cheyenne cousins: *One bullet, one enemy*

All this firepower would be unleashed on Matthew Hanchon. Killing him had become Seth Carlson's all-consuming passion, a need that ached inside him like hell-thirst.

"All right," he called out. "Prepare to mount! We'll hold double columns by sets of four. When you—"

"Sir!" the trooper named Waites shouted. "Look yonder! Emergency courier comin', Cap'n, and he's got the red flag out!"

Carlson felt his scalp prickle. He looked where the trooper pointed and saw the blue-bloused courier just then fording the creek. A small red swallow-tail guidon snapped from a short staff—every soldier on the Plains knew that red flag meant dire news.

"Sir!" An elderly corporal with a shabby and ill-fitting uniform tossed him a sloppy salute as he rode up. "Sir, it's the devil's own work! Col. Thompson just sent me on the q.t. to order you back to Fort Bates *now*! The entire Sioux camp under Red Feather is about to overrun the fort!

"They're saying the entire Indian nation is at war, sir! It come all of a sudden-like, just like an avalanche. I hear they wiped out Bighorn

Falls, left wimmin' and kids scalped in the streets! Hurry, sir! I got to ride down now and tell the log-cutters. Good luck, Captain!"

The courier saluted, gave spur to his mount, headed toward the pine ridges. Carlson had turned as pale as most of his men. Fort Bates, under attack! Civilians slaughtered in Bighorn Falls! Christ on a crutch, Carlson told himself. The great Indian war had finally come.

All of this was so shocking that even Carlson, deep in his obsessive need to kill Matthew Hanchon, forgot all about that. "You heard the man!" he shouted. "Hit leather! We're riding back to Fort Bates!"

The courier continued riding south only until the soldiers had forded the creek and were heading north again. Then he reined his mount around and dusted his hocks back toward the placer camp where he eked out his living panning for gold flake.

Curly Hupenbecker grinned to himself. He was a former soldier who had become a "snowbird"—a recruit who signs up in the winter for food and shelter, then deserts with the first spring melt. He had kept his uniform, a fact Corey knew from making his acquaintance during trips to the camp with his preacher dad.

And by God, he thought now. I'll bet that jug-eared captain never once heard them double-eagles ringing in my pocket! He was going to be madder than a badger out of his hole when he found out how he'd been hornswaggled. But nobody in that unit knew or recognized Curly. By the time they twigged the game, Curly's beard would have grown back and no one would recognize him anyway.

Goddamn Army. Goddamn little-tin-God officers. All acting high and mighty, as if *they* didn't take down their pants to crap like enlisted men did. Curly's grin widened. Well, they whipped him and shaved his head one time too many. Served them right, the stupid gazaboos.

Wolf Who Hunts Smiling seethed with anger. These hair-faced soldiers had the brains of rabbits! Where was Carlson? The Cheyenne had waited here on the ridge as long as he dared. Now the morning was waning, and soon the loggers would return to their camp to make a nooning.

Never mind Carlson. Wolf Who Hunts Smiling decided to take his chance—Woman Face had not managed to kill him yet! Let him try again now.

He made the owl hoot to get the attention of Medicine Flute. Then he pointed back toward the coulee where they'd tethered their mounts and left their weapons. They would return, mount up, conduct a lightning strike in classic Cheyenne fashion.

He led their trio up the sloping entrance of the coulee, past the spine of rocks that had hidden their mounts.

When he realized the coulee was empty, Wolf Who Hunts Smiling lost his arrogant sneer. His jaw dropped open in astonishment. And slowly, as he realized, his astonishment warmed up to rage. Once again Touch the Sky had played the crafty Indian.

"Look!" Medicine Flute pointed toward one of the rocks. Wolf Who Hunts Smiling glanced at the bold charcoal drawing, then felt his blood chill as if he'd been plunged naked into a snow bank.

The drawing depicted a wolf—a smiling wolf—with a predatory sheen to his eyes. But the detail that had momentarily frightened even Wolf Who Hunts Smiling was the fact that the wolf's smiling head was not connected to the body—it was impaled nearby on a war lance.

Chapter Twenty-one

"I'm not quite sure I understand you, Riley," Col. Thompson said. "Why, exactly, did you request commander's time? And why does Carlson have to be present?"

The two captains stood at ease before their C.O.'s desk. The hostility in Seth Carlson's face was clear. These two officers had never been able to tolerate each other. Carlson considered Riley, as a former enlisted man who had no college behind him, nothing but a hick rail-splitter from hardscrabble farm trash; Riley, in turn, considered Carlson a Tidewater snob unfit to lead real by-God men.

"I requested this meeting, sir, to inform you that I wish to press formal charges against Capt. Carlson."

Carlson stared hard at his colleague. Thompson frowned. "Now see here! What charges?"

"I'm still working on the exact wording, sir. But at this point, I'm considering one charge of bribery and another of unauthorized maneuvers."

"You fence-post digger!" Carlson exploded. "Are you daft, man?"

"Stow it, Carlson." Col. Thompson squinted, studying Riley closer. The sunburned towhead stubbornly held his ground. "Riley, you're a good officer. But do you realize how serious it is to bring charges against a fellow officer?"

"Of course I do, sir. I don't take this step lightly. Nor is this man my 'fellow.'"

"You better not take this step at all," Carlson said. "I'll—"

"*Stow* it, Carlson," the Colonel said again, a hard-edged tone of authority creeping into his voice. "Now, Riley. Tell me more about this bribery charge."

"It's my TAD orders, sir. I'm a combat officer, a platoon leader. Suddenly, for no logical reason, Maj. Kellogg, the admin officer, assigns me to noncombat duty behind a desk.

"But I've learned something from witnesses. Only forty-eight hours before my TAD orders were cut, Carlson was overheard in the sutler store, promising Maj. Kellogg several choice tracts of farmland—farmland which is presently Cheyenne hunting ground."

The Colonel shot a squinting glance at Carlson. "What about that, Captain?"

"Pack of lies, sir. Pure scuttlebutt. Personally,

I consider Riley the biggest liar since Simon Peter denied Christ."

"Leave the Lord out of this, Carlson. You're telling me you said nothing to Kellogg about giving him Indian grantland?"

"No, sir! How can I give away what's not mine? We were merely having a speculative conversation, sir. You know. We were only discussing what if. What could be done with such fertile ground if Congress had not foolishly given it to those who only waste it."

The Colonel looked at Riley. "You heard the man. You haven't got much, Tom. In fact, if you'll pardon my crudity, it sounds to me like you're grabbing at farts. What about this unauthorized maneuvers business?"

"Sir, as you well know, *any* use of troops in the field is strictly regulated and monitored by the chain-of-command according to the rules of engagement. That includes where and when they actually go and with what type of equipment.

"I think I can prove that Seth Carlson has been engaged in an ongoing pattern of abuses. He has repeatedly bypassed the chain-of-command to take his men into unauthorized sectors. He has repeatedly equipped his men for offensive combat when not authorized to do so. And he has engaged non-hostile Indians in unauthorized skirmishes."

By now Carlson was livid with rage. Col. Thompson looked at him. "Again, you heard the man. What say you?"

"Plenty, sir. To start with, maybe Capt. Riley here has forgotten that I'm presently on general scouting duty. That gives me a lot of leeway as to where my men ride. As for offensive-combat capabilities—does he think I'm going to send my men out into the field, where hostiles are active, with empty weapons? And as for engaging non-hostiles. Those who are known for fraternizing with enemies of the U.S. Government are hardly qualified to decide who is or is not 'hostile.' "

Thompson's confused frown etched itself deeper. "Gentlemen, the charges are flying thick now. What do you mean, fraternizing with enemies?"

"I'm talking about that renegade Cheyenne criminal who's tribal name is Touch the Sky. The one I already warned you about, sir. He's thick as thieves with Riley here."

"I take it, Riley, that such a preposterous charge is not true?"

Heat flowed into Riley's face. "Well, I do know him, sir. But I can tell you right now he's no kind of a criminal. The Cheyennes in this area are *not* on the warpath. Only Roman Nose of the Southern Cheyenne Dog Men."

"Like hob!" Carlson exploded. "Sir, you saw the body we found recently in Blackford Valley. Stoney MacGruder, one of Hiram Steele's workers. A harmless simpleton Steele hired out of pity. An arrow right through his head, and Cheyenne fletching on it! And then there was that sage-freighter killed a few days ago. The

259

description of the killer fits that tall Cheyenne buck like a velvet glove. And Riley here is practically his blood brother."

Riley spoke up angrily, but Col. Thompson threw his hands up in disgust. He was not corrupt, Riley knew, but he tended to think officers could go "red simple"—the frontier phrase for being too soft on Indians as the result of being around them too long.

On the other hand, Riley knew that the Colonel was not stupid. He saw clearly enough that Seth Carlson *did* often go out of his way to deal misery to the red man. Thompson did not share Carlson's opinion that Indians were merely animals to be slaughtered.

"This has become a hopeless quagmire, gentlemen. I have two competent officers, of equal rank, pressing ridiculous charges and countercharges. If I pursue this through channels, I will tie up the entire operation of this command.

"I suspect *both* of you could nick each other. But what's the point? An investigation could drag on for months. Unless either of you comes up with substantial proof, I refuse to prefer any charges. I will not let a personality clash interfere with my God-sworn military duties. That clear, Riley?"

"Yessir."

"Carlson?"

"Clear, sir."

"Good. Carlson, you may indeed be on extended scouting duty. But that's no license to rove like Texas Rangers. And that little dog-and-pony show yesterday! You and your men riding up to the post full-bore with your bugler sounding the attack. You nearly caused a panic."

"But, sir, I explained—"

"Put your 'buts' back in your pocket, Carlson. And you, Riley, I must warn you in the strictest terms. If you are truly associating with an Indian criminal, and if I receive proof of that association, I will personally rip those railroad tracks off your shoulder boards. I will bust you down to buck-private and make sure you do ten years bad time digging four-holers. Do you read me?"

"Sir, you don't understand. Carlson is—"

"*Do* you read me, Riley?"

Carlson had trouble containing his smirk so Thompson wouldn't see it. He met Riley's eye briefly. That wordless glance nonetheless sealed a promise: *Matthew Hanchon's days are numbered, Indian lover, and so are yours.*

"I read you loud and clear, sir," Riley finally replied.

When Hiram Steele was especially enraged, his face tended to bloat until it looked like a distorted image in a warped mirror. It did so now as he confronted Abbot Fontaine and Seth Carlson.

"Jesus H. Christ! If brains were horseshit, you two would have a clean corral."

Hiram paced up and down angrily in front of the desk in his library. His two interlocutors looked sullen, but also somewhat contrite. Even though Steele hired out most of his dirty work, he was neither a coward nor a small man. When he got on the peck, as he was now, it was best to tread wide of him.

"Abbot, how can you know nothing about Stoney's death? I told you not to let that simple shit run loose. You know what he did to that little girl in St. Joe."

"Aww, hell, Hiram! A man can't be another man's shadow. Stoney, he got so's he wouldn't do nothing but look for sign of them Injins. Hell, I was giving it twelve hours a day as it was. He just took off on his own."

"And you, Seth! How in the hell did you fall for that hornswaggle about an 'Indian attack' on Fort Bates? It was a simple goddamn mission! A titty baby in three-cornered britches could've handled it."

"Be fair, Hiram. The sonofabitch was in uniform. I'm a soldier, not a soothsayer. Sure I want to see Hanchon's red ass stretched on tenterhooks. But I've got friends back at the fort, I couldn't ignore the order. I'm not trained to evaluate orders, only to execute them."

"Crissakes, spare me the soldier-boy crap. West Point training is fine for combat. But we're talking about getting rich—and getting even. Duty hasn't got a damn thing to do with it."

Steele slammed a fist onto his desk so hard that a bottle of Old Crow leaped a half-inch into the air. " 'Be fair, Hiram,' " he mimicked scornfully. "You know what you two sound like, both of you? Huh? Do you? You sound like a couple of little snot-nosed brats instead of men. A bunch of goddamn *kids* always make whiny excuses. I need a couple good men with a set of stones on them."

"Now, Hiram," Abbot said placatingly, for like most brutes he respected a dangerous mood. "Course you're all riled up. You got a right to be. No white man cottons to being four-flushed by a red. But when a man's got a burr under his saddle, he needn't blame his horse."

Hiram squinted. "What the hell's that mean?"

Fontaine idly rested his palm on the butt-plate of his scattergun. The gesture was as familiar to him as a part of his body. "It means this, boss. It means that you're blaming me and Soldier Blue here for trouble what was *actually* caused by l'il sweet britches. And that carrot-top carpenter and whoever else is helping her."

Carlson had little use for this uncouth thug. But at the moment they were allies. And he was right. "Fontaine has struck a lode, Hiram," he said. "Riley has been stuck on post, I don't think he set up that masquerade with the phony courier. But I've got troopers watching his quarters, just in case. It's true, Corey Robinson visited him there recently. I'll bet my flat hat those two cooked it up and Robinson provided the false soldier."

Steele's anger had worked off its roughest edges by now. He slowly nodded, interest overcoming his foul mood. "You boys got a point. Hell, we've *all* been had. Matthew Hanchon is one slick operator, savage or no. And my own daughter has been flying his colors against us. No sense putting it all off on you boys. There's plenty of takers for the blame, including me."

Steele halted his pacing and sat on the edge of his desk. His face relaxed somewhat as he reflected on something. "Seth? Can you send that Indian scout of yours to fetch Wolf Who Hunts Smiling?"

Carlson nodded. "What's the plan?"

"You'll see soon enough. I got a couple tricks up my sleeve. Something that renegade buck said has got me thinking. He said we can hurt Hanchon more by dishonoring him in the tribe than by killing him. Well, I figure from here on out we have to try doing *both*.

"Have the Wolf meet us again near Red Shale. Our attack on the loggers never worked out. I'm tired of dragging my heels. This next strike is going to shake this entire valley up—hell, this entire territory. In fact, this time we'll enrage the entire damned nation! Even the brotherly love Quakers back East will be crying for Indian blood.

"It won't matter if Hanchon slips past us again. He'll have to ride to the moon to avoid all the soldiers and bounty hunters who're going to be after his top-knot."

"Hiram?" Fontaine prodded, idly fingering the bullet dent in his cheek.

"What?"

"What about your girl?" Fontaine gently pushed on the shotgun, making it bobble a bit in its jury-rigged sling. All three men watched it in silence.

Steele met Fontaine's eyes. "Soon," he said. "I'm holding back, out of respect for her mother's memory. But she pushes me one more time, being kin won't matter."

Chapter Twenty-two

Touch the Sky's companions agreed with him: They could not continue to ignore the dangerous situation back at their Powder River camp.

True, they had cleverly ruined the strike on the log-cutters and left Wolf Who Hunts Smiling without horses or weapons. But none of them denied their wily enemy's will to fight on, and with a renewed vengeance.

"Brothers, only think," Touch the Sky said. "While we remain here, unsure when the next trouble will come, Wolf Who Hunts Smiling is not so limited. *He* knows. This leaves him free to return to our camp at will."

"Straight-arrow, buck," Little Horse agreed. "And just as you know well the stench of a skunk, you know well how he speaks against us at camp. The damage each visit causes is great."

"While *his* filthy dishonor," Two Twists cut in angrily, "goes unmentioned by us because we are trapped here."

"Clearly," Touch the Sky said, summing up the collective will, "we are agreed we need to ride back."

All of them nodded. They had rendezvoused in a defile well back from Salt Lick Creek. Earlier all four divided to scout the entire area for Bluecoat activity. They had seen plenty of roving patrols, especially near the river. But it was impossible to deduce their enemy's next move. Nor was there any sign of Wolf Who Hunts Smiling, Swift Canoe, or Medicine Flute.

"We did not see them," Touch the Sky decided now, "because they have returned to camp. Now is the best time for us to go, too. The white-eyes will hold their treachery until their Cheyenne dog returns. Now it is time for us to take our story to the people. And with so many soldiers along the river, best if all four of us ride this time."

His companions nodded. All of this was sound counsel.

Abruptly Little Horse laughed. "I wonder if our Sioux cousins were surprised by the addition to their herd?"

The rest grinned, too. After seizing their tribal enemies's horses and weapons, they had turned the ponies loose to graze with a herd at the nearby Sioux camp at Coup Bluff.

Touch the Sky slapped the butt of the Colt Model 1855 rifle he had seized from Wolf Who

Hunts Smiling's rigging. "Brothers, only Little Horse knows this. But this weapon was once mine. I brought it with me when I left my white family to join my red one.

"You know that I was seized for a spy. My goods were divided, as is the custom. Wolf Who Hunts Smiling claimed this weapon. By our law-ways, it was his to take for I had been declared a mortal enemy of the tribe. I could not take it back, even after Arrow Keeper interfered and stopped my execution.

"But now it is mine. It is worthless to me now. I will not use it because I know it was used dishonorably. But Wolf Who Hunts Smiling is an enemy of our tribe and has quit his claim to this. He will die a hard death trying to claim it back."

"Then I hope he tries to claim it," Two Twists said fervently, and the rest nodded.

However, this solemn moment passed when Little Horse recalled their narrow escape at the mill. He burst out laughing again and grabbed young Two Twists by the shoulder. "*This* one! Brothers, you know how this fiery and sassy youth likes to taunt our white enemies, during battle, by lifting his clout at them in contempt. However, this time his clout lifted him!"

Even the embarrassed Two Twists almost fell off his pony laughing at this excellent joke. A Cheyenne warrior, snagged on a mill wheel while Bluecoats combed the bushes nearby! For that moment all danger was forgotten as the four braves were linked in tight camaraderie.

However, as they turned their ponies around and prepared to ride back to the Powder River camp, Touch the Sky reminded himself that by now that same camp was a death trap for him and his band. And he thought of Honey Eater's accusing eyes.

When he did so, he could also not help recalling Arrow Keeper's words: *Laughter, while necessary and good, always gives way to tears.*

No one greeted them when they rode in, their shadows long behind them as Sister Sun went to her bed. The crier did not race his pony up and down the camp streets, announcing their arrival. Only, thought Touch the Sky, this ominous silence.

All four braves quickly assessed the extent of the harm Wolf Who Hunts Smiling had been causing. Tension thickened the air. No young braves wrestled in the central clearing or conducted pony and foot races for bets. Gray Thunder's summer camp almost felt like two camps now, each about to spring on the other.

More weapons were carried openly now. Braves were careful to always move about in groups, seldom leaving camp alone. Brother suspected brother, clan cousins no longer gossiped freely; even the old grandmothers increased their keening wails late into the night, sensing the nearness of some great tribal catastrophe.

But the coldest welcome of all, for Touch the

Sky, came when his eyes collided with Honey Eater's.

Again, as he gauged the intensity of her hurt and disappointment, he asked himself: What had happened to convince her so deeply that *he* had killed Black Elk? Nor did it help his peace of mind to recall how sweet Kristen's treatment was compared to this bitter coldness.

All of Arrow Keeper's wisdom, all of Touch the Sky's visions and premonitions, had not told the young brave if Honey Eater would ever be his. Hitherto, hope was his only ally. But that cold look just now before she turned away— how could hope ever spring from such a well of resentment and suspicion?

"Brothers," Touch the Sky said as they turned their ponies out to graze in the common corral, "my chestnut, at least, is happy with this mission. Never has she had it so easy. Oats and river grass and plenty of rest. See? Her coat actually glows."

"Truly," Little Horse said. "But an Indian is in trouble when his pony is not."

And trouble arrived soon after the next sunrise: Wolf Who Hunts Smiling and his band, exhausted and angry from paddling a crude dugout against the current.

When the clan fires began casting lurid shadows around the camp, the vigilant Touch the Sky watched Wolf Who Hunts Smiling emerge from his tipi. Without once looking around, he began strolling purposefully toward the central clearing. The Bull Whips quickly gathered near him.

"*Now* we are in for sport, bucks," Touch the Sky told his companions. "Let us go join the fray, and cowards to the rear!"

Despite these spirited words, Touch the Sky moved somewhat gingerly, the wound over his hip still tender. By the time they joined the crowd milling in the clearing, Wolf Who Hunts Smiling had found his rhetorical stride. He stood atop the fat stump in the middle of the clearing, his lupine features dramatically outlined in the yellow-orange flames.

"Cheyenne people! You know me! Many of you men have smoked the common pipe with me. Not a woman or child or elder in this camp can say that I have not risked my life to protect them."

"Wrong, braggart!" shouted a Bow String trooper. "My son was born while you were gone!"

A few people laughed. But all smiles faded when Wolf Who Hunt Smiling sought out the face of the speaker. "And your son's father," he replied in a tone heavy with menace, "may die while I am here."

But he immediately addressed the entire crowd again.

"Cheyenne people! You saw how my band arrived here this day. Now take my words and examine them. I tell you that Woman Face and his criminal companions took our ponies and our weapons. I am a Bull Whip trooper. It is my

271

duty to watch these traitors and report on their treachery to my troop leader, Lone Bear. Knowing this, they have taken this step to hinder my duty. This is yet one more act of treason."

"Tell all of us a thing, loyal Bull Whip," Touch the Sky challenged him. "We all see clearly that you have returned by dugout."

"How else, traitor run by whites? *You* took our ponies!"

"As you say. I freely admit this. Odd, that a white man's dog could relieve such a bold killer as you of your mount. Only, tell all of us a thing. As our camp scouts will verify, the river is presently swarming with Bluecoat patrols. How is it, if I have teamed up with these soldiers, that they did not stop *you*, our common enemy? Is it perhaps because, to them, you were a familiar and welcome wolf?"

This was a sure thrust. Even the glib Wolf Who Hunts Smiling was caught without a ready reply in his parfleche. However, it was Medicine Flute who rose to the task, albeit lamely.

"Everyone knows," this lazy 'shaman' said, "that all Indians look alike to whites. No doubt, since we were in a dugout like yours, they mistook us for their dog, White Man Runs Him."

It was a weak explanation, and many were far from convinced. Using this doubt as a wedge, Touch the Sky now boldly took over and refused to fall silent until he had his say. He told the people about Wolf Who Hunts Smiling's sinister attack on the sage freighters, about the aborted raid on the Bluecoat work detail.

"This one," he concluded, "who has long accused me of being a white man's dog, now licks their hands himself! *He* is the one endangering our homeland! Just as it was he who killed our war leader."

"And *this*," Little Horse threw in, "is how they have proved Medicine Flute's pretend vision. They tell us Touch the Sky is going to join soldiers in stealing our land. Then *they* actually do this under the excuse of 'policing' us."

"People, do you hear this?" Wolf Who Hunts Smiling shouted. "These pigs' afterbirths have no shame! Gray Thunder! You and the Headmen have been foxed by the ablest spy who ever wore white man's shoes. Remember this. Uncle Pte, the buffalo, never lies. And the white man's stink on this tall intruder has scattered the herds more than once.

"He has murdered my cousin in the hope of satisfying his lust for Honey Eater. Now he attempts to destroy our homeland, to turn it into women's gardens tended by hair-faces. Bull Whips! I say there is no 'murder' possible when our very tribe is at stake! Killing them will not stain the Arrows, but *cleanse them! Let us kill them now*!"

He unsheathed his knife and prepared to leap from the stump. A great shout went up from the Whips, many of whom now brandished their weapons.

"HOLD!"

Gray Thunder's voice held the bold note of authority, and the camp quieted. Their chief stepped into the glow of a huge clan fire, and the entire assemblage gasped: Gray Thunder held the muzzle of a cocked Colt Navy pistol turned to his own temple!

"Has it come to this?" he demanded. "Must your chief leave his brains on the ground before you will listen to reason? I will not watch *any* renegades destroy the legal authority which governs our tribe. We are not heathen Comanches who murder one another in their own camp.

"The first brave—be he a Whip or a Bow String—who moves on another will also cause the unclean death of this tribe's peace chief. For I will not sing my death song before I go. You all know well what this means."

Indeed, they all certainly did. Touch the Sky, like the rest, was shocked at the very prospect. Even Wolf Who Hunts Smiling had nothing to say now. Weapons were slowly put away. Wisely, Touch the Sky caught the eye of his companions and nodded back toward his isolated tipi.

Honey Eater had been standing in the shadow cast by the council lodge. Now, as she saw Two Twists pass, his words again came back to haunt her: *Of course Touch the Sky killed our war leader so he could freely sate his loins on Honey Eater. Little Horse helped him plan it. Both are well-paid spies for the Long Knives. But this so far is nothing compared to the treachery in store for this entire village.*

She almost called out his name. She would

simply ask the young lad forthrightly if it was true. Her hand went out, and then she recalled the "white squaw" stories. Touch the Sky was with his sun-haired white woman! And truly, Two Twists was one of his cohorts—he would only lie to her.

And suddenly, her great pride made her turn away as hot tears blurred her vision.

Chapter Twenty-three

"Settle down there, you sonofabitch!" Hiram Steele growled, leaping out of harm's way just in time.

He was "lunging" a spirited dun stallion in the paddock behind his house—letting the animal burn off energy by running in circles, its lead-line secured so it slipped around a central pole. Abbot Fontaine and Seth Carlson sat nearby on the top rail of the fence. The horse clearly disliked Hiram. Every time the businessman tried to step too close, it snapped its teeth at him.

"There's no way in hell that Kristen can hear us now," Carlson remarked, glancing back toward the big, clinker-built frame house. "What's this big plan you've been holding so close to your vest? We haven't even made our play at Council Rock yet, and you've got another plan?"

"I'll get to it, Soldier Blue, don't crowd me. First, what's the word from the Indian scout of yours?"

"Lightfoot says Hanchon is on his way back to the valley. So is Wolf Who Hunts Smiling. With horses, this time," Carlson added scornfully.

"Good." Steele nodded, his eyes puckering with satisfaction as he watched the horse run itself out. "Let 'em come. Both of 'em."

"Lightfoot went to the cave where the Wolf and his band are holed up," Carlson said. "Left a sign message that we need to talk to them."

"All right. You know, Wolf Who Hunts Smiling had a good time assuring us that strike at Beaver Creek would be as easy as rolling off a log. But Hanchon gave him a comeuppance. Maybe now he won't strut around the barnyard like the head rooster."

"Oh, he'll strut," Abbot Fontaine said. "He'll strut right over our graves and piss on 'em into the deal. Ain't no humility in *that* red son."

"Abbot's struck a lode there," Hiram agreed. He looked at Carlson. "How's your C.O. taking all this?"

"He's not one to bare his soul to his subordinates. But I'd wager Col. Thompson is about half fed up with Indian criminals."

A wide smile divided Steele's big, bluff face. "Of course he is! And this next trouble will be the meal that fills him up! You talked to your men yet about filing for adjoining plots?"

"They're all for it. We'll set up our own land

office, hire a claims recorder, have the men file under summer names in civilian clothes. Then we pay each of them one dollar for his 180-acre plot. They can't legally own one, anyway, while they're serving the Stars and Bars. So they're all for it. Especially since we'll be throwing in a few barrels of whiskey to sweeten the deal."

Abbot laughed so hard he coughed up a hard loden pellet of phlegm. "Damn, old sons! I'd say you're puttin' the hay wagon in front of the team, ain't yous? You got that tall buck to send under afore you start opening up any damned land office or rolling out whiskey barrels."

Hiram frowned, the mirth deserting his eyes. "Abbot, you're a cunning old boy this morning. I don't like what you're saying, but I'm glad you're saying it. In fact, keep reminding us because we can't hear it enough. We *can't* take Hanchon too lightly, or we'll end up Shit Creek without a paddle."

Abbot dug a tick out of his grizzled beard as he nodded. "That's pure-dee fact, Hiram. That buck and his band done for Stoney. And they left old Wolf up there in the pine country with nothing but his peeder in his hand. You was right, Hiram, when you said these ain't no blanket Indians off the rez. These is crafty sonsabitches and they fear no man."

"No, they don't," Hiram agreed. "But all Indians do fear one thing—being banished forever from their tribe. That's why we're going to try the plan this Wolf Who Hunts Smiling is pushing. Hell, we can go on trying to kill Hanchon. We'll try again at Council Rock if he takes the bait and shows up.

"But we've also got to discredit him in his people's eyes. From now on we follow a double strategy. That's why we're having a phony 'meeting' tonight in my library. You boys know what to say. And Seth, this new double strategy is why I had you plant that phony order at the fort. Riley has a spy there."

Carlson looked doubtful. "I've done what you said. Of course Riley has a spy at the fort. A decoy plan is fine by me. But what if Kristen doesn't overhear us tonight?"

"Huh. She'll hear us. She missed a trick yet?"

"No, you're right. But Hiram, to hell with the decoy plan tonight. Spill your real plans for this last strike. Why are you so sure *this* will cost the savages their grantland?"

Steele said, "What do you know about Jim West, the pastor at the Methodist church?"

Carlson looked as if he wanted to spit. "A pus-gut, Indian-loving, perfumed pansy. He gives sermons all about how it was the Spaniard and the white man who taught the Indians to scalp. He's got Col. Thompson and others in his Indian-loving fold."

Steele nodded. "Exactly. So think about it. Think about how low-down awful and despicable it would be if West got killed by Cheyenne renegades—and on a Sunday morning right outside his church, in front of his congregation?"

This was so brazen that Carlson was left

speechless. But, slowly, an appreciative grin replaced his disbelief. "Hiram," he said, admiration clear in his tone, "you *do* know how to stir
up the shit."

Abbot, too, approved this with a grin. He
looked at each of the other two in turn. His eyes
revealed a mad-preacher sheen as he lightly
stroked the butt of his sawed-off. "I figure to do
for him at Council Rock. But I almost hope he
doesn't show up there so's I can watch this little
shindig at the church.

"You know, fellas? I wunner how many of
them tough Innuns got the stones to air their
own mamas like I done?"

This actually revolted Carlson, and he looked
away in disgust. Even Hiram flinched at openly
boasting of such barbarity, whether it was true
or not.

"See? *See*?" Abbot roared with laughter, almost falling off the rail. "Red men, white men,
it don't make no never-mind. *All* of you are soft
somewhere. Me? Well, Mrs. Fontaine's boy Abbot is 200 pounds of hard! See you tonight, old
sons."

No longer caring what her father did to her,
Kristen had determined to spy on his meetings
whenever possible. Too much was at stake for
her safety to matter. Now, crouched in the darkness beneath the open library window, she listened to words that pierced her heart like
shards of glass.

"Boys, it's time to fish or cut bait," her father

said. "We've got future profits to start toting up. But Seth brings a bit of bad news today from Fort Bates."

"What bad news?" Abbot Fontaine said. "Did the cook re- enlist?"

His raucous guffaw made Kristen wince. She had fixed her broken bedroom door as best she could. But Abbot Fontaine slept right across the hall. And he was not the kind of man who was easily dissuaded by mere things like doors, locks, or the word "no."

"Abbot, I'm in no funnin' mood. Now listen up and earn your keep for a change. Tom Riley will be meeting at Council Rock with a secret military courier. Day after tomorrow, toward sunset. The courier has special orders pertaining to the Cheyennes."

"What kind of orders?"

"Nobody's certain. But use your brain. If an Indian lover like Riley is involved, it won't boost our cause any. I want you to be there waiting for both of them."

"You want 'em killed?"

"I want 'em dead as last Christmas, both of them. And get those orders from the courier. We can't stall Washington off forever. But this could slow them down long enough to get the land reclamation movement going."

A cold, prickling numbness took hold of Kristen's face. They were going to kill Tom Riley! And clearly those orders were important.

She never even debated the matter, much less suspected this entire conversation was an elaborate ploy to fool her. Of course she must get word to Matthew about this fatal meeting at Council Rock. Still nonplussed by the urgency facing her, Kristen hardly noticed when a twig snapped under her shoe.

But inside the smoke-filled library, where a momentary silence punctuated the talk, that twig snapped as audibly as the shot heard round the world. Abbot Fontaine, standing near the window, glanced first at Steele, then at Carlson.

Neither man responded to his sly, exaggerated wink.

Early the next morning, even before his first cup of coffee had cooled, Riley heard a voice imploring him from the little cubbyhole window.

"Cap'n! Cap'n Riley, sir! You in there?"

The corporal named Mattson squinted in at him, having difficulty seeing into the dim interior from the bright morning sunshine suffusing the parade field.

Riley dropped the invoice he was scrutinizing and rose from the desk. "What is it, Mattson?" He crossed to the window.

"Morning, sir. Got some news you might be interested in."

Mattson glanced over his shoulder before he went on. "Sir, I overheard a sergeant in Carlson's unit giving a special order issued by Carlson himself. He's sending three sharp-shooters to Council Rock tomorrow evening."

Riley frowned. Council Rock was a huge, table-shaped granite bluff about two hours' ride north of Fort Bates. Warring tribes used to meet there to discuss terms for peace.

"Why?"

"He said a tall Cheyenne brave will be meeting with an Indian runner. I don't know why, the sergeant didn't say. But I do know that the sharp-shooters have orders to kill both Indians. Carlson didn't dare write the order down. His men made the mistake of talking about it in the First Sergeant's office. The door of the duty NCO room opens onto that area, I heard every word. Figured you'd want to know."

"You figured right, Mattson. I thank you kindly. Now you get back over there before somebody spots you talking to me."

After the trooper had scurried off, Riley paced the little room for a long time, conning the situation over. He could try catching Touch the Sky at Padgett's Mill. But Carlson's men had Blackford Valley honeycombed and were surely watching all riders from the fort.

On the other hand, the stretch north of the post would make for easy traveling. He could put in his normal workday tomorrow, then head right for Council Rock. Then he could either warn Touch the Sky or at least try to cover him. Should he risk the valley tonight or Council Rock tomorrow? If he chose the valley, he faced greater risk of encountering Carlson or his men. So he opted for Council Rock.

* * *

With both Wolf Who Hunts Smiling and Touch the Sky gone from camp, Honey Eater felt the tension ease somewhat.

But now, as the first fires of evening sprang up, she watched Medicine Flute move to the center of the clearing. This time he had not ridden out with Wolf Who Hunts Smiling. Honey Eater suspected there was a reason for this—and she further suspected the tribe was about to learn that reason, much to their chagrin.

Soon, bearing out her fear, the crier raced up and down the camp streets, summoning the people out.

"Medicine Flute has experienced a vision!" he announced. "He is about to reveal it to the people!"

Never mind, Honey Eater thought angrily, that Medicine Flute had no right to summon the people out like this. Such privileges were accorded only to tribal chiefs, soldier-troop leaders, and shamen. But Medicine Flute claimed the title of shaman, and more and more people believed it. Now everyone was streaming into the clearing, even those who did not support him. Despite her foreboding, Honey Eater knew she had to go, too.

A master of the dramatic prelude, Medicine Flute kept the entire camp in suspense. He stood deep in the shadow of the hide-covered council lodge until all were assembled.

Then, all of an instant, he stepped out into the stark firelight. At sight of his face, Honey Eater and many of the rest gasped in shock—for he had painted it garishly in the battle colors, his chin red, his forehead black, his cheeks and nose yellow.

He skipped his usual lengthy preamble, as if eager to sink the shaft of his words while the people still stared in awe. For a moment his sheening eyes dwelled on Honey Eater. Suddenly she felt as if maggots were crawling on her.

"I have previously spoken a vision to this tribe, as directed by the High Holy Ones. I have warned my tribe of the treachery of this Touch the Sky, who even now claims the title of shaman and Arrow Keeper. Many have chosen to ignore this vision warning. So be it. Those who ignore clear sign pay with their blood!

"Maiyun loves His people. He has therefore sent a second and final vision warning. Ignore it, fathers and brothers, if you wish. But this matter may soon be easily proven. For in one sleep Touch the Sky will meet secretly with his Bluecoat master at Council Rock."

"These are not 'vision words,'" Spotted Tail of the Bow Strings protested. "They are mere bubbles blown by a baby! Medicine Flute cannot know this thing. And Touch the Sky does not play the dog for Long Knives!"

"Do not even start this womanly arguing!" Lone Bear shouted. The leader of the Bull Whips had authority to speak in such a matter and did so now. "Medicine Flute has not made any 'mystical' claims here. He states a thing boldly and clearly and names a time. What boots it to debate his claim? This is child's play to prove or disprove.

"We will send a rider out to Council Rock now. A brave who is neither friend nor foe to Touch the Sky. He will be there to watch for this meeting. If it happens, Medicine Flute has proven two things. That *he* is our true shaman, and that this spy Touch the Sky quits all claim to the title of 'Cheyenne!'"

Chapter Twenty-four

"Matthew?" Kristen said. "Are you still angry with me for coming to warn you?"

"I was," he admitted. "But how could you *not* come? It would be against your nature. You'd have risked it for a stranger, I suppose. How could you let Tom Riley be ambushed? No, I'm not angry, Kristen. It just scares me, thinking about you in the middle of this god-awful mess."

"Then you know how *I* feel every time you just up and jump back into my life! It scares *me*, all the enemies you've earned, all wanting to kill you."

"Earned?" His voice took on a rare, bitter tone she seldom heard him use. "How? By choosing the color of my skin before I was born? Earned? I guess just being alive will earn any man plenty of enemies, white *or* red."

"That's not what I meant, and you know it! You *earned* them honorably, Matthew Hanchon or Touch the Sky or whoever you are, you wonderful man! You earned them because you're a man from the ground up, as tough as any and smarter than most."

They sat on a downed tree near the river, hidden by willows. Her words, so unexpected yet welcome, made him swallow a hard lump in his throat. Honey Eater, too, had once spoken similar words in open and clear admiration of her tragic warrior. Was that love and respect now gone forever, replaced by the accusing remoteness he had seen in her eyes?

"Kristen?"

"Yes?"

"Tom Riley is a fine man."

Startled, she looked up from the pollywogs she'd been watching swim in a little pool. "Yes, I'd say so, too. I don't know him very well. But I liked him instantly. He's a gentleman, but completely without pretense. An awful lot like you."

"Knowing him as I do, I take that as a compliment to me."

"To both of you." She flushed a bit, embarrassed by the topic. "Anyway," she added in a brusque, just-you-never-mind tone, "I want *both* of you to come back safe. Be careful tonight."

For a few moments Touch the Sky succumbed to the physical nearness of this beautiful young woman: the lavender scent of her perfume, the flawless skin tanned a light gold, the thick, wheat-colored hair pulled up under an amethyst comb. Several light scratches on her left cheek bore testimony to her struggle with Stoney MacGruder.

"Believe me," Touch the Sky finally answered, "I'll be nothing *but* careful."

He didn't want to worry her any more than she clearly was. So he didn't tell her how bad this whole Council Rock meeting smelled to him. That spot was excellent ambush country— he knew it well from the days of his warrior training under Black Elk, the war leader he now stood accused of killing.

But what else was there for it? He would go, and if his time to fall had come, he'd at least make sure he fell on the bones of an enemy.

About an hour before sunset, Touch the Sky crested the last rise before Council Rock.

His comrades had seethed when he ordered them to remain in the valley. But Touch the Sky's shaman sense *and* his common sense told him the same thing: In an ambush situation, the fewer targets, the better.

Council Rock rose out of the tuft-grass flats and glacial morraine surrounding it. It was that glacial morraine that worried the tall Cheyenne—hidden marksmen had excellent positions to choose from in all that jumble of rocks.

His chestnut, too, was nervous, and that worried Touch the Sky. He spoke gently to calm her, slowing her from a canter to a trot as they crossed the flat.

He felt eyes on him, felt them as real as insects crawling all over his body. Plenty of eyes. Touch the Sky had learned to scan his surroundings from an oblique angle as well as straight on. Now and then, in the gathering twilight, he caught subtle movements like shape-changing shadows.

Then his prowling eyes spotted Tom Riley, and a measure of relief surged through him. At least he was still alive! The young officer had dismounted at the base of the southern face of Council Rock. He was still stamping in his picket pin when Touch the Sky spotted him. His carbine was tucked under one arm, the leather flap over his pistol unbuttoned.

"Permission to ride in?" the Cheyenne called out.

"Stuff your permission, buck! You best ride in *and* cover down, and mighty damn quick!" Riley called back, relief warring with fear in his tone. "From what I hear, there may be a bead on you right now."

Relieved to see his friend, Tom Riley momentarily forgot the custom and offered a friendly hand for Touch the Sky to shake. Knowing it was not offered to insult him, Touch the Sky gladly took it and greeted this good friend with pleasure. Over the years, passing Indians had built rock walls around here as windbreaks.

Blood On The Arrows

Both men moved behind one now and hunkered down.

"That's damned odd," Touch the Sky finally replied. "Because Kristen warned me *you* were meeting a courier and were marked for ambush."

Neither man had liked the feel of this one from the beginning. Now they understood why. And Riley knew he wasn't just bait—not after that confrontation, in the old man's office, with Seth Carlson. He and this fugitive Cheyenne were both desirable targets.

"You thinking what I'm thinking?" Riley asked, glancing uneasily around them.

"I am if you're wondering why I haven't been killed by now."

"Give the broad-shouldered Indian a cigar. That's exactly what I'm thinking. Why? Assuming they're out there, they could have tossed lead at you when you rode in."

Could have, but didn't. The answer to that question was still only a half-formed hunch in Touch the Sky's mind. Now that hunch became a certainty. Out in the jumbled rock-and-rubble morraine, he spotted a single feather silhouetted against the pink-hued evening sky. It was cut in the distinctive deep notch of the Cheyenne Antelope-eaters Clan.

A moment later the brave stood boldly up to let Touch the Sky see him. He sat his flat buffalo-hide saddle, openly staring. And though he was one of the fairest men Touch the Sky knew, the betrayed hurt in his eyes

291

said clearly: *I saw you shake our enemy's hand!* Then River of Winds whirled his pony and rode out.

"I will tell you why they did not try to kill me right off," Touch the Sky said, "because my enemies have a clever plan with two prongs. If one does not gore me, the other will."

"I'm not the boy for riddles, pard. Not tonight. Spell it out clear."

"That brave who just rode out is the most trusted warrior in my tribe. No doubt he was sent to see if the 'spy' named Touch the Sky was meeting with his Bluecoat masters. All this is meant to make a white-livered coward named Medicine Flute look like a big shaman. See, he 'predicted' we'd be here."

Riley caught the drift immediately. "I got it. The hesitation was sort of a back-up plan to ruin you. In case they don't kill you now as you ride out, which they're itching to do as I speak. If they can't plug you, they'll at least make you a marked man without a tribe."

"You catch on quick for a paleface. And you're right. 'Itching' is the word." Touch the Sky's eyes scanned the outlying jumble of rock, narrowing to slits. But he had a feeling that Wolf Who Hunts Smiling, at least, would not be around this time. Not if he knew River of Winds or some other observer was coming—he would not risk being linked with his new white masters.

"How do we play it?" Riley said. "Wait until dark?"

That plan had its appeal. But it also left the situation in their enemy's hands. Touch the Sky's every instinct told him they must seize control of the situation, must rely on defeating their enemy by doing the unexpected. For the Indian, usually heavily out-gunned, impulse was a safer course than patience, for white soldiers were not creatures of impulse.

"We could wait," Touch the Sky agreed. "But I've got another suggestion. Let's both put our weapons away, relax, start laughing and joshing each other. Act like there's nothing out there but coyotes. You got the makings for some smokes?"

Riley nodded toward his mount. "In my *aparejo*."

"Even better. Real slow and easy, we walk over to your horse. I'll kick the picket out while you dig out the makings and build yourself a cigarette. Like we're just a couple of sightseers without a care in the world, you understand? Then, when I give the shout, we both hop our horses, hunker down, ride like hell, and throw lead anyplace where we see a muzzle flash."

It wasn't a brilliant plan. But it had the virtue of being a bold one, nothing that would pass muster at West Point. The devil-may-care warrior in Riley rose to embrace it.

He grinned. "The Smith & Wesson on my belt has got six beans in the wheel. There's no glory in peace, laddiebuck!"

They carried out the first part of the plan just

as Touch the Sky suggested it. They talked and laughed casually while Riley dug out tobacco and papers and rolled a smoke. Gesturing high with his arms to distract attention, Touch the Sky kicked out Riley's picket and worked off his chestnut's hobble.

All this time, they hardly glanced around them. The moment Touch the Sky uttered the war cry, they leaped up onto their horses and slapped their rumps hard.

"Hi-ya!" Touch the Sky yipped. "Hii-*ya*!"

Both riders surged out toward the surrounding flat. Almost immediately their worst fears were confirmed as hidden marksmen quickly recovered from their surprise and opened up from the boulders. Bullets whanged past their ears and splatted against the rocks. Touch the Sky spotted a Bluecoat marksman and snapped off a round from his Sharps. Dropping the rifle into its scabbard without bothering to see if his round scored, he snatched a handful of arrows from his quiver. Stringing and firing in one smooth movement, he sent a deadly hail of heat-tempered arrows toward the muzzle flashes.

Riley, too, laid down withering fire. He gripped his heavy frame Cavalry .44 in his right fist, muzzle spitting lead each time a capped cylinder rolled under the hammer. With his left arm he fired his Spencer carbine from the hip, cocking it with one hand by swinging it a half turn and tugging down the lever. He couldn't exactly aim, but he set up a frighteningly deadly spray of bullets and chipped rock. The number of cursing, scurrying men testified to the fire-power these two determined warriors suddenly mustered.

At the first shots, Touch the Sky's well-trained pony had gone into her evasive-riding pattern. She crow-hopped, feinted, made it difficult for marksmen to lead her. But the bigger, slower Cavalry horse made an easy target. Touch the Sky watched the big mount suddenly collapse hard, pink foam blowing from a punctured lung. Riley tumbled clear and came up in a crouch, cramming rounds into his .44.

"Tom! Head up!"

Touch the Sky whirled his mount, threw out one hand. Riley caught it and Touch the Sky gave a mighty tug. A moment later, the pony was seriously overburdened by two big men. But the game little chestnut mustang reacted by getting angry, her blood still as wild as her high-country origins. Muscles heaving like powerful machinery, she surged forward.

Their firearms were empty, and so was Touch the Sky's quiver. But somehow they had made it past the heaviest concentration of marksmen. They were about to clear a long spine of rocks when Touch the Sky saw a familiar face step out from behind a boulder: Abbot Fontaine.

What Touch the Sky witnessed next explained why Hiram had hired Fontaine. Not one spark of fear for his own safety glinted in the man's taunting eyes. The thug's weapon hung slack in its modified saber-belt sling. Without even looking down at it, Fontaine slapped the butt once. The sawed-off scattergun literally leaped up into his hand like a trained bird.

Fontaine grinned from less than 15 feet away. He pointed the twin muzzles at Touch the Sky. A heartbeat later, a desperate Tom Riley hurled his canteen. It cracked Fontaine square on the forehead, heavy enough to knock him cock-eyed for a moment.

The scattergun, knocked slightly off its bead, roared even as he staggered back. Touch the Sky's kit and rigging instantly shredded, several pellets stung at the chestnut's flank and spurred her on. Seconds later the two unbelieving men, suffering no more than a few buckshot nicks, were fleeing away from Council Rock.

They were minus one horse, but both felt very fortunate to have breath in their nostrils.

Wolf Who Hunts Smiling and Swift Canoe had holed up in their limestone cave near Blackford Valley. They waited there impatiently until a Bull Whip runner finally brought the welcome news. Although (to no one's surprise by now) Woman Face had once again evaded death at Council Rock, he had nonetheless suffered a serious blow. A blow that might prove even more devastating than death. For River of Winds had returned to the tribe with grim news. Perhaps Medicine Flute was right after all. Touch the Sky did indeed appear to be a traitor who worked secretly for Long Knives.

"I have ears for such words!" Wolf Who Hunts Smiling gloated. "Swift Canoe, count upon it. He is ruined now. We have chipped away and chipped away at the rock of his credibility. With this incident, it must finally crumble to dust! This will establish him as a white man's dog. It will also encourage the people's belief in Medicine Flute, who promised all this would come to pass."

"Truly he has fallen on grim days, Panther Clan. But this Touch the Sky has crawled out of his ashes before."

This was a barbed insight, especially coming from the slow-witted Swift Canoe. Wolf Who Hunts Smiling glanced at him with new appreciation.

"Brother, at times you stir out of your myopia and hone straight to the grain! This White Man Runs Him *does* always land on his feet. So we cannot let up now. He is down, struggling in the dirt. We must cut his throat before he can stand up and fight."

To that very end, Wolf Who Hunts Smiling was about to meet again with Hiram Steele and Seth Carlson. They had a new plan—one so damning to Touch the Sky, they boasted, that he would never be able to return to the Cheyenne tribe *or* the white man's world. A plan based on brutal sacrilege and contempt for the white man's God. In short, a plan Wolf Who

Hunts Smiling was eager to learn more about.
That plan boasted one other virtue. It would also surely lure Touch the Sky out for one more clear shot—and one shot was owed to him, Wolf Who Hunts Smiling figured, to compensate for the mistake that killed Black Elk.

Chapter Twenty-five

"I do not create the things I see," River of Winds said. "Nor do I know the secret meaning of every appearance. I am no visionary. I have told you what my eyes saw. I saw Touch the Sky meeting, in a clearly friendly manner, with a Bluecoat soldier chief at Council Rock."

"Yes. Just as Medicine Flute predicted it would pass!" Lone Bear shouted, and many of his Bull Whips chorused support. "Gray Thunder! You heard River of Winds! Touch the Sky and this soldier grabbed each other's hand in greeting, pumping them up and down as white dogs do! They laughed, thumped each other's backs."

Honey Eater felt a weary exhaustion with all of it. And she saw that same exhaustion reflected in Chief Gray Thunder's face. Only the threat of his own suicide had stopped the last rebellion. Next time, that would be useless.

Looking around the central camp clearing now, it was clear that River of Winds's careful report had made a profound impact on many. Some of Touch the Sky's most loyal supporters were visibly upset. They were finally forced to admit it among themselves: How to explain such closeness with white soldiers, such secret meetings, unless Touch the Sky were indeed playing the dog for white men?

"Cheyenne people! Have ears for my words!" shouted Spotted Tail, leader of the Bow Strings. "I confess, River of Winds's report troubles me mightily. When *he* speaks a thing, you know it flies straight-arrow. River of Winds is the brave we go to when it is time for the hunt distribution, for *no one* is more fair than he at dividing the meat equally. He never places himself or anyone else before his tribe.

"But though he speaks accurately, we cannot know the true meanings behind the apparent ones. If a brave takes to drunkenness, we cannot merely say 'he does wrong to drink.' For until we know *why* he drinks, we do not know how wrong it is. When my Uncle Sun Road found his wife and babes slain after the Washita battle, he stayed drunk for several sleeps. Who here can say he was wrong to do so?

"And so it is with Touch the Sky. Yes, he has met a soldier chief. But not *all* white soldiers hate Indians. Who knows the purpose of this meeting?"

"*This* is the voice of treason, not reason," Medicine Flute spoke up. "Never mind this verbal smokescreen about 'drunkenness.' We are not gathered here to discuss the merits of strong water. If this meeting between Touch the Sky and the Bluecoat was not for treachery, why did Maiyun bother to warn me about it? The Day Maker does not waste His time with frivolous revelations."

Honey Eater hated Medicine Flute, but she knew this was a good strategy on his part. Everyone knew that Maiyun was never capricious. Visions were serious warnings, not entertainments.

"There is no proof he *did* warn you," a Bow String spoke up boldly. "I can tell my cousin in secret to fall down at sunrise and pretend to a fit. Then when he falls, I can claim I 'predicted' this event. This is no proof."

This remark engendered more angry shouts and accusations on both sides. Honey Eater was so tired and spirit-weary from all of it that she wanted to scream at them to shut up. Before, she lent no credence to any reports of Touch the Sky's supposed treachery. She had refused to, for his enemies were too busy behind the scenes, shaping appearances against him.

But now, since accidentally overhearing Two Twists admit that Touch the Sky murdered Black Elk, she found that every new charge against Touch the Sky planted a new seed of doubt. How much faith could she have in the face of these continual charges, this constantly mounting evidence? How much battering could her love take before it finally gave way to despair?

And only look, she thought. Look around at the hatred in these faces, at the hands resting on weapons. Never before had she blamed this dangerous divisiveness on Touch the Sky. But had her love blinded her all along? Had he, after all, cleverly severed her tribe into two warring factions?

This constant worry inside her had become like a sickness, like a worm gnawing at the vital heart of a rose. Sharp Nosed Woman tried to be patient with her, but Honey Eater desperately needed counsel from someone she trusted.

Now, watching River of Winds cross toward his clan circle as the gathering broke up, she made up her mind. She hurried to catch up with him.

"River of Winds! I would speak with you."

He turned, surprise glimmering through his weariness. Like all the men in the tribe, River of Winds still wore his hair cropped short in memory of Black Elk. "When you speak, gentle sister, I always have ears."

She nodded, grateful. "I listened carefully when you described what you saw at Council Rock."

"Yes?" He was cautious.

"You were very careful, as you always are, to report fairly. Like an elder responsible for painting our winter-count pictures for future

Cheyennes, you spoke only about what happened, not what you thought it meant."

"Truly. I was sent to observe, not infer."

"Yes. But every man has a heart of hearts, true?"

Her frank question surprised him. But then again, River of Winds reminded himself, she had always been one to think about things and let her mind ask searching questions. Like most braves, he seldom spoke with the women or concerned himself with their daily activities—this was considered undignified in a warrior.

Nonetheless, one noticed things. And River of Winds had long ago noticed that this Honey Eater was as smart as she was beautiful—indeed, though he never said so to his comrades, she most reminded him of the Cheyenne sky goddess of ancient lore: *Those who beheld her lost themselves in wonder. . . .*

"Clearly, Honey Eater, every man does indeed have his heart of hearts."

"Good. Then speak from yours and tell me a thing. While you watched Touch the Sky and this blue soldier, did *you* feel he was guilty of treason? Did his manner, his gestures, his bearing, leave this impression?"

River of Winds looked off into the dark mass of the trees surrounding the camp. "Sister," he finally answered, "I cannot say such a thing to you."

"Cannot? Or will not?"

"I cannot. For saying is done with words. Manners and gestures and bearing, these are

303

not words. The word is never one with the thing. The bee does not buzz in your head, but in your bonnet."

She held him with her urgency now, respecting what he said but determined to know his mind. "You are telling me, then, that if I would have the truth from you, I must go around words? I understand. I must have another window to *your* honest soul. Forgive me, warrior, for this command, but *look* at me."

His reluctance was great. But again she bade him look, her voice heart-rending in her fearful yet determined need to know. And then he did look, meeting her eyes frankly and letting her read his soul fair and undisguised.

She stared at him hard in that flickering firelight. And though he refused to answer with talk, she saw in his eyes the answer she sought.

Despite her resolve, until now Honey Eater had held on to one slim thread of hope. Now she felt it snap, and the tears leaped from her eyes as she hurried to her tipi.

Laura Bishop knocked on the front door of the Steele residence several times. The latchstring was out, and normally on the frontier folks just came on in when the string was out. But normal didn't mean anything, Laura knew, around Hiram Steele. However, despite the fear that made her knees feel weak, she stubbornly persisted when there was no response.

She was out of touch with Kristen. Did Hiram Steele know the two girls had lied about her cousin's baby, that it was all concocted to cover a visit to wild Indians? If so, Laura realized she might as well walk into a lion's den.

But she was scared for Kristen. So when there was no response at the front door, she moved cautiously around to the side door that opened on the main parlor.

She made a fist and started to knock. Then a scorn-tipped voice drifted out of the open window to her right.

"Abbot, put a sock in it and listen to me! I don't know *what* the hell happened at Council Rock. But I do know that those two rode through a corridor of lead and didn't get a scratch! All I heard back in the settlements was about how dangerous that shotgun of yours is. I guess so. Is that how you got that bruise on your forehead?"

"There's plenty have found out how dangerous this little gal is, Hiram. Only they're resting in bone orchards now. Don't worry about me living up to my brags. I'm telling you, they were *both* warned and planned that whole escape. They was working ahead of the round-up, boss, thanks to that mouthy she-bitch daughter of yours."

"That's a possibility I'm forced to grant. Anyway, we don't have to kill the buck to get him out of the picture. We'll go ahead with the Wolf's plan to discredit him. Carlson's with the renegade right now, filling him in. As for Kristen. . . . "

Laura held one hand clutched to her throat,

head cocked like a listening bird's. *If they catch me. . . .*

"I've given her every chance to return to the straight-and-narrow path. Now I wash my hands of the Indian-loving whore. I don't know where she is right now, but she'll show up. When she does, take care of it. Do it well away from here. And just to give it some poetic justice, make it look as if Indians did it. One more brutal murder to stir up the settlers."

"Well now," Laura heard Fontaine say, "in that case, I'll have to spend a little time with her first."

Hiram snapped something curt in reply, but Laura missed it as a cold, dark panic gripped her. Kristen! She was in terrible, terrible danger. She must be warned, prevented from ever returning here again. But where was she?

Fearing that every step might give her away, Laura fled toward the front yard and the waiting landau.

The Bighorn Falls Methodist Church, Pastor James West presiding, occupied a white frame building beside a bubbling brook. A dogtrot, or covered breezeway, connected the church to the smaller parsonage. A few tombstones dotted a hillside cemetery behind the church.

"You'll attack from up there," Carlson explained to Wolf Who Hunts Smiling, pointing to a long razorback ridge behind the cemetery. "The bell will ring first, then keep ringing to cover the sound of your approach. That bell ringing means the service is over. The people will file through those big doors there. They'll stand around in a group, visiting."

The two were hidden in a cedar copse. This "attack" was going to be so easy that Wolf Who Hunts Smiling was embarrassed to be planning it. "And you say the fools will not be armed?"

Carlson shook his head impatiently. "I told you. That's a holy lodge to them. Sunday is a day of peace. No weapons."

"Sun day?" Wolf Who Hunts Smiling repeated, confused. "The sun shines almost every day, what are you talking about? As for peace, there is *no* peace west of the Great Waters."

"Yeah, whatever you say, Jo—I mean, buck. Anyway, you can't miss the shaman. He'll have on a white robe. He'll stand by the door. Kill him if you can. Kill a few of the others, too. Some women and children would be good."

Again Wolf Who Hunts Smiling felt a surge of grudging respect for this Bluecoat enemy turned temporary ally. "It does not pick at your conscience, noble warrior, this cold-blooded killing of women and children and shamen?"

Carlson shrugged, annoyed. "Why should it? My people are Episcopalians. Besides, I won't be pulling the trigger."

"Indeed. Yet you have insisted that my band must wait until you arrive before we flee. You will not kill this shaman yourself. But you will shamelessly pin his death on Woman Face. And you will play the hero and run us marauding Indians off. Do my words fly straight?"

"Something like that," Carlson conceded. He didn't want to elaborate on the impact this would have in local and national newspapers—not to mention on Col. Thompson, who would be among the churchgoers. Cold-blooded Indians violating treaties by murdering good Christians—the Red Menace would be back in force.

That Cheyenne grantland was as good as plowed and planted and heading toward first harvest. And *he* would be the soldier hero who prevented the massacre of many more civilians. Such men went on to make great strides in local politics. Hanchon, meantime, would become known to his people as the white man's spy who cost the Cheyenne their homeland.

Wolf Who Hunts Smiling, too, realized the grave consequences of this upcoming attack. Of course it would lure Woman Face out of hiding. So there would be one more good opportunity to kill him clean. Too, it would be sheer pleasure to murder a few stinking whiteskins.

But Wolf Who Hunts Smiling, even more than Carlson, knew how this attack would utterly and completely destroy Woman Face in the eyes of every decent Indian on the Great Plains.

Chapter Twenty-six

"La, Kristen! I brought what I could spare. Do you know? It's a good thing we're nearly the same size. Though, lord knows, with that hourglass figure of yours, you'll have to take in the waists."

Laura Bishop set the last carton down inside the doorway of Padgett's Mill. There were several of them, overflowing with dresses, wrappers, chemises, a corset, and other items essential to a 19th-century female's trousseau.

Kristen impulsively hugged her friend. "Laura, you're a godsend! If you hadn't met me on the road yesterday. . . ."

She trailed off, not finishing the gruesome thought.

"But what will you do now, Kristen? It's not safe for you anywhere near Blackford Valley."

Kristen glanced at Matthew. Wary since the surprise bluecoat search, the Cheyennes all shared guard duty now. Touch the Sky sat on the thick stone window sill, watching the approach from the river.

"Not safe in the valley?" she replied. "Yes, it's getting that way for plenty of us, it seems. But I might be fortunate. Tom Riley's brother, Caleb, runs a mine in the Sans Arc Mountains northwest of here. It's doing well and more and more of his married workers want to bring—or start—families out here. Caleb says there's already enough children to justify building a school and hiring a teacher."

"Oh Kristen, do it if you can! You've wanted to be a teacher, anyway. And this will get you away from—from *him*."

Laura conjured a mental image of an angry Hiram Steele, and a visible shudder passed through her. After Laura had left, promising to return when she could, Kristen wandered across to the window. Now she and Matthew were alone in the vast stone building. The river purled close by, its monotonous chuckle soothing.

"Matthew?"

He glanced back over his shoulder. "Funny. Arrow Keeper buried that name when he gave me my Cheyenne name. But it sounds natural, coming from you."

"I like both your names. But Matthew is who I met. How's the wound?"

"Fine, thanks to you."

"Matthew?"

"Hmm?"

"Do you have any idea what Carlson and my father plan next?"

"Not for sure. But Two Twists spotted Carlson and Wolf Who Hunts Smiling, both riding separately but on the same trace. It's an old game trail near Bighorn Falls, hardly used any more. So chances are good they parleyed out that way. And if Wolf Who Hunts Smiling is mixed up in this, along with Carlson, you can bet it won't be a cider party."

So far, since Kristen had been forced to shelter in the mill or face certain death, she and Matthew had carefully kept their conversations immediate and practical. But in fact, both of them had come to a disturbing realization: They were both extremely alone and needful right now, both caught in a critical period of change and uncertainty in their young lives.

Honey Eater's proud but unfair rejection had left Touch the Sky stinging with resentment, consumed by loneliness; as for Kristen, life with her father had been a prison—but fleeing from that prison left her with a whole new life to make. Facing that prospect alone was daunting. The only tender memories in her brief life were those shared with Matthew.

Now they both sensed it: They must decide if they were to revive that youthful love or let it go forever.

"Matthew? Corey has told me a little bit about—about a Cheyenne woman back at your camp. One who's special to you. Corey says she's pretty."

He maintained his silence, vigilant eyes noting every movement out on the river. He watched for the quick-darting motion of birds, the most dependable sentries on the Plains.

"She's as pretty as four aces," he finally replied. "And so are you."

A long silence until Kristen was sure of her voice. "Matthew, are you going to marry her?"

There it was, and Touch the Sky shied back from the question.

"I don't know," he replied truthfully, misery clear in his tone. "Right now, it doesn't seem likely."

"Why?"

"Why? To quote an old friend of mine, because things are the way they are."

"Oh, *why* is everything always so confused and difficult?" A tear sprang to her cheek willy-nilly. Touch the Sky felt a pang of sympathy in his heart and abruptly pulled her close. They embraced for a long time, Kristen giving up the struggle and letting her tears flow freely.

"Matthew?"

"Hmm?"

"Have you ever thought about—about what it *might* have been like? I mean, if we had gotten married and had children?"

Her frank question surprised him. But indeed he had given that plenty of thought.

"I have. And I've thought about everything I've had to go through because other people figure I don't fit neatly into one world or another. And no matter how much I loved a woman, I don't think I could bring children—mix-blood children—into this world to suffer from the unfair hatred of others."

She nodded strong assent. "I feel the same. The issue isn't just us. The purpose of any marriage should be children, among other things. And I won't ask any child of mine to take the wrong of the world onto his shoulders."

It was finally out between them, and they were of one mind. And because they did agree so strongly, neither was crippled by sadness despite their lingering love for each other. Yes, Touch the Sky told himself, right now he was lonely. But loneliness was a bump along the road of life, and men with a destiny to fulfill could not let themselves be thrown by small bumps.

Arrow Keeper had guided him to his epic vision. His destiny was to take his place, now and for all time, among the great North American Plains warriors known to friend and foe alike as the Fighting Cheyenne. Indeed, his destiny was to lead those great warriors during their finest moments in battle.

This sun-haired beauty beside him now, this decent and courageous young woman—her beauty was not the issue, nor her worth. Any man with sense would thank his God to have such a wife as she. But *he* was a Cheyenne, a leader of a proud people. And that meant taking a Cheyenne wife.

"Touch the Sky?"

It startled him, Kristen's using his Indian name. "Yes?"

"You love her, don't you?"

Had his thoughts been that obvious? Well, no matter—for through her bittersweet tears, an encouraging smile chased away his somber mood. Touch the Sky nodded. "I love her."

Kristen squeezed his hand. They spent a few more minutes there together, close but silent, each drawing hope and strength from the other.

Kristen suddenly said, "Today is Friday."

Touch the Sky grinned. "Maybe for you, white girl. I gave up naming days of the week when I threw my shoes away."

"Huh! Well, *I* still name them, you aboriginal heathen! I only thought of it because I just realized I'll have to miss church this Sunday. I daren't go, for father or Abbot Fontaine will surely be looking for me there. Still, I never miss. Pastor West will worry about me."

"So she's finally pulled her picket pin and lit out," Steele raged, throwing down in disgust Abbot Fontaine's leathery imitation of a proper biscuit. "Abbot, whoever told you you can cook is a shameless liar. This food isn't fit for a white man."

"Hell, I like it. You're just a finicky eater, Hiram."

Steele's big face wrinkled in disgust as he watched Abbot spoon greasy beans into his mouth. Juice clotted his beard, and the ever-present sawed-off shotgun jiggled in its sling while he ate.

"Finicky, my sweet aunt! This chuck would gag a buzzard off a gut wagon. But never mind that. Are you looking for her as I told you?"

Abbot sopped up some grease with a biscuit. "Li'l sweet britches?" he said while he chewed, disgusting Hiram Steele. "Course I am. Hell, Hiram—I got reasons for wanting to find her before you do."

Fontaine tossed back his head and laughed, flecks of biscuit flying across the table.

"Cover your mouth, man. Were you born in a barn?"

"Jesus was," Abbot shot back piously, grinning.

"Abbot, damnit, man! I'm in no funnin' mood. I want that little Whore of Babylon tracked down. She can't have gotten far yet. Seth's men would've spotted her if she left the valley."

"Carlson's men are just like him. They don't know their ass from their elbow."

Steele frowned. "But you do? Where's the proof? Christ, you're all talk and no walk. If I had a dollar for every brag and promise you make, I wouldn't need this damn Indian land so bad."

"No need to get all your pennies in a bunch, old son. We'll cut sign on her."

"What about Corey Robinson? You been out to his place again to see what he knows?"

"Old carrot-top lays low when Mrs. Fontaine's boy Abbot rides in. Bashful of me, I reckon. But if I have to, I'll play a little thump-thump with his old man."

"Do what you have to. At least one thing is going well. Carlson reports it looks good for the strike on the church day after tomorrow."

Fontaine grinned. "The lord moves in mysterious ways."

"That part is all set. Now I want you to concentrate on finding Kristen. You talked to Laura Bishop?"

"Not yet."

"Well, look her up. Scare the bejesus out of her if you have to. Find out what she knows about Kristen. We know now that she's a liar, so you may have to put the fear of God into her. Try not to hurt her bad if you can avoid it.

"But Kristen has to be found. I can't have her batting her gums all over hell about what we've been up to."

Chapter Twenty-seven

Little Horse kept his mustang back among the trees. He was following the crest of a long pine ridge, edging dangerously close to the whiteskin settlement at Bighorn Falls.

He was on scouting duty in unfamiliar country, and thus every sense was animal-alert. Even so, normally he would not have strayed this close to any paleface settlement. However, he thought he had glimpsed riders just beneath the crest of that razorback, the one parallel to his own course—Indian riders.

Truly, he told himself, this area was dangerous enough without worrying about a few Indians. Small patrols of soldiers were active in the vast stretch between Bighorn Falls, to the south, and Blackford Valley to the north. And twice he had spotted Abbot

Fontaine, searching for sign near the river.

But these Indians looked familiar. And now, spotting them again as they momentarily broke cover, his suspicion became a certainty.

For that was Wolf Who Hunts Smiling who led the trio. He had replaced his purloined pony with yet another pure black mustang, the only kind of pony he would ride. The two braves following him were Medicine Flute and Swift Canoe.

Little Horse's normally passive face now registered deep contempt as he watched Medicine Flute. *Shaman*. Some men were so evil and clever, Little Horse told himself, that they could piss down your back and tell you it was raining.

As he watched, Wolf Who Hunts Smiling halted his band in a sloping clearing which was partially visible from here, but not from the more heavily traveled valley floor below. When they began unrigging their ponies, Little Horse knew they were making a camp. But why here? It was an unlikely place to work mischief.

Unless. . . .

Little Horse squinted in curiosity at the gleaming white lodge down below, with its many windows and odd, pointed roof. Little Horse had seen one other like it when he and Touch the Sky sneaked into the Kansas Territory settlement of Great Bend near the Cherokee reservation. But awed—and nervous—at his first encounter with a whiteskin town, he had forgotten to ask his friend what it was.

And whatever this place was, Wolf Who

Hunts Smiling, too, was looking in that direction as he pointed out something to his companions.

Little Horse frowned. What *was* this strange lodge which clearly had piqued the interest of Wolf Who Hunts Smiling? It seemed quiet, perhaps even deserted at the moment. Did someone important, a chief perhaps, live there? For truly, Wolf Who Hunts Smiling seemed intently interested in the place.

Little Horse needed to see no more. Touch the Sky would know about this odd place. Now it was time to let the others know that their most dangerous enemy was apparently about to strike again.

Touch the Sky stared at Laura Bishop's swollen left eye without a word. His anger burned so deep into him that even his palms throbbed. But he maintained his grim silence, for indeed, what use was it to state a truth that only needed seeing?

Corey, however, was not so reticent.

"Abbot Fontaine is plug-ugly, criminal trash. He's low, dry-gulching scum, bad as that bunch that massacred the Mormon babies at Mountain Meadows. He's been out to my place again, too, only I got a Henry rifle waiting for him next time he catches me to home. He gave my pa a ration of grief, promised he'll be back. Now look how's he treated a decent woman."

"Never mind me, Corey Bryce. He did this because he's determined to find out where Kristen is," Laura said. "She *must* get out of Blackford Valley. Her father and Fontaine are determined to find her."

"Yeah," Corey said dryly, "and I got a hunch it's not because they miss her piano playing."

"Believe me, I'm working on getting out," Kristen said. "Tom Riley sent word to his brother to see if he's still interested in hiring a school teacher."

Midday sunshine illuminated even the back corners of Padgett's Mill, where cobwebs thick with dead flies still clung to the stone. A gray squirrel who had gotten used to their presence watched them from the huge, half-fallen millstone that was kept from falling all the way to the floor only by one small edge of a sturdy support beam. Little Horse had ridden out on scouting duty, Two Twists was outside in a tree on sentry duty. Tangle hair was with the ponies in their hidden copse.

Touch the Sky hated this dangerous situation and knew it could not go on much longer without a disaster. If they did not soon learn some hint as to the next incident of "Indian treachery," they would run out of time. At any moment soldiers could return to search this place.

Soldiers, he thought uneasily, or any other enemy.

And only look at Kristen's friend. Clearly Abbot Fontaine did not restrict his bullying to men. Laura had stubbornly refused to tell him anything. But, next time, would Fontaine stop after blacking an eye? Even if Kristen did get away safely, others were in trouble.

Nor were Corey and his pa safe so long as Fontaine and Steele ran a campaign of terror in this area, assisted by Seth Carlson. And there was Hiram Steele. Nothing guaranteed he would not again target Touch the Sky's white parents, John and Sarah Hanchon, for more misery.

Outside, Two Twists sounded the owl hoot three times: the signal that Little Horse was riding in.

The stout little warrior's grim news was reflected in the firm set of his jaw. "Brother," he greeted Touch the Sky the moment he stepped inside, "Wolf Who Hunts Smiling is back, and I fear his thoughts are nothing but bloody."

Quickly Little Horse reported what he had seen near Bighorn Falls. When he described the odd lodge in which Wolf Who Hunts Smiling seemed to place so much interest, Touch the Sky frowned—frowned so deeply that his eyebrows touched.

He turned to Kristen. "What day is today?"

She looked at him, startled. So far he had translated none of Little Horse's report. "Saturday," she replied. "I thought you didn't care any more about naming the days."

And suddenly Touch the Sky understood. *This* was why Seth Carlson and Wolf Who Hunts Smiling had already met near the church once before: to plan this most heinous of attacks. If it were allowed to happen, the Cheyenne homeland was hopelessly lost forever.

Never would white wrath abate after such an unspeakable crime. And this was Saturday, according to the white man's calendar—the fatal attack would come in the morning.

Quickly, speaking first in Cheyenne, he explained to Little Horse the holy significance of that lodge. He also explained how tomorrow was, for many white men, a holy day of worship. Keenly in awe of all matters spiritual, Little Horse immediately recognized the importance of preventing that attack. One-hundred white men had once tracked a Cheyenne boy for one full moon, across deserts, mountains, and plains, just to kill him for stealing a pig. What, then, would they do after Cheyennes murdered white men in their holy lodge?

Then, watching horror suffuse his white friends' faces, Touch the Sky explained in English what he feared was about to happen. Kristen, especially, seemed on the verge of hysteria.

"Not *my* church! Pastor West is my friend, and he's a friend to the Indian in his own way. I told you about him, Matthew. He has suffered more than once because of his insistence that red men have souls and rights, too, like other men. He's got so many enemies he's afraid to get married—and I know for a fact he's got a spark for Laura here, and she for him. You yourself, Matthew, called him a good man."

Touch the Sky nodded. "Believe me, lady, I

want that attack to happen even less than you do."

Touch the Sky knew they had to work quickly and take some desperate chances. "Go get Two Twists," he told Little Horse. "And then Tangle Hair, too. Bring them back here so I can fill them in. We don't know how many soldiers are in it, so we can't afford to leave one man back."

He glanced at Kristen and switched to English. "I hate leaving this place unguarded. Laura will have to leave, that landau is a dead giveaway. Kristen, it's best if you hide your stuff outside and stay on guard. Remember the tunnel. I promise I'll be back when I can."

Now he spoke to his comrades again. "We have fought many important battles. But if we do not stop that attack, brother, count upon it. Our people will not be force-marched to a reservation. The hair-faces will not rest until we are all worm fodder."

About the same time that Touch the Sky's band rode out, Abbot Fontaine spotted a familiar shape in the damp earth near Salt Lick Creek.

The notch Stoney had filed into one shoe of Kristen Steele's mare. A clear set of prints. Not made in the past few hours, but not very old, either.

Damn my eyes, Abbot cursed. For he had passed this spot a dozen times and never thought to look behind that old rotted log— there was a faint trace back there, no doubt originally started by animals coming for water and salt.

The trace was now a trail and was easy to follow, although Abbot's big claybank was famous for clearing a tight spot but not allowing room for the rider. Now and then the big man had to practically lie down ahorseback to avoid overhangs. And once his jury-rigged sling got tangled in some vines.

But soon he rounded a dog-leg bend, and immediately he spotted Kristen Steele's mare, tethered in graze. Clearly, judging from the amount of droppings and trampled grass, other horses were being kept here too, though they were gone right now. One more sharp bend, and Padgett's Mill loomed before them.

I'll be damned, Fontaine thought. He had thought about this place. But Carlson searched the area himself, declaring no Cheyenne would hole up in a building. Then again, Carlson was too damned arrogant to be smart.

Fontaine hobbled his claybank well back from the mill, letting her graze the lush river grass. He was wary of sentries, but the area seemed peaceful enough. A badger dug a hole near the river; jays chattered noisily overhead; gray squirrels dotted the area all around the mill. All these animals meant that no human was hidden nearby—not outside, anyway.

Fontaine sat down for a moment and worked his boots off, setting them behind a tree—too many dead sticks covered the ground, and the foot could feel them without thick leather soles.

He stood up. His pulse quickened slightly as he found himself hoping he was right. For it appeared that the redskins had ridden off to some mischief, leaving their white squaw behind. No doubt they all shared her before they left.

Abbot moved in closer, going slow and steady. But he left his sawed-off dangling. He had no interest in killing the girl. Not yet. No sane man wasted an opportunity like her—even if Indians *had* poked her.

He reached the half-open door and peeked cautiously around it. Then his breath snagged in his throat.

He was just in time to watch Kristen Steele hang a white cotton dress on a nail. Then she reached behind herself and began unhooking the stays of the blue dress she had on.

It took Abbot only a few seconds to verify that she was alone. Then he stepped boldly inside through the only door.

"It's just the two of us now, sweet britches."

Kristen cried out and spun around toward the door. Fontaine, backlighted by the brilliant afternoon sun, was a dark, menacing shape advancing toward her.

"Oh, I been hankerin' to get you alone, sugar scivvies," he said, his voice straining with urgent lust.

Kristen couldn't even scream. Her mouth was suddenly stuffed with the invisible cotton of fear. She began backing slowly toward the rear of the building, even as Abbot Fontaine's big-knuckled hands moved to his belt buckle.

Pastor Jim West paused for a moment in the midst of his mental labors. He loved delivering a good sermon, though he always reminded his congregation that "your religion is what you do after the sermon." But it was the devil's own work to *write* a good sermon.

He lay his quill aside and leaned his head back, massaging both eyelids with his finger tips. He still had to cut stove-lengths and feed the livestock before he made his weekly rounds of the sick and lame. And once again he would eat his supper alone and then retire to a lonely bed. But at least he knew he was doing something useful, doing the Lord's work the best way he knew how.

Seated at his desk in the parsonage, he had a good view out toward the north country. The razorback ridge that dominated that view was brilliant with verbena and columbine and mountain laurel. The day was brassy with warm sunshine, and he should have been in a better mood. But an inexplicable sadness had settled into his young bones over the past few days— inexplicable because he was a sanguine man who never suffered from melancholia.

Yet his mood these days was definitely pensive. Perhaps, after all, he needed to take a wife. Perhaps he needed to hear children playing around this quiet house where nothing ever disturbed the work of the church. Perhaps, after all, he should accept Laura Bishop's standing invitation to din—

He lost the thought as some flicker of movement outside caught his attention.

He narrowed his eyes and studied the razorback. But whatever had caught his attention was lost now. Still, as his eyes traversed the ridge, he again felt the odd premonitory sense, tasted the bitter bile of fear.

"Get thee behind me, Satan!" he said out loud, partly in jest, partly in prayerful supplication.

Then he picked up his quill, dipped it, and resumed the writing of tomorrow's sermon: "Brotherly Love on the Wild Frontier."

Chapter Twenty-eight

Only when it was too late to avoid the disaster would Touch the Sky realize it—he and his comrades were defeated by the very ruse they themselves had often employed to fox their enemies.

Riding through dense cover most of the way, they made good time covering the distance between Blackford Valley and the bluffs overlooking Bighorn Falls. Little Horse led them to his former vantage point on the pine ridge parallel to the razorback.

"There," he said pointing. "Just above where that flock of grebes is circling near that deep watershed. See? Medicine Flute's pony. They have made a camp near there, as I said."

Touch the Sky glanced down the valley at the Methodist church beside the bubbling brook. It was new, so only a few headstones dotted the cemetery out back. He couldn't help the morbid reflection that plenty of room had been left for more—and that soon, some of it might get used up.

"His pony is not rigged. As lazy as Medicine Flute is," Touch the Sky said, "I agree they have made camp."

"Brother," Little Horse said, his voice uneasy, "you speak straight, Medicine Flute is lazy. But he is above no form of base, cowardly treachery. And this thing tomorrow, if indeed they have it in mind to do—it will require no courage or skill. Just the opposite. The greater the coward, in this case, the greater the harm."

"Little Horse," Touch the Sky said admiringly, "Arrow Keeper himself could not have dug down to the nub so eloquently as you just did. Yes, count upon it. There is only one reason for them to be here so close to the whiteskin holy day. Time is a bird, and that bird is on the wing. We will have to make our move immediately.

"We will stay in the trees and circle around the valley. We will come up their ridge from the back. We will then hobble our mounts just beneath the crest and advance the rest of the way on foot. And brothers?"

Little Horse, Tangle Hair, and Two Twists all stared at him, waiting.

"Never mind the thought of the Arrows. These three are no longer Cheyennes protected by our law-ways. This treachery surpasses anything they have served up before, and their blood can no longer stain the Medicine Arrows as did that of our murdered war leader. They have quit their claim to the name of honor. Therefore, the moment any of us has a bead on any of them, shoot for their lights!"

His comrades nodded grim assent. While Sister Sun tracked further west across a flawless blue sky, they carried out Touch the Sky's hasty plan. At times they were forced to dismount and lead their ponies in the dense underbrush. But they pushed on relentlessly and made good time approaching the back slope of the steep ridge.

However, despite his efforts to attend only to his senses, Touch the Sky was also plagued by a thought. He now regretted leaving Kristen alone at the mill. In his urgent need to prevent this next critical attack, he had gone too far in not leaving a guard back there.

But such was the cruel nature of the warrior's fate—bad decisions made under pressure could not long be dwelled on. For the black warrior called Death stalked any brave who did not clear his head of thoughts and dwell in the immediate moment.

So Touch the Sky focused all his attention on the task at hand. The trio urged their mounts up the steep slope, then hobbled them when they became a noise risk. Weapons at the ready, they advanced from tree to tree until they crested the ridge.

"There," Little Horse whispered. "Medicine

Flute's pony again. But where are the rest of their mounts?"

"Hobbled separately," Tangle Hair suggested. "See how little graze there is in that spot?"

"And they are harder to spot separately," Two Twists said. "Plus, when clustered, they whinny to each other, making more noise."

"All true enough," Touch the Sky said. "But never mind the ponies. Ask instead where are their riders?"

And then, all of an instant, Touch the Sky realized their serious mistake.

"Brothers," he said, the color draining from his face, "make for our own ponies, and now. Medicine Flute's pony is only a lure. We have fallen for a false camp!"

Instantly, the others saw it, too. But even before they could whirl around, a volley of rifle shots opened up behind them. They rolled desperately for whatever cover they could manage.

"One bullet, one enemy!" Touch the Sky shouted. "No shot without a target on your bead! We cannot dig in or else the ponies are lost! Up and forward, Cheyennes! We must take the bull by the horns before he gores us!"

He led the way, leap-frogging from tree to tree while bullets zwipped through the leaves and threw chips of bark into his face. But their determined charge served to drive the attacking trio back down the ridge. Desperate, Touch the Sky broke from the trees just in time to see Swift Canoe running away from their ponies, bloody knife in hand.

At least Swift Canoe had been interrupted before his gruesome task was completed. Touch the Sky felt a surge of relief when he spotted his chestnut, apparently unharmed. Two Twists's roan, too, looked fine. But Tangle Hair's ginger and Little Horse's paint lay dead on the ground, throat-slashed!

Given the task before them, this was a tragedy. But adding insult to injury, Wolf Who Hunts Smiling's voice mocked him from the trees below them.

"Woman Face!"

For a moment the ambitious renegade broke from cover. "Look!"

His face defiant, Wolf Who Hunts Smiling raised the Colt rifle high. "Your pony still lives, but her boot is lighter by one rifle! And I see you even left a round in it for me. Soon, to repay your gallantry, I'll give that bullet back to you!"

"Brothers," Little Horse said, "we are up against it now. Four warriors and two horses."

But Touch the Sky, ignoring their fleeing enemy below, had turned to stare back in the direction of Blackford Valley and the mill.

"Should we camp near here?" Little Horse asked him.

"No," Touch the Sky decided, still looking back toward the direction of the mill. "Brothers, I have a feeling. There is no time to explain. Humor me and do as I say. Understood?"

All three recognized their shaman speaking now. As one, they nodded.

"Good enough, stout bucks! I am riding back

to the mill now. Riding fast. Little Horse, I want you to follow me on Two Twists's roan. His pony is slower than mine, but follow as best you can. Two Twists, Tangle Hair. Find a spot for a cold camp, a spot from which we can see the paleface holy lodge."

Even as he finished speaking, Touch the Sky had hurried to his pony, grabbed handfuls of coarse mane, and swung up from the right side—the Indian side, for they mounted the opposite of white men.

"Brother, hold. Wait for me!" Little Horse shouted. But Touch the Sky, his mouth a grim, determined slit, was already racing down the slope.

Kristen was scared witless. Too late, she realized she should have followed Matthew's advice about remaining vigilant. But with Abbot Fontaine rapidly closing the gap toward her, her tough frontier mind focused down to the only four words that mattered right now: *Escape to gain safety.*

With the element of surprise lost, she knew the tunnel would be sure suicide. Her only hope was to beat Fontaine to the rear window and leap out.

She willed her feet into motion. Abbot, seeing her intention instantly, angled to cut her off.

"*Got*-cha, cute corset!" he said, grabbing hold of one pleated sleeve of her dress.

But Kristen was more agile than he. She turned adeptly, spinning in a balletic movement. Fabric gave way and she tore free of his grip, baring one soft white shoulder.

"*Hell* yeah!" Abbot approved. "You done quit your grinnin', now drop your linen!"

Kristen surged ahead of him, but lost valuable time trying to clear the high, wide stone sill. She tore a fingernail out clawing for a hold, then felt a grip like eagle's talons seize her in the hips.

Kristen screamed as Fontaine, grunting in triumph, pulled her close to his stinking, unwashed body. But at the last second her groping right hand closed around a fist-sized chunk of stone that crumbled away from the sill. Fontaine easily pulled her to the floor. His breathing was rapid and hoarse now, his eyes glazed with the fire of the need in his loins. He wrapped her long hair around one wrist and jerked her head back, preparing to force his mouth on hers.

An eyeblink later, Kristen smashed the chunk of stone into his face, breaking his nose.

He roared at the fiery pain and rolled free long enough for Kristen to scramble to her feet. She ducked around the precariously propped-up millstone and shot toward the front door this time. But Abbot's left arm speared out quickly, and he grabbed hold of one slim ankle, toppling the girl again.

"I *like* a fiery wench what makes me earn my best," he assured her, blood streaming into his grizzled beard.

Kristen had been badly shaken in the hard

fall. Now, as the stinking giant began to pull himself onto her again, she unleashed a savage flurry of scratches and kicks and bites.

"*Fight*, you she-bitch from hell!" he gloated. "Cuz you're about to be tamed by a white man."

He ripped the dress away from her other shoulder, struggled to tear more of it off so he could fondle her dirty loaves, as Mama Fontaine had taught him to call them. He had just grabbed a handful of bodice when a sharp, sudden pain like rattlesnake fangs bit deep into his shoulder. Fontaine looked down and saw the bone handle of a knife protruding from the heavy biceps muscle!

Touch the Sky had thrown his knife from the doorway, drawing a perfect bead on the white man's vitals. But Fontaine had twisted around at the very moment the Cheyenne had released his throw. Now, roaring at the pain, Fontaine jerked the knife out of his arm and tossed it through the window.

Touch the Sky already had his rifle at the ready. But now Fontaine pulled Kristen up to shield himself. He moved amazingly fast for a big man—faster than Touch the Sky could believe. Fontaine scuttled backwards crabwise, pulling Kristen with him. Moments later he had ducked under the thick cover of the slanting millstone, still clutching Kristen before him. Fontaine was hidden by the stone, but Kristen was trapped in front of it, a human shield for any bullets.

"Drop your piece, John!" he roared out. "Drop

it and freeze! Nary a move, buck, or your white squaw is gonna be wallpaper!"

When Touch the Sky hesitated, Fontaine abruptly twisted one of Kristen's arms until she cried out. Touch the Sky hastily complied, tossing his Sharps out onto the floor and raising his hands.

"That's more like it. Where's the rest of your band?" Fontaine demanded.

"Gone," Touch the Sky said tersely.

"Gone where, John? Gone Wendigo? Don't get cute on me. I know them bastards're layin' for me outside."

Touch the Sky's pulse surged when Little Horse appeared in the window at the rear of the mill. The crafty young brave had seen his friend standing in the doorway with his hands up. Now his face desperately searched Touch the Sky's, trying to learn the picture inside the mill. Little Horse could see the top half of the millstone, could also see Kristen crouched out in front of it. And although he couldn't see Fontaine hunkering beneath it, using the stone and Kristen as shields, he could see the tip of the sawed-off kissing the nape of Kristen's neck.

"Let her go, Fontaine," Touch the Sky urged. "Let her go, and you walk. I give my word."

"Your word?" A harsh bark of laughter from under the huge millstone. "Your mother-ruttin' *word*? A gut-eating savage giving me his word. That's rich, John."

Touch the Sky squinted slightly, wondering what Little Horse was up to. The squat little brave had climbed silently up onto the stone sill. Now he turned his body to catch the slanting shaft of hot afternoon sunlight. Then Touch the Sky saw what his friend held in the sunlight—his magnifying glass. Little Horse was focusing sunlight on the corner of dry wood that kept the millstone from crashing the rest of the way to the floor. Already, curlicues of smoke rose from the old wood.

"Me 'n' the girl are leaving," Fontaine announced. "Together. You better tell them bucks what're hiding outside—both barrels will be pressed into her back. Deal even one card off the bottom, I'll spray her guts from here to Comanche country."

A bright little orange spear tip of flame shot up as the wood caught fire. "What's burning?" Abbot demanded suspiciously.

"That's the white man's Judgment-fire you smell," Touch the Sky assured him.

"The hell? Spell that out plain, John. Youuu—*wunh!*"

At that very moment, the fire-weakened wood snapped and the huge millstone dropped straight down on Abbot Fontaine with a reverberating thud that vibrated the floor hard under Touch the Sky's feet. Fontaine's agonized scream lasted only about a second before the heavy stone completely crushed his chest and lungs, flattening him to paste.

In a moment Kristen was in Touch the Sky's arms, sobbing hysterically. Little Horse leaped inside, glanced under the stone, and ducked outside again to vomit. Now Corey, just arrived, poked his head inside cautiously.

"God-in-whirlwinds!" he said, after realizing *who* that mess under the stone was and piecing the story together. "Well, I'm not normally one to blaspheme the dead. But *that* pile of dung"— he nodded toward Fontaine's bloody remains— "has gone to hell by now, anyway. So I guess you might say he met with a crushing defeat!"

Chapter Twenty-nine

With Abbot Fontaine dead, Corey and Touch the Sky both agreed it would be safer for Kristen to hide at Corey's house—at least until Tom Riley sent word about the teaching job at his brother's mining camp and she could flee Blackford Valley.

It was also agreed that the Cheyennes would not return to Padgett's Mill. Not only did unclean death now hang over that place, but they simply could not let this cat-and-mouse game with Wolf Who Hunts Smiling and Seth Carlson continue. All four Cheyennes had taken a vow that this last confrontation would either end the threat to their homeland or kill them.

Touch the Sky and Corey visited Old Knobby in Bighorn Falls to see about replacement mounts for the two ponies that had been throat-slashed. The former mountain man was so happy to see his old friend again that he loaned him two of his best hiring-out horses, a pair of blood geldings.

It was well after dark when the two friends prepared to slip back out of Bighorn Falls. Only one sleep now, Touch the Sky kept reminding himself, and Wolf Who Hunts Smiling's band—backed-up by blue soldiers—would strike a fatal blow to the Cheyenne homeland. He had considered every possibility to stop them, including a daring strike on their enemy's ponies.

But Touch the Sky realized ponies wouldn't even be necessary against unarmed churchgoers milling in the open. All it would take was for one Cheyenne to dart forward, show himself to the whites, then kill one of them.

It was Corey who, inadvertently, offered a faint glimmer of hope.

This came as they were each leading one of the bloods. They reached the end of the main street dividing Bighorn Falls. As in most frontier towns, the street simply ended and became deep wagon tracks. Touch the Sky reined his chestnut northwest toward Blackford Valley.

"Better hold off a bit," Corey advised. "Best to turn north after we pass Headwater Bluff. Otherwise, the horses will want to water at Red Dog Creek. But that's risky on account of they might also eat that damned Johnson grass choking the creek banks."

Touch the Sky stared at his friend in the moonlight. He knew about this so-called loco weed, of course, but had never seen horses that had consumed it.

"Corey? When a horse eats crazy weed, does it get so wild you can't mount it?"

"Sometimes. But they're just as likely to save their craziness for the rider. I've seen horses locoed a few times, but usually you couldn't tell it too much until they actually got their blood up on a ride. Pa says it's like with drunks. Leave 'em alone, and lots of them can toss back plenty of Old Busthead and still stay sweet. But get 'em agitated, and there goes the furniture."

That was exactly the answer Touch the Sky's ears ached to hear. For indeed, Wolf Who Hunts Smiling and his band could mount their raid on foot. But what if it started out on ponies and then went awry? Might that be enough to ruin the plan?

"Listen," he told Corey. "I'm playing around with a scheme that's just about as hare-brained as anything we ever pulled."

Corey's freckled face split in a wide grin. The silver moonwash clearly showed traces of Abbot Fontaine's beating. "Hare-brained, you say? Even crazier than that time I stripped bucknaked, then painted my body with claybank and pretended I was an insane white preacher?"

"Well, you pretended about the *preacher* part."

"Damn, you got a mouth on you, savage! Anyhow, them Pawnees showed the white feather and run off bawling like titty babies."

Touch the Sky grinned back. "I remember, all

right. And yeah, this new plan is even crazier."

"Sold, by God! Let's do it!"

"All right, paleface. First let's go roust out Old Knobby again. I want to borrow back some of those nosebags you returned to him."

"What the hell for?"

"You'll see when we get to Headwater Bluff. Now quit gawking and let's ride!"

The day the white man's winter-count called Sunday dawned clear and bright. But Wolf Who Hunts Smiling and his band were sound asleep, knowing they would not strike for hours yet. Red men were notorious late sleepers, and normally the braves would have drunk much water, the night before, so that aching bladders would wake them for battle.

However, Carlson had explained that the first tolling of the bells would announce that the holy rituals had begun; the strike would come soon after the bell tolled a second time. So the Cheyennes would rise at the first tolling and prepare.

Things began as planned. The early morning stillness of the ridge was shattered by a clap-booming bell. The Cheyennes rolled out of their robes, instantly alert for Woman Face.

"Remember," Wolf Who Hunts Smiling told Medicine Flute and Swift Canoe, "Carlson and his men are also waiting for that second ringing of the bells. Over there."

He pointed toward a series of folded ridges between their present location and the direction of Fort Bates. "Wait until we spot them before we attack. They will 'chase' us away. It must appear that only the Bluecoat army can save the whiteskins. Never would I have agreed to this womanly foolishness, but the soldier chief has promised powder and ball if we perform well."

By now they had reached the cup-shaped hollow where they had left their ponies. Suddenly, Wolf Who Hunts Smiling gaped in stupid astonishment: each of the ponies was wearing a nosebag! Indeed, they had been grained, judging from their nervous energy.

"Brothers?" Swift Canoe demanded. "Which of you did this thing?"

"Swift Canoe," Wolf Who Hunts Smiling said scornfully, "your name is much swifter than your brain. Did we hide these huge nosebags in our quivers or tuck them in our clouts? You fool, a hummingbird's brain is bigger than yours."

The horses were jittery, but Wolf Who Hunts Smiling reasoned that was because whoever strapped on those bags was a stranger and they were still nervous. But who had done this thing, and why?

The very moment he asked the question, an obvious answer occurred to him.

"No Indians have bags like these. Nor need for them, we have no grain or oats. Only whites use these. It was Carlson who ordered it done to keep our ponies strong and quiet. No doubt he was afraid that Woman Face was looking for them in the night. He mentioned this fear often to me. I'll wager he ordered one of his men to do this, perhaps after failing to locate us."

This was the only logical answer. Why would an enemy of their cause bother to sneak among the horses and then feed them well? The braves dropped the bags, paying scant attention to the remnants of grass still clinging to the interiors.

For a moment, only a few heartbeats, Wolf Who Hunts Smiling's black seemed to *grin* at her owner. He had never seen such a foolish look on a horses's face! But it passed quickly, and the confused brave reminded himself—this pony was new to him.

He might have noticed other odd signs, too. But very soon the bells tolled for the second time that morning. The church doors swung open below, and people began milling around in the yard.

"There!" Wolf Who Hunts Smiling pointed toward Fort Bates, grinning with anticipation. "There come the blue-bloused fools now! Such heroes. Now we may strike. Remember, kill the white-robed shaman if you can. Failing that, aim for women and children.

"And above all else, watch close for White Man Runs Him and his band. We should have seen them by now, unless Carlson got lucky and found him. Swift Canoe, now what are you doing?"

"It is my pony," he complained. "He does not want me to mount him."

"Buck, stop puling like a baby. Your pony is only eager for the charge!" Wolf Who Hunts Smiling raised the Colt rifle high over his head. "Now ride, both of you, and send some pale-faces to their funeral scaffolds!"

"Here comes their charge, brothers!" Little Horse called in a tense voice.

The four comrades had formed a hidden skirmish line between the attacking force and the church below. But they would reveal themselves and fire rifles at their enemies only as a last resort. For Touch the Sky knew how delicate this situation was. Col. Thompson himself was down there. *Any* gunfire by Cheyennes, this close to the church on a Sunday, could have serious consequences for Gray Thunder's tribe.

"Brothers, have ears for my words!" Touch the Sky called out so all could hear. "It has come down to this moment. This is no mere skirmish for bragging rights. What happens next shapes the fate of the *Shaiyena* people. I have called on you before, and always you have somehow done the impossible thing I asked you to do.

"True, these are only three braves, and only two of them worth anything, at that. But do you understand? *This* line is as far as they go, and no bullets will be fired. Bows ready!"

All four braves pulled handfuls of arrows from their quivers. The three renegades had just come into view above them, urging their mounts downslope through the trees. But clearly, the charge was not going well.

"Look!" Two Twists said. "Look at Swift Canoe's pony!"

Swift Canoe's mustang had begun rebelling as the charge heated up. She suddenly stopped, started crow-hopping, then abruptly bucked Swift Canoe off. He bounced hard off a solid tree as his pony tore off in the opposite direction.

As if triggered by Swift Canoe's pony, the other two horses emulated their four-legged comrade. Medicine Flute's mount deliberately dropped to the ground and rolled over fast. Crying out in fright, Medicine Flute barely avoided being crushed. When he jumped up, Touch the Sky saw his broken leg-bone flute protruding from the skinny brave's thigh, having skewered him in the fall.

Nor, though a much better rider, did the wily Wolf Who Hunts Smiling escape this sudden disaster. His magnificent black abruptly turned into a mankiller. It halted in mid-charge, hunkered on its hocks, then leaped straight up into the air and came down on its back to crush the rider. Only by the deftest of leaps did Wolf Who Hunts Smiling avoid being crushed to death—but he could not avoid landing with his leg turned wrong under him. Touch the Sky almost imagined he could hear the bone snap, even from here.

"Panther Clan is down!" he called triumphantly. "Injured! With a coward like Medicine Flute and a rabbit-brain like Swift Canoe to back him, we are in no danger of a further charge. But let us add some more silent persuasion."

With that, they each strung their first arrow. For the next few moments, airy *fwipps* and solid *thwaps* sounded as Touch the Sky's group turned the air deadly all around their enemy. Medicine Flute immediately deserted his fallen comrades and limped back up the ridge to safety. He glanced often at his wounded thigh and appeared on the verge of passing out from sight of his own blood.

Swift Canoe, more loyal, tried to help his leader gain safety. But evidently his head had struck the tree hard—he stumbled and fell hard on Wolf Who Hunts Smiling's broken leg, causing this fierce brave to roar with rage and pain. Touch the Sky and his band fell on the ground, helpless with laughter.

Down below, a few people had heard something and glanced up at the slope to see what it was. But Touch the Sky exalted as he realized that most of them hadn't the slightest idea what was going on only a double stone's-throw away.

But fittingly the botched strike ended on one more note of high humor for Touch the Sky and his group. For clearly Seth Carlson had not the slightest notion that the 'Indian attack' had died at birth. His bugler now blared out "Boots and Saddles" while the unit charged full bore, carbines cracking, to rescue the peaceful church.

"The cavalry saves the day, brothers!" Touch the Sky called out. "Now let *us* clear out before we are spotted and become the attackers in a lying report."

"Yes," Little Horse said, stifling a foolish grin as he watched their Cheyenne enemies disappear over the crest of the ridge. "And before we die—laughing!"

Hiram Steele had finally reached that point where rage burned itself out, leaving only a brooding disgust. Now, without a word, he traced a path around his big frame house in Blackford Valley. Seth Carlson trailed him, watching Steele empty a pail of kerosene up against the base of the house.

"Is it really necessary to burn the place?" Carlson said.

A wagon behind the two men was loaded with the only possessions Hiram cared to take. The rest would burn with the house.

Hiram heard the question, but ignored it. "They killed Stoney *and* Abbot." he lamented to no one in particular. "The land-grab scheme fell flatter than a one-sided pancake. Now I've got creditors out to skin me. Even Kristen whipped us. Christ!"

Overcome with a return of his former rage, Hiram flung the empty pail. Carlson barely ducked in time to avoid being brained by it. Hiram clawed a lucifer match out of his fob pocket.

"Well, by God, she won't be coming back to live here! I bought this place lock, stock, and barrel. She could claim it after I light out, I got no time to sell it. But I'll burn it to the ground before I'll provide the house where that Indian-kissing whore ruts with that criminal sonofa-bitch Matthew Hanchon!"

Carlson's misery, too, was acute. He had pan-icked half the church when he rode up with his saber flashing in the sun—only to realize, sheepishly, that there was no attack underway. One old woman passed out from fright, right at Col. Thompson's feet! Now, needless to say, the old man was incensed. That made two com-pletely unnecessary "rescues" in the last few days. Only green shave-tails fresh from the Point were that jumpy. At the very least, Carlson would face a review board.

Steele held the match between his fingers, watching it as if it were a nugget from the Mother Lode. "Seth? You giving up on killing Hanchon?"

Carlson's sneer of cold command suggested otherwise. "Giving up? Maybe when I'm planted in my grave! Hiram, that bastard has whipped us again. I admit it. But I'll dog his red ass from hell to breakfast and back. Kristen would be my wife by now if he hadn't turned her against me with his lies and heathen deceptions!"

Steele knew better. Kristen had despised Seth Carlson from the first day she met him, and that opinion had never wavered. But he wisely kept that to himself.

"All right then, Soldier Blue. Give me a grip!"

The two men clasped each other's hand. "I ain't much for no fancy oaths. But we two swear eternal revenge against Matthew Hanchon. So long as that red devil walks the earth, we swear never to rest in peace until he's dead. My hand to God."

"My hand to God," Seth repeated.

Hiram struck the match on his rawhide vest. Then he tossed it against the kerosene-soaked wood. With a loud, hollow *whoompf*, a necklace of dancing flames soon circled the house.

Chapter Thirty

When she heard the camp crier summoning the people out, Honey Eater's stomach filled with cold dread. Had the fatal moment finally arrived? Was the faction led by Wolf Who Hunts Smiling and Medicine Flute finally making their bloody bid for power?

Oddly, she was almost indifferent to whatever happened. In her hard life, hope had been her waking dream—hope that some day she and Touch the Sky, in spite of everything, could be together as man and wife. But recent events had sent her hope crashing. If only, deep in her heart, she could truly make herself hate and despise Touch the Sky! However, to her eternal shame, she knew she still loved him even though all the evidence of her senses said he was a liar, a murderer, a traitor.

At least she would not have to confront him. His band had still not returned. Indeed, to her shame she had been worried sick about him, just as in the old days. She joined the people streaming into the central clearing. She was relieved to see that it is Chief Gray Thunder who called the people out this time. A Sioux brave stood near Gray Thunder.

"Cheyenne people!" the chief called out. "Have ears! Crow Killer here lives at Pony Saver's camp. Many of you know him and have smoked a pipe with him. Now have ears for his words. I think you will find them interesting. Crow Killer? Tell the people what you have told me."

Crow Killer looked perplexed. He had only come to one of his friends here with an inquiry. That friend took him directly to the chief. Now here stood all the tribe, staring as if he were about to chant a blessing. He spoke in the mix of Lakota and Cheyenne which all easily understood.

"Cheyenne cousins! I recently joined others in my Spotted Owl Clan in an expedition against the mountain Utes, who have been stealing our ponies. While I was gone, an object very valuable to me was stolen from my tipi. It was a two-shot, cap-and-ball dragoon pistol. It is my prize possession because I captured it from a blue blouse in the Battle of Crying Horse Canyon."

Absolute silence greeted these words. Honey Eater suddenly attended to his every word, her lower lip caught between her teeth.

"Tell the people," Gray Thunder encouraged him, "what this pistol looked like."

"A most beautiful weapon. Indeed, almost too pretty to waste firing it. It has magnificent scrollwork all along the barrel. The metal has been polished to the gloss of a mirror, then coated with silver."

This sent an excited buzzing of whispers throughout the clearing.

"Indeed, Crow Killer," Gray Thunder said, "this sounds like a most beautiful weapon. Truly, could this be it?"

With a dramatic flourish, Gray Thunder produced the very pistol from under his Hudson's Bay blanket. Both men stood between two tall clan fires, and the reflection of the flames on the silver-coated metal seemed to make the pistol itself catch on fire as Gray Thunder handed it over.

"My pistol!" Crow Killer exclaimed, joy lighting his eyes. "But how came it to be with you, father?"

"That," Gray Thunder replied, "is the real mystery here."

"No mystery!" shouted an angry Bow String. "Ask the base plotters who follow Wolf Who Hunts Smiling!"

Whatever else was said was lost on Honey Eater. For elation was singing too loudly in her blood. No, Crow Killer's arrival did not exactly clear Touch the Sky of the charge of murdering Black Elk. He could have stolen the pistol and used it.

But, at least at first, it cleared him completely in her mind. It proved that Wolf Who Hunts Smiling and the others had viciously lied—they had claimed Touch the Sky had owned that pistol ever since the Tongue River Battle, more than two winters earlier. And if that was a lie, so was the rest of it.

In her heart, she knew what had happened. Wolf Who Hunts Smiling had stolen and fired that weapon. Aiming for Touch the Sky, he hit his cousin instead. It could never be proven, of course. And with Wolf Who Hunts Smiling now moving to seize power, it was unlikely any action would proceed against him. But never mind cruel reality. Touch the Sky did not kill her husband!

But then . . . but then, what about those words she heard Two Twists say? Those words that so clearly condemned him? Again the cold dread was back in her stomach, and the elation ceased to hum in her blood. But Honey Eater was not one to brood and hold back from a confrontation. When Two Twists arrived, she would simply trap him somewhere and ask him point blank to explain himself.

This cruel uncertainty must end. Either she would love her brave as he deserved, or she would treat him with cold contempt for the rest of her days.

"Sister," Two Twists swore, his young face as solemn as Honey Eater had ever seen it, "I speak only the straight word to you. And I tell you now, you have been the victim of a cruel misperception."

The two of them stood alone near the purling water of the Powder River. Touch the Sky's band had recently ridden back to camp, arriving only shortly after Wolf Who Hunts Smiling and his companions. Honey Eater had waited until the first opportunity to catch Two Twists alone.

"Honey Eater, my Aunt Hawk Feather once choked on a bone. She flew out of her tipi in a panic, unable to breathe. My uncle followed right behind her, swatting at her back to dislodge the bone. But two Bull Whips on soldier duty immediately began lashing him, for they assumed he was beating Hawk Feather. You see, they missed the part where she choked on the bone. And so have you.

"It is likewise with these words you overheard. Sister, I was telling Tangle Hair what Medicine Flute had said. But you heard only the words, not the original speaker. Thus you thought *I* said them."

A massive, heavy stone was suddenly lifted from Honey Eater's breast. All of an instant, she saw her cruel mistake—saw how she had been hoaxed by black appearances.

"Where is he?" she asked.

"In his tipi. And I have never seen him more despondent. Sister, I will tell you a thing that he will not tell you. While we were gone, a sun-haired white beauty was of great assistance to us. She risked her life to help us. And it was as

355

clear as a blood spoor in new snow that she loves Touch the Sky. I will not back away from the truth, it was clear he had great feelings for her, also.

"He was lonely. Rejected by his tribe, even by you. And the need was on her, too. But he holds only one woman in his heart of hearts and will forever. And I am talking to that woman now. And though I love her dearly, I also say this. She is a fool if she does not go to him now, for no better man was ever born of woman."

With that, Two Twists returned to the camp. But Honey Eater stood there for a long, long time, asking her sister the river to calm her mind and spirit, and asking the Day Maker if He could forgive the wrong she had done in her heart—asking Him, too, what she should do.

By now Touch the Sky knew about Crow Killer's visit to their camp, about how the mystery of the pistol was at least partially explained. And though Crow Killer's explanation did not clear him of the murder charge, it so weakened it that he no longer feared any official consequences. Those who supported Touch the Sky declared him innocent; his enemies countered that he could still have done the deed.

In other words, nothing had changed. He was still *in* the red man's world, but not *of* it. His enemies had suffered a temporary setback, in camp, and a major defeat at Blackford Valley. But once again few in the tribe knew how he and his loyal comrades had fought to save their homeland.

Only, one thing was very different. For some reason he had lost Honey Eater's love. And that love had been the main reason he had kept on keeping on.

He sat alone in his tipi, unable to face anyone right now. At least things had turned out better for Kristen. Caleb Riley and his wife were delighted to hire the new teacher on. Tom Riley himself escorted Kristen to the Sans Arc camp, which was becoming more and more civilized as miners brought their families out.

Touch the Sky had sensed a spark between Tom and Kristen, and he blessed the union of these two friends he dearly loved. But the blessing was bittersweet—why must he always be a witness to love but never loved himself?

Cool air suddenly kissed his cheek as the entrance flap of his tipi was thrown boldly back. Instinctively, Touch the Sky went for his knife even as he rolled sideways, expecting a shot.

Honey Eater stood in the entrance! And Touch the Sky gaped when he saw the most welcome sight of his life: fresh white columbine petals once again adorned her hair.

Still, she said not a word. But slowly, a tender smile divided her face. She raised both arms and crossed her wrists in front of her heart: Cheyenne sign talk for love.

He, too, crossed his wrists in front of his heart. Then, tears of joy streaming down her face, Honey Eater dropped the flap behind her and crossed to join her brave warrior.

It was a squaw-taking ceremony that was destined to live forever in the memory of the tribe.

Never had a marriage caused so much joy and so much hatred, and never had a marriage divided a people as this one did. Limping about camp with his broken leg in splints, Wolf Who Hunts Smiling visited all of his allies. On the morning of the ceremony, every Bull Whip trooper in camp joined Wolf Who Hunts Smiling and Medicine Flute in riding out of camp for the day. Thus, half the tribe refused to sanction this controversial marriage.

In Arrow Keeper's words, this also meant there was blood on the horizon.

But those who remained made joy ring to the very heavens.

Touch the Sky had no official clan to hand him into marriage. But his companions took over all negotiations and details usually handled by kin. A fine gift of horses was taken to the elders of Honey Eater's clan. These might easily have been refused, and the marriage denied, for Touch the Sky had few friends among these Indians. Yet, somehow Little Horse and Tangle Hair were clearly persuasive—and only long afterward would Touch the Sky learn the truth: that they had sweetened the offer considerably by throwing in furs, weapons, and other goods they had been saving for their own bride-price.

Those who remained for the ceremony honored these two young Cheyennes with a formality seldom seen except in Chief Renewals. The braves wore full war bonnets with crow feathers extending, some so rich in coups their feathers trailed on the ground. Each lodge had been decorated with totems and scalp locks stretched over little willow hoops to avoid shrinking. Each blooded warrior carried his decorated buffalo-hide shield.

The simple exchange of vows was routine, save in two respects. In front of everyone, before the exchange, Honey Eater produced a gift for Touch the Sky—a gift she had made herself. When it was passed around for all to admire, a respectful hush fell over the people. For it was an exquisite necklace made of the foreclaws of the grizzly bear. Every Cheyenne knew the significance of this, for the foreclaws were the killing claws—and the grizzly the fiercest warrior in Maiyun's kingdom.

A more spontaneous event occurred, too. One so touching, so simple and yet powerful, that even blooded warriors swiped at their eyes.

Ever since the cloud of murder had hung over Touch the Sky, the young girls had stopped singing their favorite song in their sewing lodge—an inspiring song about a fine Cheyenne maiden and her brave warrior, who overcome all odds to unite in marriage. Everyone knew, though it did not name them, that the song was about Touch the Sky and Honey Eater. And suddenly, just as they finished the exchange of vows, Honey Eater's niece Laughing Brook began singing it in a fine, clear voice. Tears of joy streaming, every girl—and even some old grandmothers—joined Laughing Brook and raised their voices in singing this love to heaven.

"Brother," Little Horse said awkwardly, "it is not nearly so fine as both of you deserve. But your comrades have done what they could."

No ponies this time. Touch the Sky and Honey Eater, accompanied by his three fellow warriors, had come to this place on foot: a private willow copse well away from camp. And in the center, a fine bride-lodge of hides stretched over a sapling frame had been erected.

"As always," Touch the Sky replied with a smile, "my comrades have done what they could. And what they can do is awesome indeed. I thank you, brothers."

During this exchange, Honey Eater had watched Two Twists slip around behind Little Horse. Suddenly Honey Eater gasped when Little Horse's clan feather erupted in flames! Her surprise turned to outright astonishment when Two Twists, Tangle Hair, and even Touch the Sky laughed so hard they fell upon the ground. Two Twists ran back toward camp, brandishing Little Horse's magnifying glass and still hooting in derision. Little Horse chased him, vowing—between spasms of laughter—to add the young brave's scalp to his clout.

"Brother," Tangle Hair said awkwardly, realizing he was the only one left, "when we built this bride-lodge, we made the entrance tall, for we knew *you* would be passing through. And none taller than the woman on your arm."

With those fine words, spoken on behalf of all in Touch the Sky's band, Tangle Hair turned and left these two alone. There was no awkwardness between them, nor any hurry. How many cruel years had they suffered for this moment?

Nor, they both realized, was the suffering even close to being over. Even now their determined enemies were planning their next move. Arrow Keeper was right—there was blood on the horizon. There had been unity in camp today only because their enemies were missing. But they would return, and the bloody power struggle would continue. However, just as goodbyes are more poignant before a battle, this rare time of privacy and solitude was even sweeter for the dangers they faced.

"You taught me the white man's custom of kissing," she told him when they were alone inside. "You made me like it and want more of it. When you first arrived at our tribe, we accidentally saw each other naked. I liked what I saw, and I liked watching you watch me. Watch me now, Touch the Sky."

She stood before him and slipped off her beaded bride-shawl, her fine calico wedding dress, and dropped them in a puddle at her feet. Sunlight pierced the opening at the top of the lodge and lit her flawless skin in a topaz hue.

Honey Eater reached up, taut and full breasts swaying heavily, and pulled the comb from her hair. The thick tresses poured down over her shoulders.

She stood before him naked. Her breathing had begun to quicken as the desire long pent up inside her now clamored for release.

"Do you like what you see?" she asked him frankly.

He nodded, past all words now as the need to merge with her seized hold of him and pinched his throat closed. He pulled her down, their lips met, and in that moment all time and all places meant nothing as the entire universe closed down to them and their great need and the little world they made together, joined as one.

CHEYENNE
WENDIGO MOUNTAIN
DEATH CAMP
JUDD COLE

Wendigo Mountain. A Cheyenne warrior raised by white settlers, Touch the Sky is blessed with strong medicine. Yet his powers as a shaman cannot help him foretell that his tribe's sacred arrows will be stolen—or that his enemies will demand his head for their return. To save his tribe from utter destruction, the young brave will wage a battle like none he's ever fought.

And in the same action-packed volume . . .

Death Camp. Touch the Sky will gladly give his life to protect his tribe. Yet not even he can save them from an outbreak of deadly disease. Racing against time and brutal enemies, Touch the Sky has to either forsake his heritage and trust the white man's medicine—or prove his loyalty even as he watches his proud people die.

___4479-X $4.99 US/$5.99 CAN

CHEYENNE

Double Edition:
Pathfinder/ Buffalo Hiders
JUDD COLE

Pathfinder. Touch the Sky never forgot the kindness of the settlers, and tried to help them whenever possible. But an old friend's request to negotiate a treaty between the Cheyenne and gold miners brings the young brave face-to-face with a cunning warrior. If Touch the Sky can't defeat his new enemy, the territory will never again be safe for pioneers. *And in the same action-packed volume...*

Buffalo Hiders. Once, mighty herds of buffalo provided the Cheyenne with food, clothing and skins for shelter. Then the white hunters appeared and the slaughter began. Still, few herds remain, and Touch the Sky swears he will protect them. But two hundred veteran mountain men and Indian killers are bent on wiping out the remaining buffalo—and anyone who stands in their way.

___4413-7 $4.99 US/$5.99 CAN

Dorchester Publishing Co., Inc.
P.O. Box 6640
Wayne, PA 19087-8640

Please add $1.75 for shipping and handling for the first book and $.50 for each book thereafter. NY, NYC, and PA residents, please add appropriate sales tax. No cash, stamps, or C.O.D.s. All orders shipped within 6 weeks via postal service book rate. Canadian orders require $2.00 extra postage and must be paid in U.S. dollars through a U.S. banking facility.

Name_____
Address_____
City_____ State_____ Zip_____
I have enclosed $_____ in payment for the checked book(s).
Payment <u>must</u> accompany all orders. ❑ Please send a free catalog.
CHECK OUT OUR WEBSITE! www.dorchesterpub.com

CHEYENNE

BLOODY BONES CANYON/ RENEGADE SIEGE

JUDD COLE

Bloody Bones Canyon. Only Touch the Sky can defend them from the warriors that threaten to take over the camp. But when his people need him most, the mighty shaman is forced to avenge the slaughter of their peace chief. Even Touch the Sky cannot fight two battles at once, and without his powerful magic his people will be doomed.

And in the same action-packed volume . . .

Renegade Siege. Touch the Sky's blood enemies have surrounded a pioneer mining camp and are preparing to sweep down on it like a killing wind. If the mighty shaman cannot hold off the murderous attack, the settlers will be wiped out . . . and Touch the Sky's own camp will be next!

___4586-9 $4.99 US/$5.99 CAN

Dorchester Publishing Co., Inc.
P.O. Box 6640
Wayne, PA 19087-8640

Please add $1.75 for shipping and handling for the first book and $.50 for each book thereafter. NY, NYC, and PA residents, please add appropriate sales tax. No cash, stamps, or C.O.D.s. All orders shipped within 6 weeks via postal service book rate. Canadian orders require $2.00 extra postage and must be paid in U.S. dollars through a U.S. banking facility.

Name_____
Address_____
City_____ State_____ Zip_____
I have enclosed $_____ in payment for the checked book(s).
Payment <u>must</u> accompany all orders. ☐ Please send a free catalog.
CHECK OUT OUR WEBSITE! www.dorchesterpub.com